Secrets
at
Sweetwater Cove

Sally Roseveare

INFINITY
PUBLISHING.COM

ISBN 0-7414-5451-3

Published by:

INFINITY
PUBLISHING.COM

1094 New DeHaven Street, Suite 100
West Conshohocken, PA 19428-2713
Info@buybooksontheweb.com
www.buybooksontheweb.com
Toll-free (877) BUY BOOK
Local Phone (610) 941-9999
Fax (610) 941-9959

Printed in the United States of America

Published July 2009

In memory of my grandson
Jonathan Stephen Joseph
Born December 27, 2003
Entered heaven January 13, 2006

ACKNOWLEDGMENTS

Many thanks to Marilee Earle, Louis and Charlotte Fischer, my high school English teacher Dr. W. Frank Landing and his wife Carolyn, Micki and John Singer, Peg Breiholz, my daughter Christine Joseph, and my granddaughter Bailey Roseveare for reading my manuscript. I appreciate so much the editorial input, encouragement and suggestions all of you offered me. Thanks also to my friend Martha Stokes for a really cool idea, and to Amy Thomas for giving me more time to write.

The gals in my real-life bridge club—Mary "Boo" Bane, Sue Griggs, and Helen Guthrie—are the complete opposite of the bridge club in my novel. For this I am truly grateful! Thanks, girls, for all the fun and laughter at the bridge table and elsewhere.

The Lake Writers, sponsored by the Smith Mountain Arts Council, encouraged me and let me bounce ideas off them. Betsy Ashton, Becky Mushko, and Bruce Rae—fellow Lake Writers—read my manuscript and offered excellent advice. As with my first novel "Secrets at Spawning Run," I laughed and learned every time Becky used her red pen to scrawl "Aaarrrggghhh!" and "Cliché!" Betsy and Marilee Earle also have active red pens. I honestly like red pens!

I have a vivid imagination. At times it isn't easy being around me, much less living with me. To my husband Ron Roseveare, thanks so much for your incredible patience and perseverance, your support, and for listening to all my "What ifs."

If not for all of you listed above, I may not have finished this novel.

CHAPTER ONE

Friday, September 22

He turned left and drove past her car. Their eyes met. She shuddered, blinked, and he was gone, lost in the five o'clock traffic. Behind her, horns blared when the light changed to green. The black Lab in the back seat whined. Aurora Harris glanced in the rear view mirror. A driver yelled and shook his fist. Embarrassed, Aurora steered her Jeep through the intersection.

She drove into a parking lot and shut off the engine, her knuckles white from gripping the steering wheel. Never before had she looked into such eyes—cold, calculating, dangerous. The eyes of the devil, she thought. Eyes she'd never forget.

At home that evening, Aurora told her husband about the fleeting encounter.

"So what color was his hair?" Sam asked.

"I don't know."

"Was he short, fat, what?"

"I don't know."

"Black? White? Mexican? Chinese? An extra-terrestrial being? Come on, Aurora."

"Sam, I'm sorry. I just don't know."

"So you're telling me that even though this man's eyes scared you half to death, you have no clue what he looks like?"

"Right. But if I ever see those eyes again, I'll know him. He's evil, Sam. And dangerous."

CHAPTER TWO

Friday, October 13

Carole looked up from her desk and stared at the man in the doorway.

"Well, hello there." He flashed a toothpaste-commercial smile and closed the door. "I'm Winston—I. Winston Ford. Friends call me Win. Because I always do. Win, I mean." He crossed the room, extended his hand over the desk. "And you are . . .?"

"I'm Carole Barco." Carole shook his hand. It was smooth, soft, perfectly manicured. Not like Luke's work-worn hands. "Is there something I can do for you?" She fingered the diamond ring on her left hand.

"I'm sure there is." He removed his sunglasses, smiled again and looked at her through gray eyes. "Actually, I'm here to buy some property. A lady I met at Gifts Ahoy suggested I come see you." He handed her a box. "She said to give you this fudge, said it would sweeten you up."

"How nice." Carole laughed, opened the box. Taking the plastic knife that came with the fudge, she cut off several pieces. "Help yourself, Mr. Ford. Their fudge is delicious."

"Thanks." Win reached in the box, popped a piece in his mouth.

"I'm sure we can find something to suit you, Mr. Ford. Please have a seat." She gestured to the chair on the other side of her desk.

"Call me Win. I intend to call you Carole. Only when a meeting's all business do I call a foxy lady by her last name." He sat, crossed his legs, looked into her eyes. "And I hope this meeting won't be all business."

Carole ignored his comment. "What type of property do you want, Mr., uh, Winston?"

"Win, remember?"

"Oh, sorry, uh, Win." She blushed, tucked a strand of chestnut hair behind her right ear.

"I'm interested in something on the water, preferably four or five bedrooms with private baths, a great room with high ceilings. I own a big powerboat, so a large boathouse or covered dock is imperative. Can you find that for me?"

"I'm sure I can, but it'll be expensive. Smith Mountain Lake is one of the fastest growing areas in Virginia. Waterfront property here is pricey."

"The price isn't a problem, Carole. I'm picky. I can afford to be." He stared at her. "If I want something badly enough, I don't stop until I get it."

Carole felt her cheeks turning pink. "Okay, then." She put her palms together, touched her chin with her fingertips. "Sweetwater Cove has single-family homes and condos, all with great floor plans. New ones are being built all the time. Do you have a preference for new houses or older homes?"

"Probably older ones that people are still living in. That way I can see how their boats fit the docks, get a better idea of how my boat will work. But I'm open to new homes, too."

Carol opened her planner, clicked keys on the computer. Options to select virtual tours appeared on the screen. "You can view some homes on my computer right now. Then this afternoon we'll look at the ones you're interested in seeing."

"I'm not a virtual tour kind of guy. I need to see actual houses. And what's wrong with seeing them right now? No point in putting it off."

Carole looked at the wall clock and frowned. "I'm meeting someone in forty-five minutes."

Win reached for the phone on Carole's desk and held it out to her. "Call him and cancel. It *is* a man, right?" She nodded and took the phone.

"He's not there," Carole said after the sixth ring. "I'll try his cell." When Luke still didn't answer, she hung up. She glanced at the clock again, then opened a yellow legal pad and started writing.

"What are you doing now?" Win stood, jingled the keys and coins in his pocket, sat back down. "I'm ready to go."

"I'm leaving Luke a note in case he comes while I'm gone. I'll be ready in a minute."

"Does this man, this Luke, have a key?" Carole nodded. "He must rate pretty highly, then."

"He does. We're engaged."

"Pity." Win picked up Luke's picture on the desk, studied it, set it back down.

"I'm almost ready. Just let me get a few things from the file room and I'll be right with you."

After a visit to the bathroom, Carole retrieved her purse and keys from a file cabinet. She hesitated before shutting the drawer. Should she slip her .22 in her purse? After all, she reasoned, I know nothing about this man. He's too cocky, too sure of himself. There's something about him that bothers me. He could even be an axe murderer or something.

"Carole, are you coming?" Win said from close behind her.

Startled, she jumped and slammed the drawer shut. Her opportunity to carry a gun had passed.

Win stared at Carol, shook his head. "Hmm-um," he said.

"What's wrong?" She twisted around as best she could and looked behind her. "Please don't tell me toilet paper is hanging out of my slacks."

He laughed. "No, there's no toilet paper. And there's not a damn thing wrong with you. From where I stand, everything looks absolutely perfect." He licked his lips. Carole blushed and picked up her jacket.

"You blush a lot, don't you, Carole?"

Her cheeks turned even redder. "Yes. I don't like it, but I can't help it."

"I think it's charming." Win took the jacket from her. When she slipped her arms into the sleeves, his hand brushed hers. She trembled.

"That shade of brown looks good on you, goes well with your brown tweed slacks. You have excellent taste."

"Thanks." She doubted Luke would have ever noticed that her outfit matched perfectly.

"Let's go. Time's flying, and I want to find the perfect waterfront house. You can try your fiancé from the car if it makes you feel better." Win held out his hand. She pretended not to see it and walked past him.

"Good idea." She opened the door and nearly bumped into Luke.

"Hey," she said. "I just tried to call you."

Luke kissed her gently on the lips. "Forgot my cell again." He smiled sheepishly, looked from Carole to Win. "Going somewhere?"

"I'm afraid so. Luke, this is Winston Ford." Luke and Win shook hands. "Mr. Ford, uh, Win, this is Luke Stancill. Luke, Win wants to look at waterfront property. Thought I'd show him around Sweetwater Cove. I can't go to brunch with you. That's why I was trying to reach you. I'm sorry." She saw the disappointment in his eyes. "Want to come for dinner tonight, instead? Around 8:00? I'll cook something special."

"I'd like that. See you then."

"We better go," Win said. Carole nodded and headed toward her car. Win grabbed her arm. "We'll take mine." He put his hand on Carole's back, steered her toward his black Porsche.

Win called out the window to Luke as the Porsche pulled onto the highway, "I'll take real good care of her."

"That's what I'm afraid of," Luke mumbled as he memorized the Porsche's license number.

CHAPTER THREE

At 8:45 p.m., a black-paneled van backed down the rutted drive to the garage. The driver shut off the engine and listened for several minutes. Satisfied he and his two buddies wouldn't be discovered, he opened the door and climbed out. "Let's go," he said.

Inside the nearly completed house, the men turned on their flashlights. "Keep 'em beamed low. Don't want anybody driving by to get suspicious," said Butch.

"So who does this house belong to?"

"To the contractor himself, so let's give him some extra special surprises besides the usual vandalism. Let's go do some damage." He grinned.

Otis wrapped a hammer in a towel and hurried upstairs. Downstairs, Shorty yahooed each time he heard Otis knock a hole in a wall. Meanwhile, Shorty beat the heart pine floor in the great room with a chain, poured bleach on it.

"Okay, Butch, we've left our surprises. You got anything else planned?" asked Shorty.

Butch grinned. "Yep. You'll like this one. Wait here." He hurried out to the van and returned with a plastic grocery bag, pulled out raw chicken parts.

"Where'd that come from?" asked Otis.

"Grocery store."

"Whatcha gonna do with it? Cook supper for the man?"

"Nope, just you watch." In the master bedroom, Butch removed the covers from two heat vents and stuffed the chicken down the holes. "That fowl's gonna smell mighty foul when the heat comes on." They laughed.

A few minutes later, the three men stood together in the kitchen. "Should we bust the gas lines?"

"Nah," said Butch. "We got the appliances. Been here long enough. Don't wanna git caught. Let's go."

In the van's front seat, Butch laughed. "Good job tonight. They'll get a big surprise come Monday when they discover the appliances delivered today are missin'."

"Hey, my girlfriend Monique's been wantin' a freezer. Maybe the boss will let me have this one instead of us selling it or tossin' it down a ravine," said Otis.

"Maybe so. He could call it a 'fridge' benefit." They laughed.

"I'd give anything to see Southerland's face when and if it dawns on him that the fire last month was no accident," Butch said. "You know, Southerland should appreciate the fact that we didn't burn his house down tonight."

"But Butch, he don't even know how the other fire started."

"Right. And we ain't gonna tell him. Open that jar of 'shine. We'll have a quick one or two to celebrate the lootin' of another house in Sweetwater Cove."

Half a mile away at Sweetwater Country Club, a man tapped his wife on the shoulder. She finished dealing and glanced up at him. "What is it, Tom?"

"How much longer will you girls be playing?"

Blanche looked at her three companions. "It's nine now. Probably another hour, don't you think?" The women nodded.

"About an hour," she said to her husband. "Why?" She finished dealing, organized the cards into suits and counted her points.

"I'm going outside for a smoke," he said. "Might drive over to the house to check on things. Be back by ten or a little before."

"Okay, 'bye. I bid one spade," Blanche said to her friends. She didn't look at her husband as he left.

"How's the house coming, Blanche?" asked Mary Ann. "Will you be moving in soon?" She studied her cards, bid two hearts.

Blanche's partner bid two spades. "We only need two for game," Lillian explained.

"Pass," said Estelle.

"I don't know," said Blanche. "We've had one problem after another with that house. I thought it would be my dream home; it's turned out to be a nightmare." She looked at her hand again and passed. Mary Ann led the ten of diamonds. The board played a low diamond. Estelle, her hand poised to scoop up the cards, threw the ace of diamonds on the table and smiled.

"Not so fast," said Blanche. She laughed and put a low trump on the trick.

"That wasn't nice," Estelle said.

"You know I'm not always nice." Blanche sipped her third Margarita. "Back to your question about the house, Mary Ann. One of the subs working on it suggested it was built on an old Indian burial ground."

"You don't believe that."

"Of course not. Tom's had trouble with many of the homes he's building here. They couldn't all be built on burial grounds. Could they?"

"Wasn't the house that burned a few weeks ago one of Tom's?" asked Lillian.

"I'm afraid so," Blanche answered. "Glad no one had moved in yet."

"There's a rumor that the construction problems and delays in Sweetwater are because Tom hires inferior subs to save money," said Mary Ann. She fiddled with her cards, sipped her gin and tonic, and sneaked a peek at Blanche.

"That's not true. If you're insinuating Tom's a bad builder, you're out of line. And I don't like it one bit."

"My husband is Tom's foreman. Both men have years of experience," Estelle said.

"If they're so good, then why have they had so many problems with the homes in Sweetwater?" Mary Ann smiled sweetly.

Blanche slapped her cards down on the table. "You will not talk to me that way if you know what's good for you." She glared at Mary Ann. "And don't you forget, Mary Ann, that Tom helps butter your husband's bread—yours, too. Tom buys all the appliances—overpriced ones, I might add—for Sweetwater Cove from your husband's business. So don't you act so high and mighty with me."

"I didn't mean to offend you, Blanche. I was only repeating what I'd heard."

"Now, girls, let's don't go saying things we'll regret," said Lillian. "Besides, we need to finish this rubber. Let's play bridge."

Across the room, Sam Harris smiled at his wife. "Come on, Aurora. That's a cha-cha the band's playing."

"Thought you'd never ask." They pushed their chairs away from the table.

"Hey, Sam," Blanche said when the couple walked past her table. "I saw you sitting over there with this lovely lady. Who is she?" She flashed an icy smile at Aurora.

"Good to see you again, Blanche. This is Aurora, my wife. Aurora, this is Blanche Southerland, one of the best golfers at the club."

"Oh, Sam, how you do go on." Blanche put her hand on Sam's arm, stroked it. "Aurora, you are the envy of all us ladies. Each of us would like to take your husband home. But, of course, he isn't interested."

"I'm glad." And this is probably the only cha-cha the band will play all night and I'm missing it, she thought.

Sensing Aurora's aggravation, Sam said, "I'll see you around, Blanche, ladies. Must get my charming wife to the dance floor or she'll find someone else to be her partner. 'Bye."

"'Bye, Sam," the four women said in unison.

"Who's that woman?" Aurora asked. They reached the dance floor as the music stopped. "We missed a cha-cha because of her."

"That's Blanche Southerland. Her husband's the general contractor building the houses, town houses and condos in Sweetwater Cove. I'm sure you've seen his name in the *Smith Mountain Eagle*. He's a big shot. So is Blanche. But enough about the Southerlands. Did anyone tell you you're the prettiest lady in the house?"

CHAPTER FOUR

Saturday Morning

The Lab whined and looked up at Aurora. She reached over the side of the bed and massaged his big black head. "You're the best dog in the whole world, King. But you already know that." King barked. She looked at the clock. "Good heavens, it's 8:00. Sam didn't wake me."

King yelped, trotted across the room, whined, pawed the bedroom door.

"All right already. I'm coming as fast as I can. Wonder where Sam is." Aurora slid her feet into her slippers and hurried to catch up with her dog.

Aurora put King outside. "Sam, where are you?" she called, then closed the door when she received no answer. She sniffed, smelled coffee, followed the aroma into the kitchen. A note from Sam lay on the counter beside the coffee maker. She reached in the cabinet for her favorite mug, poured herself a cup, and read Sam's note.

> *Good morning, Susie-Q. Hope you slept late. I woke around 5:30, was just sitting down to eat an omelet when Blanche Southerland called. Tom didn't pick her up last night at the club; she had to catch a ride with Estelle. Blanche said that last night she was furious. Now she's worried. Tom still hasn't come home. She asked if I'd go look for him—don't know why she chose me. Anyhow, I didn't wake you; figured you could use the sleep after last*

night—which, by the way, was spectacular. Call me on the cell phone if you need me. I love you. Sam.

Aurora sipped her coffee. "Yum. Strong. Exactly what I need." She thought about last night and how much fun they'd had. Picking up the phone, she dialed Sam.

"Hey, Susie-Q," he said. "What's up?"

Aurora smiled when she heard the nickname he'd given her on their first date. "Hey, handsome. Just wanted to let you know how much I enjoyed last night." She sipped her coffee. "You're a great dancer."

"You're pretty good yourself. Remember the first time we danced together?"

"How could I forget our first date? We went to the Peaks of Otter for dinner, and on the way home you pulled onto one of the overlooks and we danced. I love you, Sam."

"And I love you, too, Susie-Q. How about we have another incredible evening tonight?"

"I'd like that very much." She carried the phone and coffee mug with her to the bedroom. "I'll fix shrimp and grits. That suit you?"

"Shrimp and grits and you. Yum. Does it get any better than that? See you later."

Aurora quickly spread moisturizer on her face, brushed her blonde hair, dressed in gray sweats, and hurried outside. She stretched, then looked around for her dog.

"King, want to go for a run?" she called. Seconds later he dashed around the corner of the house and sat in front of Aurora, his eyes sparkling, a big dog-smile covering his face. She laughed, leaned over and hugged his thick neck. He licked her cheek, and she laughed again.

"Everyone should have a friend like you, boy." This dog, this loyal, loving friend, had helped her survive the sorrows of the past year and a half. King offered his paw and she shook it. "Okay, let's jog." They headed down the drive past the barn and paddocks where she'd kept her dapple-gray pony years ago, and onto Spawning Run Road. King ran ahead.

"Only half a mile to go," she said to King after a mile. They always turned around at the end of Spawning Run. The next road, which formed a "T" at the stop sign, carried too much lake traffic to suit her.

She jumped at the sound of screeching tires around the curve ahead. A horn blared and someone shouted. Aurora called King and they hurried toward the commotion.

"Old woman, are you nuts?" The man screamed at the white-haired lady standing in the middle of the street, his van only two feet from her. He climbed out of the van, shook his fist at her. "I almost wrecked my van 'cause of you. You're a damn idiot. You oughta be locked up some place."

Aurora hurried to the woman's side, touched her shoulder. "Are you hurt?"

"Hello, little girl. What's your name?" the elderly lady asked, a vacant look in her eyes.

Aurora recognized a sign of dementia; she'd seen that same confused expression too many times in her own mother's eyes. "I'm Aurora. I'd like to be your friend." Gently she took the woman's arm and guided her toward the van.

"Can she sit in your van for a few minutes while I call 911? I think she's lost," Aurora said to the man.

"Hell, no." He blocked their way. "Get that old retard away from me."

Aurora glared at him. King growled, moved between them. Cursing, the man returned to his van and drove off.

An antique store across the street had Adirondack chairs in the yard, and Aurora said to the old woman, "Let's go sit over there. Those chairs look so comfortable. Let's see if they really are. Wouldn't that be fun?" The woman nodded.

"What's your name, little girl?" she asked again as Aurora lowered her into a chair.

CHAPTER FIVE

"I'm Aurora. Aurora Harris. What's your name?" She held the old woman's hand, massaged it gently.

A pale green Camry drove up, braked and stopped. A woman jumped out. "Hessie, are you all right? I've been so worried about you."

Hessie stared straight ahead. Her thin lips formed a pout. "I want a cookie. I said I want a cookie!" she yelled.

"Okay, Hessie, I have some cookies in my purse. See?" The lady offered her a chocolate chip cookie. Hessie snatched it.

"I'm Dixie Lee Cunningham," the woman said to Aurora.

Aurora held out her hand. "Hey, Dixie Lee, I'm Aurora Harris." The two women shook hands. Aurora judged the woman to be between 60 and 65 years old.

"This is Hessie Davis," said Dixie Lee. "I'm one of her caregivers. I thought it would be good for her to get out of the house, let her breathe in some fresh air, watch the boats, and maybe get a bite to eat at Bridgewater Plaza. On the way, she demanded a cookie, so we stopped at a convenience store. She promised she'd wait in the car while I ran in to get some cookies. I shouldn't have trusted her. When I returned, she'd disappeared." She handed Hessie another treat. "I wasn't gone long. What happened?" She guided Hessie toward the Camry and helped her into the car.

Aurora told Dixie Lee about the van nearly hitting Hessie. "The man driving the van treated her terribly. I felt like clobbering him. King was ready to attack. I almost let him. I just don't understand people like that man."

"Thank you for intervening, Aurora. I'm quite fond of Hessie. She's fun to be with when she's having a good day. This isn't one of those. The poor thing has had a hard time. Three years ago Hessie developed Alzheimer's. Then her husband died a year ago, five years after they'd moved into Sweetwater Cove." She looked at Aurora. "Do you know where that is?"

Aurora nodded. She smiled and pointed to Hessie who was snoozing in the car.

Dixie Lee smiled back. "Good, she's asleep. By the time I get her home and she awakens, all she'll remember is that she had some cookies. At least I hope she'll remember the cookies. Thanks so much for your help." She looked at King. "Thank you, too, King." King offered Dixie Lee a paw. She shook it and laughed.

"Hope to see you again, Aurora." Dixie Lee waved and drove away.

"Let's go home, King. I don't know about you, but I'm exhausted."

CHAPTER SIX

In Sweetwater Cove, Sam pulled his cell phone from his belt clip and called Blanche. "Tom's not at your house or any of the other houses under construction," he said.

"Did you look everywhere?"

"Everywhere you told me. Your new house is locked, so I couldn't go inside. I banged on the door, though, but Tom didn't come. Is there any place he frequents other than the club?"

"No. And Tom doesn't use the club much. That's my thing, and he just goes along with me. His work is his life. I wish I'd known that when I married him. Oh, Sam, I'm so very lonely. Tom's, well, our needs aren't the same. I want some romance in my life."

Sam couldn't believe what he was hearing. Your husband's missing and you're coming on to me? he wanted to ask. Instead, he said, "Blanche, I know this is difficult for you, but I have to know. Is there someone he visits occasionally, a friend or, or something?"

"Are you suggesting there's another woman? How could you?" Sam didn't answer. "Well, I guess you would think that of most men, but Tom isn't most men. He loves his work and me. As you're probably interested only in your work and Aurora?"

Sam heard the question in her voice. "Yes, Blanche. From the first day I saw Aurora sunning on the dock. She's the only woman for me, more important than my work. Or anything else, for that matter." He wanted this conversation to end.

"Oh, I see. Well, then, if that's the way it is, I won't keep you any longer. I'd planned to go to the house, help you hunt for my husband, but I'll stay here instead. I'll call the Sweetwater Cove clubhouse and tell them you'll pick up a key to the house. I keep

15

one there for convenience. Let me know when you find Tom."
Blanche slammed down the phone.

Sam stared at the phone in his hand. "What does she think I am?
Her private detective? No way. And that's what that crazy woman
needs." He hung up. "And maybe a good scolding. And a marriage
counselor wouldn't hurt, either."

CHAPTER SEVEN

In his office, Luke Stancill sat at his desk and frowned. Dinner last night at Carole's hadn't gone well. Instead of fixing her usual semi-gourmet meal, she'd popped a frozen lasagna in the oven, opened a bag of spinach salad, and twisted the lid off a jar of applesauce. And she'd seemed distant, pensive, not her usual fun-loving, Luke-loving self. At ten o'clock she'd even implied that Luke should go home.

Uh-oh. Maybe she was coming down with a cold, not feeling well. Flu season was here. Had she remembered to get her flu shot? He'd call and check on her.

"This is Carole Barco. Thank you for calling Your Real Estate Agency. I'm out of the office right now, but I'd love to help you with all of your real estate needs. Please leave your name and phone number and I'll return your call as soon as possible. Or you may call my cell at 540...."

Luke hung up. Maybe she was sick in bed, unable to come to the phone. Visions of Carole up-chucking into the toilet ran through his mind. He'd better go check on her. He picked up his car keys but stopped. A client was due at 9:30. That gave Luke only 15 minutes, not enough time to get to Carole's and back. He dialed her cell phone.

"Hey, Luke. What's up?" Carole said.

"Carole, are you okay?" He looked at the picture of her on his desk.

"I'm fine. Why shouldn't I be?"

"I called your other phone and you didn't answer. Didn't know if you were downstairs in your office or upstairs sick or

17

something. I was concerned about you." A ladybug crawled across the photo. He flicked it off.

"A client called early this morning and wanted me to show him more houses."

Luke heard laughter and voices in the background. "Where are you now?"

"We're at Diamond Hill General Store. Win hadn't eaten breakfast, so we stopped for a quick bite. We'll be leaving in a few minutes. Was there something you needed?"

"No, I just called to say I love you."

"Me, too. Gotta go. I'll call you later. 'Bye, Luke."

Win. Carole's with Win. Luke didn't like the man. He's too rich, too good-looking, too smooth. Too damn perfect. And too interested in Carole.

CHAPTER EIGHT

Back home, Aurora showered, cleaned the kitchen, unloaded the dishwasher, made the bed, and tossed a load of whites in the washing machine.

She retrieved the newspaper from the kitchen counter, flipped through the pages. The headline "Boats Missing" caught her eye. She read the article.

> *Sheriff Paul Jones reported yesterday that there have been no leads in the missing boat cases. Four boats, each valued at $65,000 or more, have disappeared within the past two months from boathouses while the owners were either on vacation or at their primary residences. Sheriff Jones said that he, the state police, and the law enforcement agencies in the two other counties around the lake are working together to solve the mysteries. "We don't know yet how the boats were taken," said the sheriff. "Photos and descriptions have gone out to all law enforcement agencies in the Eastern US. A breakthrough is expected any time."*

Right, thought Aurora. But I won't hold my breath. She folded the paper and put it in the recycle bin.

She noticed a dirty smudge on a sliding glass door and wagged a finger at King. "Looks like your nose print. And I just scrubbed that slider yesterday."

She started to the pantry for window cleaner but stopped. No, she thought, I don't want to do housework today. I want to spend the day with Sam. But he's not here.

In the bedroom, she sat on the chaise lounge facing the lake and pulled a cross-stitch project from her tote bag. She'd designed the pattern from a scene in the Lexington, Virginia, travelogue she was creating. The City of Lexington had called in June and asked her to produce the travelogue, said they wanted footage from all four seasons, so she could take her time. She'd jumped at the chance to portray one of her favorite cities for all to see.

Years ago her mother had suggested that Aurora design a cross-stitch kit from each travelogue, commercial, or promotional film she produced. Aurora agreed, and the kits quickly became sought-after items in upscale gift and needlework shops. This kit, a picture of horses grazing in the foreground with the Blue Ridge Mountains as a backdrop, would be one of at least four in the Lexington area.

She stitched a row, didn't like the color, pulled it out. She looked at the framed and hanging cross-stitch of the shoreline of the Pamlico Sound in North Carolina. Her dad had framed it for her. Memories of her dad's murder in January and her mother's death in April from Alzheimer's disease surfaced. Meeting Hessie Davis hadn't helped her emotions, either.

"I can't do this right now," she said to King. "I've gotta get outside, do something to occupy my mind. I can work on the cross-stitch later when Sam's home."

King whined and licked her hand.

Aurora called Sam. "Where are you?" she asked.

"I'm back at Tom Southerland's house in Sweetwater Cove. Just got back from picking up a key at the clubhouse. Still can't find Tom. Seems as though he's just vanished."

"Want some help? King and I can be there in about twenty minutes." She opened the closet door, pulled out the dark yellow L.L. Bean jacket that Sam had bought for her because it matched the color of her hair.

"I'd love to have your help and your company. King's, too." He gave her the address.

"Okay. We'll see you soon." Aurora tossed her jacket on the sofa and hurried to the kitchen. She dropped two packages of peanut butter crackers, a couple bottles of water and two apples into a plastic bag. She put on her jacket, grabbed the car keys, called King, and left the house.

*

"Tom, if you can hear me, yell!" hollered Sam for what seemed like the umpteenth time. He'd searched Sweetwater for hours, but hadn't found Tom or his white truck. Finally inside Tom's house, Sam saw scuff marks and footprints in the construction dust. Holes were punched in the drywall. Miscellaneous tools were scattered around. He shook his head when he saw the damage done to the floors in the living room.

He fingered an old jacket on the kitchen counter. Was the jacket Tom's? It could belong to one of the construction workers. He'd ask when the workers showed up this morning. Sam knew the house was weeks behind, so some of the subcontractors should be working today to catch up. He also knew that bow-hunting season had recently opened. Trying to get a dedicated deer hunter from this area to work during hunting season was next to impossible, especially on a Saturday.

Tires crunched on the driveway. "Hey," Aurora said when Sam stuck his head out the kitchen door. King jumped out and ran to greet him.

"Hey, Aurora." Sam patted King's head. "Glad you're both here."

Aurora kissed Sam. "Me, too." She pulled a well-used tennis ball from her jacket pocket and threw it. "Fetch, King." The dog dashed after the ball. "Any news about Tom yet?"

"Nope. Maybe you'll find something I overlooked. You have a good eye for detail." He held the door open for her. "There's an old jacket over there on the kitchen counter, but it could be anyone's."

Aurora glanced around the kitchen. The drywall was up, cabinets in, ceilings stippled. "If it weren't for all the holes in the walls, the kitchen is finished. Except for the appliances."

"Yeah, you're right. Looks like not-very-nice people had a good time. Wait until you see the living room."

"What a shame. This is a great kitchen, lots of counter space. Nice view of the lake, too." She rubbed her hands over the granite countertops. "What happened to the countertops? There are lots of bad dings in them. Think the same folks are responsible?"

"That'd be my guess."

She picked up the jacket, smelled it and checked the pockets. "Do you know if Tom smokes?" She handed Sam an almost empty pack of Marlboros and a lighter.

"I think he does." Sam turned the lighter over. "It looks like the initials T. S. engraved on this side."

"Then it could be Tom's jacket. Let's see if King can find him." Aurora opened the kitchen door and called. King came running around the corner of the house. A boy jogged behind him.

"Is this your dog?" the boy asked.

"It is. His name is King. I'm Aurora Harris."

"King's a nice dog." The boy plopped down on the ground. King dropped the slobbery tennis ball in his hands. "Yuck." He wiped his hands on his jeans, patted King. "I've always wanted a dog, but Mom's allergic. Okay if I throw the ball for him?"

"In a little while. Right now King has work to do. Do you live around here?"

"Yes, ma'am. My name's Kurt Karver. I live next door." He pointed at the house to the left of the Southerland property, then handed Aurora the ball. "What kind of work?"

"Well, the man who's building this house is missing. My husband and I—that's Sam over there—are going to let King smell this jacket and see if he can find Mr. Southerland." She introduced Sam to Kurt. "We think Mr. Southerland came here last night, but we can't find him."

"Does he drive a white four-wheel-drive truck with a shell?" Kurt leaned over and scratched King's head.

Sam and Aurora looked at each other. "Yes," said Sam.

"Kurt, did you see a white truck here last night or this morning?" Aurora asked.

"Yes, ma'am. A white pickup was here last night." King whined. Kurt scratched the dog's back. "A black van was here, too."

"A black van? Did you see any people?"

"I saw three men. They loaded stuff in the van."

"Stuff? What kind of stuff?" Aurora asked.

"Don't know. Some of it was in big cardboard boxes. Took all three guys to carry 'em." He thought for a second. "The white truck belongs to Tom. I've talked to him lots of times. He's nice."

"Let's put King to work," Sam said, holding the jacket out for the dog to smell.

"Can I watch?" asked Kurt.

"You sure can," said Sam.

Aurora signaled King, and soon he was casting about for a scent. Fifteen minutes later the Lab had tracked the entire house and grounds.

"This is hard; Tom's scent is everywhere, of course." Sam scratched King's head.

"How old are you, Kurt?" asked Aurora.

"I'm thirteen. I'm in eighth grade."

"What are your favorite things to do?"

"I like computers, playing Game Boy, D.S., Wii, fishing. In fact, I was fishing from our dock last night. Striper fishing's good around here; lots of people fish at night. Anyhow, I had just caught a small one and thrown him back in the water when the black van drove in. About an hour later the white truck drove up."

"What happened when the white truck came?" asked Sam.

"At first there was some yelling and cussing, then everything calmed down."

Sam motioned to Aurora, and the two stepped inside the house. "So what do you think happened to Tom?" Aurora asked.

"Remember all the theft and vandalism that's been going on in Sweetwater for ages?" Aurora nodded. "I think Tom surprised the vandals and they got rid of him."

"That's an awful thought, but I bet you're right." Aurora pulled out her cell phone and dialed the police.

Kurt asked Sam if he could throw the ball a few times for King. When Sam nodded, Kurt said to King, "Wanna fetch the ball?" The dog answered with a high-pitched yelp. "Okay, King. Sit."

King sat, anticipation glowing in his eyes. His muscles twitched. When Kurt threw the ball, the dog barked and galloped across the yard. Kurt looked at Sam. "King's fast."

"He certainly is." Sam watched King snatch up the rolling ball and trot back toward them. "He'll fetch all day long if someone will throw the ball for him."

"Okay if I throw it a few more times?" asked Kurt.

"Certainly. King would love that," said Sam.

"How long do you think it'll take the cops to get here?" Aurora asked Sam.

"Depends. If they're in the vicinity, we shouldn't have to wait too long.

CHAPTER NINE

On the other side of the Southerland house, Carole explained that the Sweetwater Cove house she was showing him would be complete in about two months. There was still time for Win to choose his colors, appliances, flooring, light fixtures, cabinets and counter tops. "The developer will soon move in the house that he's building next door, and. . . ."

"What the hell?" Win galloped down the stairs.

"What's wrong?" Carole called after him.

"My car alarm's going off!"

With a wet tennis ball in his hand, Kurt stood in the driveway near the gleaming black Porsche.

"Hey, kid! What the hell did you do to my car?" Win grabbed Kurt's shoulder with one hand, drew his other arm back, balled up his fist.

"Don't hit me, mister!" said Kurt. "The ball hit your car, but the car's not hurt. I checked. Honest."

"Turn the boy loose. Do it now," said a furious Sam. King growled. His lips curled, his teeth looked like ivory daggers.

Win relaxed his grip, stared at Sam and King. "That kid hit my car with a ball. And this is none of your business."

"Win, let him go!" Carole hurried into the yard.

"Carole, what's going on?" asked Aurora, running toward them. She clutched a-two-by four.

Win stared at the man ready to defend the boy, at the woman holding a board, at the dog poised to attack. "Hey, I wasn't going to hurt the kid. Just wanted to scare him a little, teach him it's not polite to throw balls at expensive cars." He released Kurt, laughed.

24

"Aurora, Sam, this is Win Ford, a client. Win, meet Aurora and Sam Harris. Aurora's my best friend." Carole looked at Win. "Would you please shut that car alarm off?"

She turned to Kurt. "I'm sure this was an accident. Right?"

"Yes, ma'am. I was throwing the ball for King and aimed wrong. I didn't mean to hit the car. There's no dent or anything, see?" He touched a damp spot above the door handle.

Win examined the door, ran his hand over it, pulled a linen handkerchief from his back pocket and wiped a piece of grass off the door. "No harm done," he said in a now charming voice. "Can we be friends?" He held out a hand to Kurt.

Kurt looked from Aurora to Sam. "I, I guess so." He shook Win's offered hand.

"Now that we're all buddies, why don't I take everybody out for lunch?" Win said. "To show there're no hard feelings. Hey, even the mutt can go."

"Sorry," said Sam and Aurora in unison. "We have things to do."

"But I'll treat you to the most expensive place on the lake."

"Sorry, but no."

"Okay, then. Suit yourself. Maybe some other time."

"I doubt it," Aurora said.

"Aurora, be polite," Sam muttered. She glared at him.

Win opened the car door. "Get in, Carole. I'm not interested in this house. Take me to the next one on your list." He gunned the engine and waited for Carole to buckle up.

"I'll call you tomorrow, Aurora," said Carole. The Porsche squealed out of the driveway.

King sniffed. His nostrils twitched. With nose to ground, he trotted around the side of the house.

"He's picked up a scent." Aurora hurried after her dog. Seconds later King stopped in front of a mud-colored portable toilet in the back yard. He sat, barked three times, pawed the closed, battered door. Aurora grabbed his collar.

Sam studied the door. "Nobody could have any privacy in there. The door's barely hanging on. The lock's broken, too. I'm going to open it. Stand back, this might be ugly." He opened the creaking door.

Aurora wanted to cover her eyes, but she couldn't look away. Had King found Tom Southerland?

CHAPTER TEN

An hour away at Ivy Hill Golf Club in Forest, Charlie Anderson wiped a speck of tuna salad off his mouth and pushed away from the table. He'd enjoyed the nine holes of golf with his retired buddies earlier this morning, had liked their companionship, stimulating conversations and off-color jokes during lunch. Now they were eager to play another nine. But Charlie didn't feel like playing and he didn't know why. After all, one of the reasons he'd retired from the bench was to golf with his friends. And to see more of his love-her-like-a-daughter niece. Maybe he just needed to spend some time with Aurora.

He'd been on the links at Ivy Hill in May when Aurora called to say that she and Sam were leaving Augusta, and moving to Smith Mountain Lake. He smiled, remembering the loud "Yahoo!" he'd yelled in the middle of a fellow golfer's swing and his friend's reaction when the ball flew into the rough.

"You coming, Charlie?" that same golfer asked now.

"Nope. I think I'll call Aurora and see if I can visit with Sam and her tonight, maybe take them out to dinner." He slung his golf bag over his shoulder.

"How does she like living in her parents' house?"

"She likes it fine." Charlie knew Aurora's emotions had bothered her at first, that memories of her parents were bittersweet. But he said only, "She's happy to be at the lake. She grew up in that house, you know."

"Glad to hear it's working out okay."

The four buddies discussed which course they'd play the next day, decided on New London, tee off at 9:30. Charlie declined.

26

He liked the New London course, usually jumped at the chance to golf with these three men. But something in his life was missing. It was time to find out what.

CHAPTER ELEVEN

In Sweetwater Cove, Field Lieutenant Ian Conner tapped Aurora on the shoulder. She jumped. "Sorry, Ms. Harris. I didn't mean to startle you."

Aurora switched her attention from the portable toilet to the deputy.

"Lieutenant Conner, it's nice to see you again. And call me Aurora." She smiled, remembering how he helped her a few months ago. "How'd you get here so quickly?"

"I was only a couple miles away when I got the call." He turned to watch Sam fish a tan cap from the toilet. Across the front of the cap was printed "Sweetwater Cove."

Aurora told Lieutenant Conner about Tom Southerland's disappearance, the vandalism in the house, and Kurt seeing Tom's white truck and a black van the night before. "Neither vehicle was here when Sam arrived earlier this morning." She pointed to the toilet. "King tracked Tom Southerland here; Sam's found what I'm guessing is Tom's cap. Don't know if his body is in there, though."

"Looks like the door took a whacking," Lieutenant Conner said. He peered into the toilet. "Hey, Sam. Found anything else?"

"Nope. I've felt around with Aurora's two-by-four, but haven't hit anything. Except for this cap—and it may not be Tom's—I think the toilet's clean. Figuratively speaking, that is."

"I'll get my guys to check. But even if King tracked Southerland here, the man could have just needed to use the john."

"Except that there's a portable potty at his house next door. And it was night. Why would he walk all the way across two large yards in the dark to use this one? Doesn't make sense to me," Sam said.

CHAPTER TWELVE

That evening at Smith Mountain Lake, Aurora hugged Uncle Charlie. To most folks in the Lynchburg area, Uncle Charlie was either "Judge Anderson," "Judge Charles," "Charlie," or simply "Charles." It just depended on how close—or in what capacity—the person knew him. When he had asked if he could take Sam and her out to dinner, she insisted they eat at the house. Unfortunately, most of the home-cooked meals Uncle Charlie had eaten since his wife Annie died from cancer five years earlier were either those Aurora cooked or the ones his widow neighbor insisted he share with her. Aurora knew Uncle Charlie missed Annie terribly. She made a silent vow to call him more often, invite him to spend more time at the lake.

So many things about him reminded her of her dad, Jack Anderson. She missed her dad. Her mother, too. Aurora had fond memories of her parents and Uncle Charlie and Aunt Annie as they gathered around the piano and sang songs from the Big Band era, as well as '50s and '60s tunes. The family spent most holidays together. Since Aurora had no siblings, she'd often wished her aunt and uncle had produced cousins for her to play with. But they never had. Aurora didn't know if they couldn't, or if they just didn't want any. She'd never asked.

As though reading her thoughts, King poked Aurora's leg with his nose, stretched out beside her. She smiled at him.

"Let me look at you," Uncle Charlie said, grabbing both her hands. Aurora smiled at the same greeting he'd given her for as long as she could remember. She waited for him to finish.

"I declare, girl, you keep getting prettier and prettier. Are you taking pretty pills?"

Aurora laughed, gave the expected response. "Uncle Charlie, you're the bestest uncle any girl could have." They both grinned and hugged.

Sam welcomed him. "I need to pick your brain, Charlie. That okay?"

"Fine with me. I'm always glad to help if I can." Charlie liked being needed, appreciated it when anyone considered his opinion worthwhile.

"Let's eat in the sunroom," Sam said. He carried the three place settings of silverware and napkins Aurora handed him to the porch.

As he set the table, Sam told Uncle Charlie about Tom Southerland's disappearance and finding his cap, but not Tom, in the portable toilet.

"How do you know the cap belonged to Tom?" Charlie asked.

"His wife Blanche identified it a few hours ago." Sam frowned. "That woman's another story. Maybe even a horror story." He told Charlie how Blanche had acted that morning.

"Hey, you guys, dinner's ready," Aurora called. "Come fill your plates." She pointed to the bowls of shrimp, grits, and asparagus on the kitchen counter, then carried the French bread and an open bottle of Hickory Hill Winery's Vidal Blanc to the porch and set them on the table.

Over dinner, the three discussed Win Ford and his explosive temper. "Sounds like a rich, spoiled jerk to me," Uncle Charlie said. "Did he say why he wanted a house at the lake?"

"I asked Carole that same question a little while ago," Aurora said. "Seems one of Win's rich, boat-crazed buddies told him about the annual Poker Run held here and invited Win to help crew a powerboat this past May. He did, and now he's hooked. Carole said Win's looking for a house of his own and a faster boat than his friend's. According to Carole, his wealth is as big as his ego. Which must mean he's loaded."

"I didn't think the Poker Run was a race. Isn't the object to draw a card from each of the participating marinas? Best hand wins?" asked Uncle Charlie.

"Yeah. But try telling that to some of the skippers." Sam knew many of the locals were against the Poker Run. He had mixed emotions. The sleek, fast boats excited him. He owned a classic '50s Chris-Craft, knew the thrill of opening her up, seeing her perform. And he also understood how folks in small boats would feel threatened when a 35-foot or larger craft zoomed by, its wake nearly swamping them. Then again, the Poker Run raised thousands of dollars for charity each year. And wasn't that a good thing?

The phone interrupted Sam's thoughts. He started to ignore the ringing, but figured it might be the cops or Blanche Southerland reporting on Tom, so he answered it.

"Aurora, it's for you—a Dixie Lee Cunningham. I told her you'd call back after dinner, but she said it was urgent." He handed the phone to Aurora.

"Dixie Lee, what can I do for you?" Aurora asked.

"I'm sorry to bother you, dear. I know you're eating dinner. But Hessie is carrying on about a van, probably the one you told me nearly hit her. She said the van was black."

"She's right."

"She rattled off a license number, swore it was correct."

"You're kidding. This morning she couldn't even remember my name," Aurora said.

"I know. And get this. She said she's seen the van driver before in Sweetwater and in her house. And, according to Hessie, he called her a 'retard.'"

"He did. Doesn't she have Alzheimer's?"

"That's what the doctors say. But they don't really know, do they? I thought an autopsy was the only way to know for sure, although I understand the medical people have come up with some pretty accurate tests. She hasn't had the tests, and of course, she hasn't had an autopsy."

"Sometimes the mind does strange things, Dixie Lee. I remember when Mother was in the nursing home. We didn't think she could still use a phone, but we kept it in the room for our convenience when we were there. She didn't even have a phone book in her room. But on my birthday I received a phone call from her. 'Happy Birthday, Aurora. I love you,' she said. And then she hung up."

For a moment Aurora fought to control her emotions.

"Tell you what, Dixie Lee. Give me the license number and I'll see what I can find out." Sam handed Aurora a pen from his shirt pocket. She scribbled the number on her paper napkin. "I'll let you know."

Sam noticed a puzzled look on Charlie's face. "Anything wrong, Charlie?"

Charlie sipped his wine, buttered a piece of garlic bread. "I knew a Dixie Lee Cunningham. Annie and I played bridge twice a month with a Dixie Lee and her husband Ernie when we guys were young lawyers practicing in Lynchburg. Then they moved west to Washington. To the Sequim area, I think. We lost touch." He closed his eyes for a moment, embracing the memories. "But that was a lifetime ago, before you and Aurora came into the world. Couldn't be the same Dixie Lee."

"Maybe it is, Uncle Charlie. After all, how many Dixie Lee Cunninghams could there be?" She looked at her uncle, saw a spark in his eyes she'd not seen often since Annie had died.

"What did this Dixie Lee look like? Not that my Dixie Lee would look the same after all these years. I certainly don't." Charlie took a bite of bread.

Aurora tried not to grin. She wondered if Uncle Charlie realized he was referring to the lady as *my* Dixie Lee. "She's slim. Her hair's kind of a strawberry blonde with some gray mingled in. She's a pretty lady."

"My Dixie Lee's hair was strawberry blonde. She wore it chin length, as did Annie. Those gals enjoyed each other so much. I remember them lugging portable sewing machines to each other's homes. Sometimes they'd sew together all day. Dixie Lee and Annie were the same size, used each other's patterns. Annie made most of her clothes, you know." Aurora nodded.

"Maybe you should call Dixie Lee and find out if she's your long-lost friend."

"I'll think about it."

CHAPTER THIRTEEN

Sunday Morning

The doorbell interrupted Aurora's quiet time in the sunroom. She laid her book on the chaise lounge and hurried to the front door. Usually on Sundays she and Sam went to church, but with Uncle Charlie visiting, she wanted to spend every possible minute enjoying his company. Aurora smiled, her irritation vanishing when she heard King's high-pitched bark and an answering yap-yap of equal intensity. King had just identified the bell ringer. Still smiling, Aurora yanked open the door.

"Jill! Robert!" The three friends hugged. "It's so good to see you." Aurora reached over to pet the ecstatic Jack Russell terrier. "Little Guy, you haven't changed a bit."

Yelps and barks from King and Little Guy drowned out all chance of conversation. King whined and looked at Aurora.

"Okay, the two of you can go play. Just don't get in any trouble."

The two canine buddies first ran in circles, then dashed toward the lake.

"Have you had breakfast?" Aurora asked her friends. They shook their heads. "Well, we'll remedy that right now. Bacon's cooked; I'll scramble some eggs while you keep me company. Bring me up to date on what's happening with you two. Haven't seen you since the wedding. How was the honeymoon?"

Sam, followed by Uncle Charlie, entered the kitchen. "Charlie and I were fishing on the dock when King and Little Guy came running to greet us. Figured you were here when they ran back to the house," said Sam. "Good to see you."

Aurora cracked a dozen eggs into the frying pan, buttered some English muffins and popped them in the oven, and put on a fresh pot of coffee. When everything was ready, they took their plates to the table. The dogs, their energy depleted, stretched out under the table and slept.

Jill and Robert assured their friends that their month-long honeymoon on the French Riviera was everything they thought it would be.

"And I'm pregnant," said Jill.

"We're thrilled," said Robert. He squeezed his wife's hand.

Sam glanced at Aurora, saw the emotions on her face. He knew she was happy for their friends. He also knew she was a tiny bit jealous. He was, too. They'd wanted so badly to have a child, maybe even two or three, and the one time Aurora had gotten pregnant she'd miscarried. She'd be a fantastic mother, Sam thought. And I'd be a great dad. He wondered if time would dim their pain. Could the memories of life—and death—ever be erased? Did he want them to be?

"A baby. I'm so happy for you both." Aurora hid her emotions behind a smiling face. She murmured an excuse and left the room. "I'll be back in a minute."

In the bathroom, she blew her nose, wiped her eyes, told herself to get a grip and to stop wallowing in self-pity, and returned to the dining room.

Jill and Robert, floating on their happiness of wedded bliss and pregnancy, couldn't stop talking. They described in detail the French Riviera villa in *Villefranche sur Mer* from which Robert's house next door had been modeled.

"You need to see it for yourself," said Robert. "I can get you a good rate if you ever want to go."

"Thanks. We may take you up on your offer one day," said Sam.

CHAPTER FOURTEEN

Inside a metal building in Franklin County, three men worried.

"She saw me. The old retard can identify me. I'm toast." Butch lit a cigarette, inhaled, exhaled. He frowned. His hand shook slightly.

"I told you before not to worry about her. Everyone knows she's got Alzheimer's. Why would anybody believe anything she says?" said Shorty. "Hell, even she probably don't believe what she thinks she seen. If she can even think."

"Easy for you to say. I did some work inside her house right after her and her husband bought the place. She's seen me up close." Butch ground out his cigarette on a pine board.

"She almost got inside the van yesterday. Can you believe what could've happened if them two women had seen what was in the van?" asked Butch.

"Damn it, Butch, you had your gun on the seat. If they'd done got inside you coulda just blowed their brains out." Shorty grinned, bit off a chew of tobacco. "I'd of just kilt 'em both. You're too uptight. Ain't no way she'll remember you now. Not with her memory."

"Hey, you're not the one she saw. And why'd you stop by, anyhow, Shorty?"

"Things are gittin' a little too hot around here. I heard the cops are startin' to ask questions 'bout me. So I'm moving, going West. Won't be around to help you with your dirty work no more." Shorty looked at his watch. "I'm late. Gotta go."

After Shorty drove off, Butch opened the back of the van. He looked at Otis. "You got rid of the body, I hope."

"Of course I did. Just 'cause I'm a red-neck don't mean I ain't got good sense," said Otis. "I put him in—"

"No, don't tell me where he's at. As long as you're sure we cain't be connected if anybody finds him, then I'm satisfied. And the boss will be, too. Now let's unload this stuff."

CHAPTER FIFTEEN

From the passenger seat, Carole studied the man driving the Porsche. This was the third day in a row they'd been together. Granted, they were looking at real estate, and she often drove clients around for a week before they found property they thought they couldn't live without. But her time spent with Win Ford was different, almost like pleasure instead of business. And Win exuded charm, charisma—and sex appeal. Watch it, Carole, she thought. You're engaged to a fine man. Don't fall for Win's charm.

As though reading her thoughts, Win glanced at Carole and said in his deep voice, "So what happens when you find that perfect house for me?"

"What do you mean? My thought was that you'd buy it."

"Of course I'll buy the house. I mean what will happen to us?" Win reached across the seat, cupped his hand over hers.

"What do you mean?" She pulled her hand away. You love Luke, Carole. Remember that, she reminded herself.

"That's the second time in thirty seconds you've asked me that question. You know exactly what I mean." He looked at her, licked his lips.

"Win, I'm engaged. You're my client. That's all." She looked away from him, folded her arms. Warning bells sounded in her brain. Remember Luke, remember Luke, remember sweet Luke, she thought.

Win started to respond, but Carole interrupted him. "Turn left here, then take the second right. The property I want to show you is the last one on the right in the cul-de-sac."

Win turned into the driveway and shut off the engine. Carole opened her door and hurried toward the house. Win sat for a minute in the driver's seat and watched her. He didn't understand. Surely she knew he wanted their relationship to go further. Why didn't she jump at the chance? Any other woman would have. It couldn't be Luke. Hell, Luke could never shower expensive gifts on Carole or take her on exotic trips the way Win could. And Luke didn't have the class a woman like Carole needed. He smiled. Carole was a challenge. Win liked challenges.

On the porch, Carole opened the front door. "Win, you coming or not?"

Win grinned. Now he understood. Carole was playing hard to get. Of course she wanted him. All women wanted him. His name was Win—and he would. He always did. Or else.

CHAPTER SIXTEEN

In her Sweetwater Cove condo, Dixie Lee Cunningham brushed away a tear. Lord, she was lonesome. Sure, she had her part-time job—if there really was such a thing. Being a caregiver to Hessie Davis kept her busy about 40 hours a week. Hessie's nephew only paid Dixie Lee to work 25 hours, but somehow she put in extra time (no pay, of course), often overlapping with other caregivers. Besides, she liked Hessie. And Dixie Lee felt that now was her chance to pay back some of the help her mother had received when her dad was so ill.

Dixie Lee had lived in Sequim, Washington, when her dad was diagnosed with lung cancer. She'd hated being unable to help her mother care for him. But Dixie Lee worked full time as a registered nurse and couldn't get back to Virginia often. Ernie, her husband, had urged her to quit her job or ask for a leave of absence, to take all the time she needed to help her mother. But life and her job kept throwing surprises at her, and when Dixie Lee finally gave her notice and quit, her dad was in a hospice house. He didn't last long after that. And neither did her mother. Now she wondered if all the attention she lavished on Hessie was an attempt to rid herself of all the guilt she'd felt for not being there for her parents when they'd needed her.

The pain she had felt after losing her parents had slowly diminished. Now she remembered mostly the good times.

It was a different story where Ernie was concerned. Dixie Lee remembered the day the two cops had appeared at her door and told her that her husband had died in a plane crash. "We think a flock of geese flew into the engine on your husband's Cessna. He didn't stand a chance," they'd said. She remembered how they'd looked standing on the front porch, their hats in their hands, their eyes brimming with tears. They'd loved Ernie, too. "We'll never find another District Attorney like him. They don't make 'em like Ernie Cunningham anymore."

That was two years ago.

She banged her fist on the kitchen counter. "Ernie asked me to fly to Seattle with him that weekend, but I was too busy. I should have been on that plane. I *wish* I'd been on that plane. I wish I'd died, too." She hadn't said that for probably four or five months. Would the experts tell her that she was coming out of her depression? It didn't feel like it.

Dixie Lee walked over to the sliding glass door and stepped onto the porch five stories above the lake. Seven months ago, when she could no longer stand to wallow in her own self-pity, she returned to Lynchburg, looked at property at Smith Mountain Lake, and bought this condo.

For several minutes she watched the boats—not nearly as many since Labor Day—skim over the glistening water. She liked the designs their wakes left behind.

Dixie Lee frowned when the phone rang, thought about not answering it. After the third ring, she sighed and stepped back inside. "Hello?" she said.

CHAPTER SEVENTEEN

"Breakfast was delicious, Aurora. Thank you. You and Sam look great. I can't tell you how good it is to see you again."

Aurora put the last plate in the drainboard. Jill dried and stacked it with the others.

"It's nice to see you, too, Jill. And I'm so happy for you and Robert." She looked at her friend. "Honestly, I'm thrilled for you." She started a fresh pot of coffee.

"I'm so relieved. As soon as we announced our pregnancy to you and Sam, I realized the news was upsetting you. And I believe I understand how you feel. If I should lose this baby, Robert and I would be devastated."

"Sam and I will pray for you, Robert, and the baby. In my heart, I believe you'll deliver a strong, healthy child." And, God willing, one day I will, too, Aurora thought. The two friends hugged.

In the den, a grinning Charlie hung up the phone. Hurrying to the kitchen, he grabbed his coat and hat off the coat rack, hugged Aurora and gave her a quick peck on her cheek.

"Can't stay for lunch, Aurora." Charlie put on his coat, pulled his car keys from his pocket.

"Why not? Where are you rushing off to?"

"I've got a date. I took your advice and called the number you gave me for Dixie Lee Cunningham."

"And?"

"You were right. She's *my* Dixie Lee. We're meeting for lunch." Charlie put his hand on the doorknob, then hurried back to Aurora and kissed her cheek again. "I love you, girl."

She laughed when he hugged and kissed Jill, too.

"I'll call you later," he said, as he dashed out the door.

"Uncle Charlie, its only 10:30."

"I know, girl, but I don't want to be late. Goodbye," he called back to her.

"What was that all about?" asked Jill, laughing.

Aurora explained to Jill the events leading up to Uncle Charlie's quick departure. "Did you see the gleam in his eyes and the spring in his step? I haven't seen him this excited since I told him I was pregnant." She didn't mention Uncle Charlie's despair when she miscarried.

The friends refilled their coffee cups and took them to the sunroom. The trees were at their full, glorious color.

"I think fall is my favorite season," said Jill. "I love the shades of red, gold, orange and green. Soon only dry brown oak leaves will be left clinging defiantly to the branches."

"You're right. And fall is my favorite season, too," said Aurora. "Look."

She pointed to the great blue heron standing on the floating dock.

CHAPTER EIGHTEEN

Sunday night

On the Leesville Lake side of Smith Mountain, two weary coon hounds—one a male blue tick, the other a female red bone—waited beside the rutted trail. They knew their owner would come back for them. He always did. During the night, he and his buddy had driven a four-wheel drive truck loaded with five hounds to the mountain for training. The two experienced hounds had picked up the scent of a raccoon and treed him; the three young ones had run a deer.

The female whined, looked at the male. Both dogs stood, sniffed the morning air and howled. From the ridge came an answering bay. Soon two of the missing hounds trotted down the mountain, touched noses with the other two, and dropped exhausted on the cold ground. The blue tick barked, listened, nudged the female. The four hounds stood, cocked their ears to the sound of a truck grinding gears.

The mud-splattered truck appeared around the curve and stopped near the hounds.

"Told you they'd be here," said the driver. "Blue and Maggie know their stuff. And they always manage to bring in the others."

"Ain't but four hounds here, Jude," said the friend. He glanced around the clearing. "Where's number five?"

"Wish I knew, Elton." Jude pulled a whistle from his shirt pocket and blew. The sound echoed across the mountain. Men and dogs cocked their ears, listened for an answering bark. Jude blew three more times. No answer.

"Wuz hopin' that young bitch would git herself back up this mountain. I ain't in no mood to go traipsin' 'cross this rough ground. She's always been an ornery cuss." Jude looked at his friend. "You want her, Elton? She's got real good bloodlines. I'll sell her to you cheap. But you gotta go find her yourself."

Elton laughed. "Naw, don't reckon I do. Now if you wuz to go find her for me. . . ."

"Ain't gonna happen. If I go looking for her, you ain't gonna git her." Jude looked at his watch. "Okay, let's git to it. Put the two young 'uns in the crate, leave 'em some food and water. Maggie and Blue are good trackers. They'll come with us."

Blue and Maggie pulled at their leashes. Jude and Elton stumbled, recovered, fended off pine branches that slapped their faces as they tried to keep pace with the hounds. Jude pulled Blue to a stop, blew his whistle. Nothing.

"Last night was a blast, Jude," said Elton. "Today ain't so good. How come you ain't got all that new-fangled huntin' stuff them guys at the Corner Store's always going on 'bout?" He wiped his brow with a grimey handkerchief, stuffed it back in his pocket.

"You mean all that 'lectronic junk like radios on the hounds' collars and a truck horn what beeps every ten minutes or so to help you find your way back?" Elton nodded. "I ain't never gonna get none of that stuff. Don't need it. Takes all the fun outta coon huntin'. Besides, I could buy me two more well-broke hounds for what it'd cost me to buy all that stuff." Jude blew his whistle again.

Blue cocked his head, stuck his nose in the air, sniffed. Elton jumped when a deep hound-dog bay rumbled from Blue's throat. In the distance, they heard an answering bark. The hounds tugged on their leashes.

"Hot damn," said Jude. He unleashed Blue. "They's got her now. Turn Maggie loose, Elton."

Once free, the hounds bounded down the rocky mountain. Soon the dogs' voices changed to frantic barking. The hunters slipped and slid their way down Smith Mountain. All three hounds' barks blended into a fevered pitch.

"They's got somethin' down by the water," hollered Elton. "Cain't see what it is, though."

"I kin tell you this; it ain't no coon they's after." Jude called the dogs. Only Blue bothered to even look at him. "Careful, Elton. There's somethin' mighty strange 'bout this."

The men continued down the mountain, grabbed the hounds, snapped the leads on their collars. The dogs whined, pulled against their restraints. Jude and Elton stared at the object in front of them. The dented freezer, its door cracked partially open, lay half in Smith Mountain Lake. A mangled shoe stuck out of the freezer. Inside the torn remains of the shoe was a human foot. Blood oozed from the big toe.

Elton puked. He could hardly breathe. He wondered what Jude had gotten him into this time. Why had he ever accepted Jude's invitation? He'd hunted with Jude before, knew his reputation. Not good. Now he wondered if he'd survive this.

His wife had told him not to go. "The astrological signs are not in your favor," she'd said as she'd sipped her green tea. "Stay home. Please."

Elton had laughed at her, blew off her warnings. She was too wrapped up in all that gobbledygook horoscope stuff. Until then he'd thought they were only superstitions. Now he wasn't sure. Would he ever see her again? Would he see his five kids?

Elton puked again, wiped his mouth with his sleeve, and scrambled up the mountain. He stumbled, regained his footing, lost the leash.

Jude glanced once more at the freezer—and the foot. "Wait for me!" he hollered to Elton. Tripping over roots, rocks, and fallen trees, he hurried after his friend as best he could. The three hounds followed close behind.

Elton lost his footing, fell backwards. "Watch out!" he yelled to Jude.

Jude stopped, looked up. Elton's falling body knocked Jude to the ground. Both men tumbled down the mountain. *Thwack.* Elton's body slammed against a boulder. He didn't move.

Farther down the mountain, Jude's high-pitched scream as he hit the pine stump echoed across the mountain. Maggie ran to him, whined, tugged on his jacket. When he didn't move, she stretched out beside her master.

An hour before Monday's sunrise, Elton stirred, groaned. He moved his arms, tried to move his legs. His right leg refused. He winced, screamed. He couldn't believe the pain. He touched his knee, felt blood, torn flesh and bone. His head hurt like hell. But he was alive.

"Jude!" he hollered. "Where are you?"

His buddy didn't answer. But Maggie did. Elton yelled for Jude again. Maggie's answering howl was the only sound.

"Maggie, come here, girl." A mournful howl answered. "Maggie, Blue, come." Maggie barked but didn't come.

Elton flinched when Blue's tongue touched his forehead, licked the blood. Elton figured Jude was seriously injured or dead. Otherwise, he would have answered Elton's shouts. He needed to get to Jude's truck, call for help from the cell phone they'd left on the front seat. Elton wondered how he could have been so stupid. Of course, Jude didn't like new-fangled contraptions, usually left his cell in the truck's glove compartment, kept it for emergencies only.

"Well, if this don't count as a 'mergency, I don't know what does," Elton said. Blue licked his forehead again. Elton pushed Blue off of him, grabbed his collar, worked his hand down to the end of the leash. "Don't wanna lose you, boy. You just might be my only way outta here."

CHAPTER NINETEEN

Monday morning

First King whined, then nudged Aurora's knee and trotted to the door. When she let him out, she heard the rain. There wouldn't be a run for King and her this morning. Aurora considered herself a fair-weather runner; King had learned to accept that.

Aurora stepped onto the covered porch—her mother had called it the veranda—and listened. The sound of sirens was not a welcome one. She had hated them ever since she was a little girl, when the family had lived in Lynchburg. An ambulance, with sirens blasting, had gone to the house next door. While trying to adjust a TV antenna, the man who lived there had fallen from his slate roof to the cement walk two stories below. He'd died instantly. Aurora had seen him fall, had heard his scream and the thud when his body hit. She'd dreamed of the blood for months.

Pulling herself together, Aurora tried to concentrate. She hadn't heard this many sirens since the boating accident when two people and their dog were killed by a drunk driver in a powerboat.

With her imagination running overtime, she wondered if terrorists had attacked Smith Mountain Dam, but quickly dismissed the idea. Besides, she'd have heard a loud boom. Maybe the accident would be on the news.

Sam drove to work amidst a pouring rain. Some folks asked how he could stand the 45-minute commute to Bedford every day, but he liked driving the curvy country roads with their rolling hills and flat fields—many now yellowed because of the drought—and catching sight of turkeys and deer crossing the road, watching the ever-changing shades of blue in the Blue Ridge Mountains.

He switched the windshield wipers from intermittent to high. Lots of rain would help the drought. He laughed, realizing he was humming "Drip Drip, Drippety Drop." This 1958 Drifters song would run through his mind all day unless another tune or something important took its place. His co-workers wouldn't like it, but by the end of the day they'd all be humming the same tune.

Sam liked his engineering job. From his office window he could see the Peaks of Otter. Before they moved to Augusta, he and Aurora had enjoyed many picnics and hikes on Sharp Top and Flat Top. They surprised everybody when they honeymooned at the Peaks of Otter Lodge.

"Why in the world did you go there?" friends had asked.

"Because the Lodge is quiet—no TV or phone to disrupt nature's song—and because no other spot can equal the Blue Ridge Mountains," they'd answered.

Sam smiled, remembering his and Aurora's first date. He'd fallen for her when he saw her sunning one steamy August day. In his Chris-Craft, he and his friends had stopped to ask her for directions. The next day he'd driven to her house, asked her for a date. That evening they ate dinner at the Peaks of Otter Restaurant, then stopped at an overlook and danced to beach music. Even though he'd known her less than 24 hours, he'd wanted right then to ask her to marry him, but figured she'd think he was weird and never want to see him again. So he waited a year to pop the question. He discovered then that her answer to his proposal on their first date would have been a resounding "Yes!" He knew he was a lucky and blessed man.

Sam rounded a sharp curve. Flashing lights on two rescue squad vehicles, two police cars and a state police car warned him to pull over. With sirens blaring, the emergency entourage whizzed by. Seconds after he pulled back onto the road, he met three volunteer rescue vehicles and another police car.

Something big must have happened, he thought. Bet there's been another boating accident on the lake or a wreck on 122.

Maybe Aurora had seen something about the accident on TV after he left this morning. Sam reached for his cell phone, called the house. When she didn't answer, he switched on the radio.

*

Aurora hurried back inside, turned on the TV. She poured a second cup of coffee, sliced a small piece of leftover chocolate meringue pie, and sat down to watch. King stretched out beside her, one paw across her foot.

Aurora switched back and forth among the two Roanoke channels and the Lynchburg one. On ABC, Diane Sawyer and a fashion designer were discussing fall fashions. On NBC, Meredith Vieira and Dr. Nancy Snyderman talked about head lice and the need to use a nit-picker. CBS flashed pictures of heavy flooding in Washington and Oregon. Nothing about the lake flashed across the screen.

The telephone rang. Jill didn't bother to even say hello. "Aurora, Robert just called me from D.C. A ham radio friend of his heard that a body has been found on Smith Mountain. The friend called Robert because he knew we own a house on the lake. He's not sure where on the mountain the body was found, though." Before Aurora could respond, Jill said, "And get this. The body is in a *freezer*! And the freezer is partly in the lake."

"When did this happen?"

"This morning, some time before eight."

"Did the friend say what happened?"

"At this point, I don't think anyone knows. According to Robert's friend, the authorities don't know much yet. A couple of coon hunters and their dogs found the freezer. Did you hear a lot of sirens a little while ago?"

"Yeah, I did. Bet they're related." Aurora thought for a second. "And you know what else? There's no way a person could do that to himself, not if he's in a freezer that's in the lake. Was it a man or woman?" She looked out the window at Smith Mountain shrouded in fog. Rain drummed on the skylights overhead.

"I don't know; I assume a man. So what do you think happened to freezer man?"

"I think freezer man was murdered."

CHAPTER TWENTY

When the phone rang, Charlie Anderson put down the newspaper and checked caller ID. "Dixie Lee. I'm so glad you called," he answered.

Charlie was more than glad; he was ecstatic. He couldn't believe how he and this lady from his past had clicked, how they'd enjoyed reminiscing about the old times and their departed spouses. Each understood the love and respect the other felt for their deceased partner. After all, they'd both been in loving marriages, were childless, and were devastated when their spouses died. Charlie was sure his beloved Annie would understand and applaud his feelings for Dixie Lee. He believed his old friend Ernie would feel the same.

"Charlie, something's happened." Her voice shook. "I'm really worried. Hessie's missing."

"Whoa, Dixie Lee. Slow down. Why do you think Hessie's missing?" He picked up the coffee pot, refilled his mug.

"Because she's gone. I came to work this morning. There's no sign of Hessie anywhere. I've called her nephew. He told me he talked to her at ten last night when her nighttime caregiver arrived."

"Maybe Hessie just wandered off," he said. "Does she wear an ID bracelet?"

"I've thought of that. And yes, she does."

"What time did you get to her house? Where are you now? Give me details."

As she talked, Charlie took notes. Dixie Lee had arrived at Hessie's house at 7:45, 15 minutes before her scheduled time. A large vase was missing, but she'd found no sign of a struggle, no doors left open, no sign of the nighttime caregiver. After checking all the rooms in the house, even looking under beds, in closets, and in the basement, she had called Hessie's guardian—who accused Dixie Lee of arriving late. The man said he'd scheduled her for 7:00, that Hessie's nighttime caretaker probably left, maybe took Hessie with her when Dixie Lee failed to show up.

"Charlie, he called me irresponsible. I'm not." She burst into tears. "Nobody's ever talked to me the way he did."

Charlie knew the drive from the Boonesboro area of Lynchburg would take him an hour. Someone needed to be with Dixie Lee now.

"Honey, I'll call Aurora. If I can reach her, I'm sure she'll gladly go stay with you until I get there. See you in about an hour." He didn't realize he'd called her "honey."

Aurora assured Uncle Charlie that she and King could be at Dixie Lee's condo in about 15 minutes. What a morning, she thought when she hung up. First she heard all the sirens, then. . . .

A horrible thought hit her. Was Hessie Davis the dead body in the freezer?

On the mountain, Special Operations Command leader Mike shouted orders to rescue workers. "Jim, load the litter and ropes on your four-wheeler and head on up the mountain." He pushed a button on his radio, barked into the mouthpiece. "Stan, Jim's on his way with ropes and a litter. Where'd you say the injured man is?"

"Halfway down the Smith Mountain Lake side of the mountain. We may be only a few miles from civilization, but believe me, this is still a backcountry rescue. Tell Jim to drive to the first tower and unload his gear. From there he may need to repel. Be better if several others come, too. I'd go help, but this man's in bad shape. Got a damn broken pine branch sticking all the way through his right thigh."

No matter how many calls he answered, Mike never got used to the injuries, the deaths. Every time he thought about quitting he remembered the day of his son's motorcycle accident, how the 17-year-old would have bled to death if not for the care of dedicated EMTs. No, he could never quit. "You're saying he's impaled?"

"Yeah. And his head's bleeding, and he's unconscious. His vitals aren't good. He needs help ASAP." Mike looked around.

"Would be good if we could fly him out of here. Maybe somebody up top can scout around for a possible chopper landing site. And we need a saw, too.

"A saw? Why?"

"To cut off the branch that's stickin' through his leg."

"Is the branch still attached to the tree?"

"Yep."

"You gonna stabilize it first?"

"Yep."

"Gotcha. I'll send a saw," said Mike.

Down by the lake, members of the Smith Mountain Marine Fire Department tied up their boat and stepped on shore. "Hell, it's a freezer! The body's in a freezer!"

"That's what I told you when I made the call," said Bob, another EMT. "And we don't know if the body is intact or, or . . ."

"Is 'mutilated' the word you're looking for?"

"Yeah. Mutilated. Did you bring the crowbar like I said?"

"Right here."

"Then let's get at it."

CHAPTER TWENTY-ONE

In Carole's office, Luke stood with his arms folded. He could barely control the fury raging inside him. Things between them had changed drastically in the last four days. He didn't like it worth a damn. And he didn't want to lose Carole. Especially to a man like Winston Ford—a man who would wine, dine, and charm her, then leave her with a broken heart as he moved on to his next conquest. The man was a sleazeball. Couldn't Carole see through him?

Luke willed his temper to calm down. Trying to ignore Win who stood behind her, Luke faced Carole at her desk. "Why can't you take half a day off, Carole?" He pointed to Win and said, "You've worked with him every day since Friday. I've only seen you once, and then for only a couple of hours. You've spent most evenings with him. Hell, you've eaten almost every meal with him. For heaven's sake, Carole. We're *engaged*! Start acting like it." ·

Carole looked up at him, shook her head. "I'm showing him property, Luke. So far nothing has suited him. It's business. And don't tell me what to do."

Smiling, Win walked around from behind Carole's desk, stopped in front of Luke. "Whether it's business or pleasure, old man, Carole's doing exactly what she wants to do. And if you lose her because of your jealousy—well then, the best man will win."

Win flicked a hair off Luke's denim jacket. "And I assure you, I always win."

Luke's right fist slammed into Win's jaw. A follow-up with his left knocked Win to the floor.

"Stop it, Luke!" Carole screamed. She knelt beside Win, stared at the blood on his lip. "Luke, you're acting like a damn fool!"

Win pushed himself into a sitting position, wiped his mouth with a handkerchief, grinned at Luke. "Thanks, old man. You just lost."

Luke spun around, slammed the door on his way out. He stood on the porch, breathed deeply. Smart, Luke. You just drove Carole into Win's eager arms. She's right. You're a damn fool.

On the fifth floor of The View, King and Aurora stepped off the elevator. Minutes later they stood in Dixie Lee's condominium. With a big dog smile on his face, King sat and offered his paw to Dixie Lee. She wiped away her tears and shook hands with him.

"Aurora, thank you for coming. And thanks for bringing King, too." She rubbed the Lab's head.

"Dixie Lee, why don't you sit down. I'll fix us both a cup of coffee. Or tea. Whichever you prefer."

"Thank you, dear. Tea would be wonderful." Dixie Lee told Aurora where she kept the tea, sugar, and cups.

"You have a gorgeous place here," Aurora said. They sat on the love seat facing the water and sipped Earl Grey. "Your view is incredible."

"Thank you. Guess that's why they named this building The View." She spooned sugar into her cup, stirred it, watched the honey-colored liquid swirl round and round.

Aurora recognized that Dixie Lee was upset. Maybe instead of side-stepping around Hessie's disappearance, they should just talk about it. Right or wrong, Aurora forged ahead.

"Dixie Lee, Uncle Charlie told me about Hessie. Do you have any idea what happened? Do you want to talk about it?"

"All I know is that I arrived for work 15 minutes earlier than necessary. I almost always get to Hessie's house early. And I usually leave late. And contrary to what her guardian says, I was not told to be there at 7:00." Dixie Lee set her cup on the coffee table, stood, and shuffled through some papers on her desk. "Look here." She pointed to the paper in her hand. "My schedule for this week says I'm to work five hours per day, Monday through Friday, from 8:00 to 1:00. This came from Hessie's nephew last Friday. Look, he even signed and dated it." She handed the schedule to Aurora.

"You're right. This clearly gives your hours and days. I don't see how Mr., uh," she read the man's name on the paper, "Mr. Smoot can say otherwise."

"That Mr. Smoot infuriates me. Would you believe he threatened to fire me? I've never liked him. I would have quit working for him a month ago when he started yelling at me over the phone, but I'm fond of Hessie. And I honestly think she needs me." Dixie Lee reached for a tissue, blew her nose. "I haven't mentioned this to anyone else, but I think Mr. Smoot's stealing from Hessie. And I don't believe she's safe under his care. But please don't repeat this."

"I won't." Aurora watched a bass boat zip across the water. "Do you know if Mr. Smoot called either the night person or the police?"

"I don't know. Probably."

King barked, ran to the door seconds before the doorbell rang. Aurora let Uncle Charlie in. He gave her a quick hug and rushed to Dixie Lee, folded his arms around her. His gentleness with the distraught lady told Aurora that these old friends would not lose touch with each other again. She smiled. Time to go. Uncle Charlie could handle things from now on.

Aurora retrieved her jacket, said her goodbyes, told Uncle Charlie and Dixie Lee to call if they needed her, whistled for King, and slipped out of the condo. In the hallway, she paused for a moment and smiled. At least something was going right. And now she was going to the grocery store.

King whined, ran to the condo next to Dixie Lee's and scratched on the door. When Carole poked her head out the door and saw Aurora, she stepped into the hallway.

"Aurora, hey. What are you doing here?"

"I was visiting a friend next door. She's the lady I told you about, the one who helps look after the elderly woman who nearly got run over the other day. What are you up to?"

Carole explained that she'd finally convinced Win to look at a condo, hoped he'd like it and buy it. She told Aurora that Win was beginning to get on her nerves, that she missed Luke a lot.

"Carole, what are you . . . ?" Win walked into the hall, saw Aurora and stopped. "Aurora, it's you. Why are you here?" Win stared at her. King growled, moved in front of Aurora.

"I'm just leaving, Win." Aurora's green eyes looked into his grays. Only sheer willpower kept her from screaming. She said goodbye to Carole, called King, and walked away. Around the corner, she leaned against the wall and closed her eyes. Her hands shook.

Win had been wearing sunglasses when she saw him the day he lost his temper with Kurt. He wasn't wearing them today. And that's what scared her. She'd seen those eyes at the intersection in Lynchburg. Her sixth sense told her what he was capable of. And she was terrified for Carole.

She must warn her friend. She reached for her cell phone and stopped. What could she tell her? That Win had scary eyes, eyes that screamed to Aurora that he was dangerous, maybe a killer? She had no proof that he'd ever done anything against the law. Carole knew Aurora didn't like Win, but she'd never believe such a story based only on what Aurora thought of his eyes. She dropped the phone back in her purse.

CHAPTER TWENTY-TWO

Back home, Aurora didn't notice the blinking light on the answering machine until she'd unloaded the groceries and put away the cold and frozen foods. She pushed the "Play" button. After listening to the first message, she wished she had never discarded the old beep-when-there's-a-message machine for this silent one that lights up. She replayed the message.

Ms. Harris, this is Kurt. You know that black van I saw at Mr. Southerland's house? Well, I saw it last night parked across the street where an old lady lives. It was in her driveway up by the garage. I started to call you then, but figured I shouldn't disturb you 'cause it was so late, around 2:30 in the morning. Probably not important, anyhow, but I thought you'd like to know. It's like 7:45 now, I'll leave for school in five minutes. Hope you get this before I go. Anyhow, I'll be home around 4:30. Oh, a couple cars are parked in her driveway now. My phone number's . . . .

Aurora's watch read 2:00. She figured she'd been outside listening to the sirens when Kurt called that morning. What should she do? Should she call the school and get Kurt out of class, call the police, what?

If only I'd checked for messages earlier, she thought. If I'd answered Jill's call on this phone instead of the portable, I'd have seen the blinking light. Still would have been too late, though. She wondered who the old lady was. Her intuition nagged at her. She had a horrible thought. Was the lady who lived in the house across from Kurt Hessie Davis? She dialed the number Kurt had left.

"Karver residence," the voice said. "Can I help you?"

"Hello, I'm Aurora Harris. I'm trying to reach Mr. or Mrs. Karver."

"They're both at work. I'm the maid. I clean for the Karvers two days a week, usually every Monday and Friday. Do you want to leave a message?"

Aurora almost shouted that the maid was inviting a burglar when she announced what days she worked. Instead, she asked when the Karvers would be home, then requested their work numbers.

"Ma'am, I'm real sorry, but unless this is an emergency or Kurt's school calling, I'm not allowed to give out that information. Is this an emergency?"

"Well, I don't know." Aurora explained about Kurt's phone call and why she was hoping one of his parents could help her. "What I'd really like to know is the name of the elderly woman who owns the house across the street."

"I can tell you that. I'm friends with one of the lady's caregivers, Dixie Lee Cunningham. The old woman is Ms. Davis."

Aurora thanked her, hung up and dropped in a chair. Picking up the phone again, she dialed the sheriff's office and left a message for either Field Lieutenant Conner or Sergeant Johnson to call her as soon as possible.

And what the heck was Kurt doing up at 2:30 in the morning on a school night?

Squench. The crowbar tore at the freezer door. *Squench.* The three men looked at each other, pulled again. The door popped loose. They stared at the body inside. Bob, the EMT, leaned over the body, held his ear close to the man's mouth, looked for a rise and fall in his chest.

"You gotta be kidding," said one man.

"Hey, we don't know how long he's been here. Cold weather and water will slow body functions. Even though I don't expect to, I may be able to revive him," he answered. Bob held two fingers against the victim's carotid artery. "Holy cow! You guys ain't gonna believe this. He's alive! Barely, but he's alive." He pulled out his radio.

"Mike, freezer guy's got a faint pulse. I'll call dispatch, ask them to have a medical unit meet us at the nearest boat ramp. Which ramp do you suggest?"

"Let dispatch decide. They have all the lake maps and data there. Good job, Bob."

Bob called dispatch and requested Advanced Life Support personnel to meet them with the medical unit. "This guy's in bad shape," Bob said. "If Lifeguard 10 is available, it would be good to fly the patient to the hospital."

"We'll see what we can do," said the dispatcher. He instructed the three men to transport the patient to Parkway Marina. They backboarded the patient, covered him with blankets, loaded him on the boat, and sped off to meet the medical unit.

CHAPTER TWENTY-THREE

At Sweetwater Cove Country Club, Estelle spread her cards on the table in suits and looked at her partner. "How's that?"

"Here, look at my hand, see what you think." Lillian passed her cards to Estelle, watched her partner silently count the points.

"Has possibilities," Estelle said as she handed the cards back to Lillian.

"You shouldn't have stopped at three," said Blanche. "Lillian re-bid her suit, so you know she has at least five diamonds." She counted Estelle's points. "And you have eight points and three diamonds. Whatever were you thinking, Estelle?"

"It's my hand, Blanche. Not yours. I'll have you know I'll bid it the way I wish." She pushed herself away from the card table. "I'll be back."

"Where are you going?" Blanche asked. Estelle didn't answer.

"I asked you where you're going!" Blanche stomped her foot.

"I'm the dummy. And where I'm going is none of your business. I could be going to the bathroom, or to the bar, or home. Or I could be going to get my gun to shoot you." Estelle smiled at Blanche, pointed a finger at her and said, "Pow, you're dead!"

"Ew! Did I make you mad? Look, girls, Estelle doesn't like me any more." Blanche laughed, pretended to pout. "And by the way, Estelle, don't forget that your husband works for Tom."

In the ladies room, Estelle fumed. Blanche's big mouth and superior attitude always infuriated her. Until today, she'd kept her feelings under control, played the necessary dishrag role when around Tom and Blanche. Her husband was a better man, a better builder than Tom Southerland could ever be. Dave had helped start Sweetwater Cove, had worked as foreman for the contractor for six years. When that contractor had a heart attack on the job and died three years ago, Dave had expected to take his place. Instead, the dimwit owner of Sweetwater had offered the position to Tom Southerland, an old college roommate. Tom had majored in accounting in college, couldn't keep a job, changed to insurance. Failing at that, he'd accepted the contractor job when it was offered even though he knew zilch about building houses. Estelle never could understand how Dave could put up with Tom, could let Tom take the credit for the good construction and pass the blame to Dave when bad things happened. No, Tom Southerland was not qualified for the job he now held. But, she admitted to herself, Tom was a lot nicer than Blanche.

Estelle had attended Lynchburg College, gotten pregnant, and dropped out at the end of her sophomore year to marry the father of her unborn son. A year later, she gave birth to a second son. When the boys were two and three years old, their father graduated, thanked Estelle for financing his college education, and walked out of her life. She had worked two jobs to put him through college, had dreamed of how life would change when he got his degree and found a high-paying job. In her mind, she saw herself as a stay-at-home mom looking after the kids, making the house they'd buy a true home. A delicious dinner would be ready every evening when he opened the door and called, "Honey, I'm home!"

Instead, for six years after he left she struggled to pay rent and put food on the table, clothes on her kids and herself. When she met Dave on a blind date and he proposed three months later, she accepted, even though she didn't love him. She liked him a lot, however, and hoped that eventually she'd learn to love him. Dave worshiped the boys, adored Estelle, was kind and fair in his dealings with his family and with others. One morning when Estelle awakened, she realized that not only did she like Dave, she also loved him. And wanted only the best for him.

Estelle looked in the mirror, applied lipstick, ran a comb through her hair, and headed back to the bridge game.

"Speaking of Tom, have you found him yet, Blanche?" asked Mary Ann. Blanche shook her head, played a jack of clubs. Lillian took the trick with the queen, led with the ten.

"If my husband were missing, I'd be knocking on doors, making phone calls," Mary Ann said. "I wouldn't be sitting at the club playing bridge. When did you last see Tom?"

"When we played bridge Friday night. He left to check on the new house, never came home."

"Have you gone to the bank and made sure that you still have some money?" Mary Ann asked. She stifled a giggle. Blanche glared at her.

"I'm guessing you've called his office and made sure his secretary hasn't disappeared, too," said Mary Ann.

"Mary Ann, that's not a nice thing to say," said Lillian.

"I'm not worried about Tom leaving town with anyone but me, if that's what you're implying, Mary Ann," Blanche said. She would never admit that she had indeed called Tom's office and checked on the whereabouts of his young secretary. She really didn't care if Tom left her as long as he didn't clean out their bank accounts. She'd called the banks, too, verified that she was still a wealthy woman. She also had her own secret mad-money account just in case, had invested a large portion of it in CDs in her own name, was getting a good return on her money. And if by chance Tom met with a terrible accident and died, there was the five million dollar life insurance policy on him she'd collect. No, Blanche wasn't worried about money, although more would be nice.

Lillian looked at the bridge girls and wondered how they ever became a foursome. Individually they were nice. Except for Blanche. Together they were a disaster. Did they even have anything in common except for the love of bridge? She wished they could just play bridge, have fun and chat like normal bridge clubs some of her friends were in, not get into all the squabbles and adverse personality stuff like members of a dysfunctional family. What was wrong with them?

Mary Ann was catty, vicious, but she'd stick by you if you needed her. Blanche's every word carried an unseen dagger ready to thrust into anyone's back. Estelle was normally quiet, a yes-girl to anything Blanche said or suggested. But then, Estelle's husband Dave worked for Tom Southerland. Lillian had never known Estelle to react the way she just did.

Mary Ann and Lillian had attended the University of Virginia, were in the same sorority there, dated UVA guys who'd gone to high school with Tom. Blanche had graduated from Sweet Briar College in Amherst, Virginia, thought she was something special. She'd never worked a day in her life, never even made a bed. Her parents were stinking rich and flaunted their wealth. Lillian remembered the short vacation the bridge girls took to Blanche's parents' summer home in Newport, Rhode Island, two years ago. That fiasco had been a vacation from hell. Maybe Estelle felt like she didn't fit in with the three college grads.

Mary Ann interrupted her thoughts. "Lillian, for heaven's sake, play a card. Please."

Lillian looked at the three cards already played, trumped with a low diamond and scooped up the last trick. "Good bidding, partner. We made three exactly," she said as Estelle returned from the ladies' room and sat down. Estelle nodded.

"What, no gun to shoot me with, Estelle?" Blanche laughed. "Or were you out of bullets?" She looked at Lillian and Mary Ann and grinned.

"Blanche, you know I love you too much to shoot you." Estelle smiled sweetly at Blanche.

"I know you do, sugar. And I love you, too."

CHAPTER TWENTY-FOUR

Monday

Jasper Smoot checked caller ID when his office phone rang. "I told you not to call me here," he said into the mouthpiece.

"Yeah, well, I called you anyhow. You gonna fire me?" Butch pulled a cigarette out of his shirt pocket, lit it.

Jasper ignored Butch's comment. "This had better be important."

"We took the old lady last night."

"You what?" Jasper looked around his office, saw the secretary using the copy machine in the next room. "Why the hell did you do that?"

"My girlfriend Etta's a substitute night babysitter for the old woman, fills in when the regular one wants off. She called me 'round midnight, said she was lonesome, and that the old woman was asleep. Since I was kinda lonesome, too, I just took myself over to the house for a little visit. I've done that lots of times." He took a drag on the cigarette.

"You're an idiot. You know that, Butch? A damn idiot." Jasper glanced at the still busy secretary, lowered his voice. "So what happened?"

"Well, Etta and me was visitin' when the old retard walked in the room. She knowed me, told me so, called me Butch, called Etta trash, told us to git outta her house. She got Etta all riled up and cryin' and all. Then the old woman started screamin'. Etta was screamin' and cryin', too, and I just couldn't take no more."

"What'd you do?" Jasper stood up, sat back down.

"I slapped Etta to git her to calm down. The old woman picked up a vase and threw it at me. She shouldn't a done that. Made me mad. So I punched her hard in the face. Knocked her out. Wuz gonna slit her throat with my huntin' knife, but Etta grabbed holt of my arm, begged me not to. Said blood would be all over the room, that she'd get blamed."

"So what did you do with Hessie?"

"Etta helped me load her into the van. After that, Etta cleaned up the broken vase and lit outta there like a bat outta hell. Said she warn't gonna be here when somebody came 'round askin' questions. I got the retard with me in the farm building right now."

"Well, she can't stay there, stupid."

"Don't you think I know that? And don't call me stupid no more." He ground out his cigarette. "So can I kill her or what? And what do I do with her body?"

"Is she conscious?"

"Yeah."

"Think she recognizes you now?"

"Naw, she's back to her crazy old self, don't remember nuthin'."

As Hessie's guardian and beneficiary—thanks to a local banker who'd invested heavily in Sweetwater Cove—Jasper's long-term plan had been to have Hessie admitted to a cheap nursing home, sell her house, keep out just enough to pay for Hessie's keep, and invest the rest in high-interest bonds. He'd reap huge benefits after she died. But now he needed lots of cash. He'd had his eye on a 25-acre waterfront parcel that came on the market a month ago on nearby Leesville Lake. He didn't have the funds to buy it, but if Hessie died and her house sold for the recently appraised value, then he could easily swing the deal. And when she died, he'd inherit her estate and the money from the large life insurance policy he'd talked her into taking out—with him as the beneficiary, of course. Unfortunately, he couldn't get to it until she expired. This unexpected dilemma might just work to his advantage.

"Take her over to the part of the mountain on one of the dirt roads, about a 20-minute drive from her house, and put her out. Wait until tonight, though. Make sure nobody sees you. If anybody finds her they'll think she just wandered away and got lost. She has a history of wandering. I'll have a good reason to put her in a nursing home. If nobody finds her, well, tough luck."

CHAPTER TWENTY-FIVE

Luke guided his water taxi into a boat slip at Bridgewater Plaza, assisted the middle-aged couple from the boat, thanked them for their generous tip, and waved goodbye. Usually he enjoyed showing folks different waterfront developments around the lake, the cliffs, and some of the other attractions. This time was different. When he'd met them at Bridgewater four hours ago, he'd not been in the best mood. He was angry at himself for losing his cool earlier in the day and socking Win. Luke couldn't get Carole's reaction—or Win's—out of his mind. *Maybe Win's right,* he thought. *Maybe my actions will drive Carole into his welcoming arms. I'm an idiot.*

Fifteen minutes later Luke stepped onto his own dock and secured the boat. He looked at his watch—4:15. Maybe Carole was home. Probably a good time to call, he figured. When he entered his office, he checked the messages on his answering machine, decided they could wait, and dashed upstairs to his apartment and picked up the phone. No answer at Carole's office. He didn't leave a message, nor did he call her cell. He needed to see her in person—without Win hanging all over her—and apologize, tell her he was sorry, that he loved her more than anything in the world. After showering, he splashed on the after shave Carole liked so much, put on a pair of slacks, a nice shirt and tie (he hated ties, but Carole liked them), and took a sports jacket out of the closet.

"Look out, Carole. You're not done with me yet." Grabbing his car keys, Luke rushed out the door.

Luke stopped at a flower shop and hurried inside. "Give me a dozen long-stemmed red roses, the finest you have," he said.

The lady behind the counter looked at the handsome young man, smiled knowingly, and soon handed Luke twelve velvety-soft red roses, their stems wrapped in green tissue paper. "Would you like a card with them?"

"Good idea, thanks." He took the small card she offered and quickly wrote "Carole, please forgive me. I'm sorry and I love you."

"Good luck," she called after him as he hurried out the door.

"Thanks."

Still at The View in the Sweetwater development, Carole showed Win the two-story condo with its three spacious bedrooms, each with private bath, and powder room. The kitchen and living room combination was to die for. She pointed out the gas fireplace flanked on each side by bookshelves, told him how nice it would be to cook in such an efficient kitchen. A screened porch, accessible from the great room and from the small office, overlooked the lake and offered an ever-changing view. How could he not like living here?

"And Win, it comes completely furnished. What do you think?"

Win didn't answer her. He was still angry with himself for letting Aurora see him without his sunglasses. He'd recognized her the first time he saw her in Sweetwater Cove; he had seen her once before that. For some reason his instinct told him when their eyes met at the intersection that September day that she knew what he had done. How she knew, he didn't have a clue. He hoped that today she hadn't remembered their previous brief encounter.

"Win, are you listening to me? I asked you what you thought. Do you want to make an offer?"

Pushing his thoughts about Aurora out of his mind, he looked at Carole. "What?"

"I asked if you want to make an offer. On the condo."

When he told her it wasn't what he was looking for, Carole fought to control her temper. She'd shown him brand new houses, older homes, contemporary, traditional and eclectic homes, some fully furnished, most with large covered docks. A few even included the boat and jet ski. How could anyone who said price was no problem turn down every single house she'd shown him without even having to think about it?

"I have shown you 27 fantastic properties, all on the water, each different in some way or another." Carole sighed. "Have you seen a single thing that's interested you at all?"

"Yeah, I have. And it's standing right in front of me." He put his arms around her, pulled her close to him, kissed her.

Carole pushed away from him.

Win reached for her again. "Come on, Carole."

Carole sidestepped him, reached the door and hurried into the hall. She nearly bumped into Aurora's Uncle Charlie.

"Well hey, Carole. You don't live here, do you?"

"Hey, Uncle Charlie. No, I couldn't afford this place. I was showing the condo to a client."

"Anthony, is that you?" Charlie asked when Win looked around the door.

"Charlie, meet Winston Ford. Win, this is Judge Charlie Anderson. He's Aurora's uncle."

Charlie stared at Win. "Winston Ford, huh? You're the spitting image of a man who's been in my court. That man was charged with assault and grand theft, but the jury let him off. A mistake in my opinion."

Win smiled. "Nope, sorry to disappoint you. I've never been in a Lynchburg court—or any court, for that matter—never been charged with grand theft or assault, and my name's always been Winston Ford. I've heard there's a double for everybody somewhere. Would like to see this Anthony guy. Must be a handsome fellow."

"My mistake," said Charlie, a frown on his face.

Charlie and Carole talked for a couple of minutes. He told her about Dixie Lee who lived next door and how Hessie had disappeared. Win interrupted their conversation.

"Sorry to have to leave, but Carole and I are going to dinner. Nice to have met you, Judge Anderson. Coming, Carole?"

Carole said goodbye to Charlie and hurried to catch up with Win. "I'm not going to dinner with you. Why did you say that?"

"You're afraid to be alone with me." Win grinned at her.

"No, I'm not. I'm tired. Take me back to the office, please."

They rode in silence until they reached the real estate office.

Win drove his Porsche into the parking lot and looked at Carole. "What can I say to convince you to eat dinner with me?" he asked.

Carole gave him a tired smile. "Nothing. I told you that already. There's nothing you can say that will tempt me, Win. I'm exhausted. I need some down time."

"I would love to be down with you."

"Don't you even think about it. I'm serious. I'm so tired I'm not thinking straight. I just want to go to bed."

"Why didn't you say so? I'd love—"

"Don't go there, Win." Carole looked at him, put her hand on the door handle. It was locked. "Unlock the door, Win."

"What if I refuse?" Win leaned toward her, put his arm around her shoulders, caressed her neck. "I know you want me, Carole. Don't play hard to get. And remember, Carole. I always win—one way or the other."

The first thing Luke saw when he drove into the parking lot was the black Porsche. He thought about leaving. He stopped, uncertain of what to do next. When he saw Carole slap Win hard across the face, he smiled and turned off the ignition. "Atta girl, Carole!" he wanted to yell, but he didn't.

Seconds later Carole stood beside the Porsche, Luke at her side. "Go somewhere and cool off, Win," she said. "And take a cold shower."

"Yeah," said Luke, grinning. The Porsche screeched across the parking lot and onto the road.

Inside her apartment, Luke knelt on one knee and held the roses out to Carole. She took them and laughed. "You've already proposed, Luke, and I accepted."

"Yeah, I know. But I'm an idiot who doesn't handle things right and I'm not sure you still mean it."

Carole knelt in front of him. "I said yes the first time, Luke. And yes, you're an idiot sometimes. And yes, I still want to marry you."

CHAPTER TWENTY-SIX

Monday, 4:45 p.m.

Jill pushed the grocery cart through the produce aisle, dropped a bag of carrots, a pound of broccoli, and two sweet potatoes in the cart, and hurried to check out. She was thankful the lines were short. She felt nauseous, a little dizzy, too. Looking at all this food hadn't helped. The morning sickness was much worse than she'd ever expected. She couldn't understand why folks called it morning sickness. Hers lasted all day. She scrounged through her purse and pulled the last saltine cracker from a Ziploc bag. Her hand trembled as she gulped the cracker down in two bites. She hoped she wouldn't throw up. She wanted to go home, crawl into bed near a bathroom and go to sleep. She wanted none of the healthy foods she'd dropped in her grocery cart, but she knew that the blessed baby she carried inside her needed wholesome nourishment. Surely this malady wouldn't last much longer. She wondered how women who had multiple pregnancies coped. How could they allow themselves to get pregnant more than once when they knew how awful they'd feel?

Jill remembered the day Poppa came home from the hospital with the newborn baby and told his other children that Momma had died in childbirth. For two days, 10-year-old Jill, the oldest child in the family, had resented the baby boy, wouldn't look at him. After all, she'd reasoned, Momma would be alive if not for him.

The night she heard the creak-creak-creak of the old rocking chair, she padded into the hall and peeped into Poppa's bedroom. In the chair sat Poppa, tears streaming down his face, the baby snuggled lovingly in his arms. Jill ran into the room, hugged Poppa. He pulled her onto his lap, and the three of them rocked until Jill fell asleep. From that day on, Jill had loved the baby with all her heart, understood what a precious gift Momma had left them.

And now she and Robert would have a baby all their own.

Jill loaded the groceries in the car, started the engine, and drove to the traffic light. When the light turned green, she steered her sedan into the intersection. Seconds before a speeding car ran the stoplight and slammed into her front fender, she looked into the eyes of the driver and screamed. Her car careened into the air. Jill screamed again. Before she lost consciousness, she prayed for the life of her unborn baby.

At 5:50, Aurora covered the chicken casserole with aluminum foil, put it in the oven, and set the timer for 40 minutes. Sam would be home at 6:30. When he walked through the front door, she'd remove the foil and cook the casserole 20 minutes longer. They'd have time to unwind with a glass of wine, catch up on each other's day before sitting down to eat.

Maybe Kurt was home. She reached for the telephone to call him at the same time the phone rang. Aurora jumped, answered it. She hardly recognized Robert Reeves' distraught voice.

"Aurora, Jill's had an accident. A car ran a light, slammed into hers. They're taking her to the Emergency Room in Roanoke right now. I arrived in Madrid on business 45 minutes ago. I'm boarding a private jet as we speak, but won't arrive in Roanoke for hours." His voice broke.

"Do you want me to go to the hospital? I can be on the road in five minutes."

"Thanks, but my secretary in D.C. is already on the company jet. She should land soon. I've told her to call you as soon as she hears anything." He sighed. "I just thought you'd want to hear it from me first, before you saw it on the news."

"Absolutely. Thank you, Robert. How is Jill? Do you know anything about her condition?"

"I know she's alive." He swallowed a sob. "I'm scared, Aurora. So very scared."

"Sam and I will pray for her, Robert."

"Thank you. And please pray for the baby, too."

"You can count on that. Do you want me to get Little Guy and bring him to our house?"

"Little Guy. I forgot all about him. That would be a tremendous help. Could you keep him until Jill's home and doing well? You still have a key to the house, right?"

"I do. And it will be a pleasure to have Little Guy with us again. You know we love him."

"Thanks for helping, Aurora. I'll call you when I know something."

Aurora rummaged through the junk drawer in the kitchen for the key to Robert's house. As she latched on to the key ring, her hand brushed against a familiar object—her Dad's old Boy Scout knife. The Boy Scout motto "Be Prepared" rang through her head. Was her Dad trying to tell her she needed to be prepared, that she should carry the knife? She picked it up, stared at it. "Nah," she said. She tossed it back in the drawer. King whined. Aurora looked at him, shrugged, picked up the knife and dropped it in her jeans pocket.

"Satisfied?" King nudged her leg.

The five-minute walk to Robert's house helped drain some of Aurora's tension. She relaxed, secure in the knowledge that Jill was in good hands, would receive excellent medical care. She said a silent prayer for Jill and the baby. For Robert, too.

A high-pitched bark from inside the Reeves house answered King's excited woofs. When Aurora opened the back door, Little Guy dashed out, ran around the walled flower bed, back to King, then to Aurora.

"They should have named you Yo Yo! Stop jumping so I can love on you a little," she said to the Jack Russell terrier. She collected Little Guy's bag of dog food and food bowls. His dog bed could wait until later. The two canine buddies romped in the yard.

Aurora looked around. Except for the October colors in the landscape, Robert's five-acre lot and house looked the same as they had several months ago. Something's different, though, she thought. She stood still a minute, then smiled. "Of course. There's love here now. You can't see it, but you can feel it. Lord, please don't let their love be replaced with grief," she said.

She glimpsed a streak of red as Sam's car drove up Spawning Run Road. If she didn't hurry he'd be parked and inside the house before she made it home. Some folks thought her old-fashioned because Aurora liked to greet her husband with a smile and a kiss when he walked through the door. Of course, that wasn't always possible, but today she could reach the house before Sam if she cut through the woods at a run. She had fond memories of her mother greeting her father that way for as long as she could remember. She wondered if that was why their marriage had been so successful.

By the time Aurora had crossed the two acres separating her house and Robert's, she was out of breath. She leaned over, breathed hard, and said a silent thanks to her dad for building his house on this side of his 21 acres. She walked through the side porch door the same time Sam entered the kitchen.

"Aurora," he hollered, "turn on the TV! I just heard on the car radio that there's been a bad wreck at Westlake."

She picked up the remote, aimed it at the television. Sam put his arm around her, kissed her. "Don't know any details or names yet," he said.

"Sam, I . . . "

"There! I think the reporter's talking about it now." He perched on the love seat, stared at the screen.

"Sam, I know what . . . "

"Oh, geez! Would you look at that car. It's totaled. How could anyone survive that?"

"Sam!" He looked at her. "That's Jill's car."

"What? What did you say?"

"I've been trying to tell you. That's Jill's car. Robert called me a little while ago." She moved over and sat beside him.

"Oh, no. Is she . . . ?"

"She was alive and being transported to the hospital when Robert called." She willed herself not to cry. "They don't know about the baby." Her bottom lip trembled.

The timer went off in the kitchen. Aurora squeezed Sam's hand, hurried to the stove and removed the casserole.

"What should we do?" Sam asked from close behind her. "Should we go to the hospital?"

Aurora pulled off the aluminum foil and put the casserole back in the oven. "I think we should eat first, then think this through. Robert said his secretary would call us when she knew more." She set the timer for 20 minutes. "Little Guy's dog bed is still at the house, so we'll need to get that."

"Why don't we get the prayer chain activated?" Sam suggested. "I'll fetch Little Guy's bed if you'll start calling."

"Great idea. Prayer never hurts." Aurora flipped to the list of committee chairs in the church directory and dialed.

CHAPTER TWENTY-SEVEN

7:30 p.m.

Finally home from school, Kurt rinsed off his dinner plate and stuck it in the dishwasher. He'd just finished wolfing down the two hamburgers his mom had picked up for him at the drive-through on their way home. Earlier that day, she had called the school and told them not to let Kurt ride the bus home, that she would pick him up instead. He'd groaned when he'd read the message. Most times when she wanted to pick him up, it meant that she had someplace to take him—almost always somewhere Kurt didn't want to go. Usually he didn't mind too awful much, but he never let his mom know that. Today, though, he had really wanted to go straight home.

"Hey, Kurt, how was your day?" his mom had asked when he opened the car door and climbed in the front seat at 3:10.

"Okay, I guess." He tossed his backpack into the seat behind him and looked out the window.

"That's good." She patted his leg. "You're growing so fast I can hardly keep you in clothes. The stores at River Ridge are having great sales," she'd announced, "so I took off early from work. We are going shopping." She beamed at him.

"Aw, Mom. I have plans," he'd said.

"Well, they'll just have to wait."

That was four hours ago. Now he hurried to the phone and dialed the number for the umpteenth time. "Mrs. Harris," he said when Aurora finally answered the phone, "I've been trying to call you for an hour, but your line's been busy. Oh, this is Kurt."

"Hey, Kurt. I'm sorry. Our phone's been tied up. I didn't get your message from this morning until after you left for school."

"Like I said in the phone message, I saw the black van at 2:30 this morning. What I forgot to tell you was that after I saw the van, I sneaked in my parents' bedroom and took my dad's night vision goggles out of his closet."

Goosebumps raced down Aurora's arms. "Surely you didn't get close enough to get the license number."

"Yes, ma'am, I did. Got it written right here on this piece of envelope." He grinned when he heard Aurora's shout. "You want it?"

"Would you like to catch a 50-pound striper? What do you think? Of course I want the license number. Hold on a sec while I find a pencil with a point."

With the phone still to his ear, Kurt grabbed his backpack and hurried upstairs to his bedroom. He had a lot of homework tonight.

"I'm back," said Aurora.

Kurt read off the license number. "And guess what else? It's a Chevy cargo van. Don't know the year, though."

"I owe you a big one, Kurt. Thanks a lot."

"No problem. Uh, I mean you're welcome." His grandmother had fussed at him for saying "no problem" instead of "you're welcome," said it was bad manners. He thought about trying to break the habit, but decided he wouldn't say it when she was around. She lived out of state. How hard could that be?

"One more thing before we hang up. What were you doing up at 2:30?"

"I was working on a science project that's due tomorrow. Still have more to do, so I'd better go." He plopped down on his bed and pulled a notebook from the backpack.

"Okay. Thanks again, Kurt. I'll let you know what develops." As she hung up the phone, she hoped if she ever had a son he'd grow into the kind of kid Kurt was.

"Aurora, you'd better stay off the phone. Robert's secretary might call you any minute," Sam said when his wife started dialing again. He opened the kitchen door and let the dogs in.

"You're right. I'll use my cell." Quickly she located her cell phone and called Dixie Lee.

"Hello, Aurora dear," answered Dixie Lee as soon as she recognized her new friend's voice. "How are you?"

"I'm fine. But I have an important question to ask you. Do you still have the license number Hessie blurted out a day or so ago? You know, the one she said was on the black van?"

"I'm not sure, dear. Maybe. Why?"

Aurora told her about Kurt's message that morning, about talking to the cleaning lady at Kurt's house and discovering that she knew Dixie Lee. "I just hung up from talking to Kurt. He has the license number of the black van. I know you already gave the number to me, but I can't find the napkin I wrote it on. I want to see if his numbers match Hessie's."

"Well, so do I. Now wouldn't that be exciting. Hold on and I'll go look in my purse." Aurora heard "How Sweet It Is to Be Loved by You" by James Taylor playing in the background at Dixie Lee's house. She tapped her foot to the beat.

"I'm back. Would you like me to read it to you?"

"You found it! You are one amazing lady. Yes, please do." Each number and letter Dixie Lee read off matched Kurt's except for the last number, which was missing.

"You know, dear, I bet your Uncle Charlie would think it's interesting that we have a license number for that van. Do you think I should call him?"

"I think he'd like to know about the license number, too, Dixie Lee. Yes, why don't you call him?" Aurora guessed that Uncle Charlie would feign interest just to hear from Dixie Lee.

"Thanks again, Dixie Lee. I'll call Lieutenant Conner right now."

The minute Aurora started dialing the cell phone, the other phone rang. Sam answered and passed the phone to his wife. "It's the call you've been waiting for." Aurora turned off the cell.

"Ms. Harris, this is Georgeanne, Robert Reeves' secretary. I have a report on Jill. And the baby, too."

Aurora sat down on the sofa. Sam moved over beside her. "I'm ready," Aurora said into the mouthpiece.

When she hung up a few minutes later, Sam handed his wife a tissue, cradled her in his arms. She wiped her eyes.

"I'm so sorry, Susie-Q. I know more bad news is hard for you to take."

Aurora lifted her head, smiled at him. "The news is good." She blew her nose.

"Good? Then why are you crying?"

"Because I'm so happy." She laughed, wiped tears from her cheeks. "I'm sorry, but you know I cry when I'm happy or sad. I can't help it."

"True. So what's the word on Jill and the baby?"

"Georgeanne told me that the front and side air bags saved Jill's life. The baby's, too. Jill has some bruises from the force of the bags, a black eye, a concussion, and her left wrist is broken. The baby—a boy, by the way—seems to be doing fine. Jill will remain in the hospital for a few days just to be on the safe side." She patted the two dogs' heads when they rubbed against her leg. "And that's good. We don't want her developing complications."

CHAPTER TWENTY-EIGHT

Tuesday Morning

"Field Lieutenant Conner isn't in right now," said the receptionist. "Sergeant Johnson, his partner, is available. Would you like to speak with him?"

"Please," said Aurora.

When Sergeant Johnson picked up the phone, Aurora identified herself and told him that Kurt saw a black cargo van across the street at Hessie Davis' house at 2:30 Monday morning, and that he had the van's license number.

"Not only that," she said, "but now Hessie is missing."

"Yeah, Lieutenant Conner and I have been looking into that. This is the first I've heard that a black van may be involved, though." He wrote the license number on a piece of paper. "I'll run a check on it right away."

"You do know Hessie has Alzheimer's, don't you?" Aurora asked.

"Yeah, we've been operating on the premise that she just plain wandered off. Happens often. We've been searching within a one-mile radius. She's old; we didn't think she could've gone far. Guess now we'd better enlarge the search parameters."

"The other interesting thing that I haven't told you or Lieutenant Conner is that Hessie was almost hit by a black cargo van near the intersection of Spawning Run Road on Saturday morning." She shifted the phone to her other ear.

"You're kidding."

"Nope. The driver was rude and hateful to her, called her a retard. King and I witnessed the way he treated her. Dixie Lee

Cunningham, Hessie's caretaker, told me that later on Saturday Hessie blurted out a license number—the same number I just gave you except for the last digit—and she also remembered that the man was driving a black van. And Hessie hadn't forgotten that the man had called her a retard, either."

"Thanks for the info, Ms. Harris. I'll call you when we find the the van's owner. You can help identify him."

"Okay. And it's Aurora, remember?"

After hanging up she wished she'd thought to ask Sergeant Johnson about the hit and run driver who had totaled Jill's car and nearly killed her and the unborn baby. Had they found him? Had they located any witnesses? She called him back and told him about Jill.

"Yeah, we're investigating the accident, too. Haven't found a witness yet, but we will eventually. I'm heading to Westlake in a few minutes to see if I can dig up some witnesses." He thanked Aurora again for her interest and hung up.

Aurora looked at the kitchen clock, drummed her fingers on the counter, poured a third cup of coffee. She took a couple of swallows and dumped the rest in the sink. She needed to be doing something. Beside her, King whined, rubbed his head against her knee. Little Guy whined. She decided to work on the Lexington travelogue project for a while.

CHAPTER TWENTY-NINE

Tuesday, 10:15 a.m.

At Sweetwater Cove Country Club, Blanche sipped on a Bloody Mary, glanced at her diamond-encrusted gold watch. So what if it was only a little past ten on Tuesday morning. She didn't give a hoot. Tomato juice and V-8 juice were breakfast drinks, right? The vodka just added a little kick, a kick she seemed to need more often these days. She was antsy, different, but she didn't know why. Could it possibly be because Tom was gone? Surely she couldn't miss him so much. For all these years she'd thought of Tom as a meal ticket, someone to pamper her, shower her with trinkets, smother her with the finer things in life. And, in her opinion, she deserved the attention Tom gave her. She was spoiled; she always had been. Her parents had seen to that. She enjoyed being spoiled, liked having underlings kowtow to her every whim. But without Tom, something was missing. Could she actually care about him? Miss him just a teeny bit? Or maybe a lot?

The club bartender appeared at her shoulder, refilled her glass, stuck a fresh celery stick in it. "Any word on Mr. Southerland?" he asked.

"No, Jip. But my fingers are crossed." She smiled at him.

The buzzer signaling other arrivals sounded and in walked Lillian, Mary Ann, and Estelle. "It's chilly in here, don't you think?" asked Estelle. She rubbed her hands together.

Both Mary Ann and Lillian agreed.

"Not to me," quipped Blanche.

"You're never cold, Blanche," said Mary Ann. Except in your heart, she thought, as she laid the cards on the table and the four of them drew for deal.

"Looks like I deal," said Lillian, as she turned over the five of diamonds. She wondered if the three of hearts, the four of hearts, and the two of clubs the other three had drawn meant the cards would be lousy today. Or would it be a bad day period? She shivered.

The bartender interrupted their conversation. "Mrs. Southerland, you have a call." He handed her a portable phone. "It's your housekeeper."

Blanche frowned. Maria had orders to never call her at the club. "This had better be important," she said.

"Yes, ma'am, it is. The sheriff called here. He's been trying to find you. He asked if I knew where you were. I know you don't like nobody calling you at the club, so I figured I'd pass the message on and you can call him back if you want to." She paused, dreading the string of expletives that would fly out of the receiver. "It's about Mr. Southerland."

"About Tom?" The color drained from Blanche's face. "Did the sheriff say what?"

"No, ma'am. But he gave me a number for you to call."

Blanche grabbed the score pad and pencil, jotted down the number, and hung up. She picked up her Bloody Mary and the portable, walked away from the bridge table. She identified herself to the woman who answered the phone and was connected to the sheriff immediately.

"Mrs. Southerland, we found your husband," he said. He heard her gasp. "He's alive."

"That's wonderful." Blanche sank into an overstuffed chair, fought to control her emotions. She didn't want the bridge girls to see her crying.

"He's in a coma. But for right now, he's alive."

"Where is Tom? And where did you find him?" Suspicions of Tom being found in some kind of love nest ran through her brain. Could she ever forgive him for that? And what would her friends think?

"I'm not sure we should go into detail right now. Is anybody there with you?"

"My three bridge buddies are here. I'll call them." Blanche gestured frantically to Mary Ann, Lillian and Estelle to come. They hurried to her side, and Blanche quickly told them about the phone call.

"Sheriff, what's wrong with my husband?" Her hand shook as she raised the Bloody Mary to her lips. The celery stick bumped her nose.

"Mrs. Southerland, your husband is at a hospital in Charlottesville."

"How in heaven's name did he get there?"

"He was airlifted off Smith Mountain. The EMTs on the scene thought it best that he go there immediately."

"What was he doing on Smith Mountain?" Blanche asked.

"We don't know why he was on Smith Mountain. He can't tell us anything; he's in a coma, remember?" He didn't mention that Tom had been found in a freezer, that part of a toe had been chewed off, and that he wasn't expected to survive. She'd learn that soon enough. "His condition is critical."

"Oh, my," said Blanche. She stared at her friends, took a sip from her glass. "I'm going to Charlottesville."

"Are you up to driving yourself?" the sheriff asked.

"Estelle will take me." She looked at Estelle. "Right?"

"Well. . . ."

Estelle didn't want to drive Blanche to Charlottesville. Each way would take over two hours, not counting the time she'd have to spend waiting in the hospital. And she'd be with Blanche, a person she could barely stand, the entire time. The one thing that would make the trip to Charlottesville tolerable would be if Tom died and she'd no longer need to pretend when around Blanche. She had nothing against Tom. He was a nice, honest man. But he was incompetent. He never deserved the contractor job. And if Tom died, her husband Dave would be the contractor—a position that should have been awarded to him three years ago.

"Right, Estelle?"

"I'll need to make a few phone calls first," Estelle said.

CHAPTER THIRTY

Tuesday, 10:30 a.m.

"No, deputy, I didn't see a thing. I heard the crash, though. It was loud. Made me jump. Figured surely someone was killed in the wreck," said the shop employee to Sergeant Johnson. She put her waiting customer's purchase in a bag, smiled, told her to have a nice day, and turned her attention back to the deputy. "Surely someone shopping or working here witnessed the accident, though."

A frustrated Sergeant Johnson was beginning to think everyone who came to Westlake wore blinders. He'd checked twelve stores so far. Nothing.

The employee rang up another customer, told her how much she'd enjoy the Halloween sweater and said goodbye. "Have you thought about leaving flyers in the shops? Or handing them out as people come out of the grocery stores? Maybe if you checked around the same time the wreck occurred, you'd run into people who saw something," she said.

"The department's working on flyers right now. Should be ready soon. A deputy will come back later to distribute them. Thanks for your help." He left the store.

Outside, he drove to a parking space near the traffic light at Booker T. Washington Highway and the entrance to Westlake Center. He studied the intersection Jill Reeves had pulled into when she left Westlake. Traffic, this time of day, was light. He thought about the pictures he'd seen of Jill's wrecked car, marveled at how she'd survived the impact. That meant the hit and run vehicle had been heading north. A thought occurred to him.

Had the "bad" car turned right at the next light? If so, maybe someone in one of the shops on Scruggs Road had seen the car.

He drove into the intersection and took a right. He made another right at the next light, and parked at the first strip mall. He stopped in each shop and asked if anyone had seen a badly damaged vehicle pass the store on Monday afternoon between 4:45 and 5:15. No one remembered seeing anything. Sergeant Johnson continued to each store in the other shopping strips, asked the same question. No luck. He sighed, crossed Scruggs Road and into The General Store's parking lot.

"Ma'am," he said to the woman behind the counter, "I'm Sergeant Johnson. I'm hoping you can help me." He told her about the wreck.

"I saw it on the 11:00 news last night. This morning, too. They said the driver of the one car is alive," she said. Sergeant Johnson nodded. "It's a miracle she survived," said the clerk. "I can't believe the other car didn't even stop."

"Do you remember seeing a car that looked as though it had been in a wreck drive by here late yesterday?"

"I didn't, but let me go ask the girls downstairs." She returned a few minutes later with another woman. "Ruby, this is Deputy Johnson. Tell him what you just told me."

"Lessee. I'm guessing it was a little after five. I'd left a little early—we close at 5:30—and I pulled out of the parking lot onto Scruggs Road. This car came up behind me, real close, you know. The driver blew his horn like a crazy person. I could see in my rearview mirror that the front end was all bashed in. The driver sure was in a hurry. He couldn't pass me because cars were coming in the other lane. I turned into the Dairy Queen's parking lot to get out of his way. When I did, he floored it, 'cause the car sped out of sight. That's when I saw that the front right side was messed up, too."

"Did you see his license number? Could you tell what kind of car it was?" Sergeant Johnson could hardly contain his excitement. This was the news he'd been searching for, not much information so far, but at least something.

"The car was dark, black, or dark gray. I didn't see a license plate on the front." She smiled at a customer who walked by. "I don't know what kind of car it was. Not a truck or an SUV or a minivan, though. I'm sure of that. My guess is it was some kind of small car. At least it looked pretty low to the ground to me."

"You've been a big help, Ruby. We'll probably want to talk to you again." He started to leave.

"Wait. You asked earlier if I saw the license number. I didn't see the front plate. But I saw the first digit on the back plate. It was either the number '1' or the letter 'I'."

CHAPTER THIRTY-ONE

Wednesday morning

Carole retrieved the mail and the *Smith Mountain Eagle* from her mailbox. She would read the *Eagle* while waiting for eager clients to rush to her door. Ha! I wish, she thought. Even though she didn't like Win Ford, if she could sell him a house, she'd be able to pay her bills the rest of the year and into next year. The commission on a $1,000,000 plus house would be significant. Until he'd shown up, she'd worried about making her payments. Now if Win would just buy a house. . . .

Carole had seen the for-sale sign on the real estate property a year ago when she drove home after work. Never had she dreamed of owning a real estate agency, but teaching high school math had lost its appeal. Seemed like most of the kids these days had no desire to learn. And what had happened to students' manners?

Owning a real estate agency appealed to her. She liked challenges, enjoyed taking something that didn't work and fixing it. Now she wondered if buying this nearly bankrupt business had been a good choice. She'd made a few sales and rented some vacation homes. But now it was October. Sales and rentals wouldn't pick up again until late spring, perhaps not even then. Because of the economy, prospective buyers were having trouble getting mortgages. No, the slump in the housing market wasn't helping. Could she hang on? Probably not if Win didn't buy a house.

And where was Win? It wasn't like him not to call or be pounding on her door by 9:00 a.m. at the latest. He hadn't called yesterday, either. He'd been furious when she'd refused his unwanted advances on Monday. But what else could she have done? He'd acted like a jerk. No, she told herself, I did the right thing. If he called her again, she'd insist they take her car from now on. That way she would have more control over any situation that arose. She dialed his number. No answer.

That should make Aurora happy, she thought. Her friend had called Monday night, warned Carole to stay away from Win.

"He's bad news, Carole, dangerous. What does he do for a living? He must have a lot of money to be looking at such expensive houses."

"He told me that he deals in big ticket commodities. I don't know what specifically."

"Like I said before, he's dangerous. I should have warned you sooner. Please don't do business with him."

Carole unfolded the newspaper, checked to see if her real estate ad was correct, read about the progress on the retirement complex under construction near the lake. She looked at the picture of the Fountain powerboat on the front page. The caption underneath read, "Have you seen this boat? New Jersey resident discovers boat missing when he returns to lake home."

Carole opened the magazine insert and sighed. So many homes for sale. So many real estate agents competing for clients. So many bills to pay. She jumped when the phone rang. The sound of Win's voice excited—and scared—her.

"Hi, Carole," he said.

"Win. It's you."

"Carole, I'm sorry. I owe you an apology."

Carole said nothing.

"I acted like a jerk Monday evening. I'm so sorry." He waited. When she said nothing, he continued. "It's just that you are everything I want in a woman: smart, gorgeous, sexy, and I love the way you smile, and . . . . Sorry. I'm not helping matters, am I?"

"'I'm sorry' was a good start."

"I'm relieved. At least you're speaking to me. I came on too strong. I didn't take into consideration that you're engaged to Luke, that you have feelings for him."

"Win, do you plan to purchase property or not? I need to know. There are other clients who need my services. To put it bluntly, if you have no intention of buying, then we can end this conversation right now." Carole crossed her fingers. She needed his business desperately.

"I intend to buy a house in the next couple of days, and I want to purchase it from you. Unless you say otherwise, starting now, you and I will be on business terms only."

Whew, she thought. "Okay, Win, I can work with that. But from now on we take my car. Agreed?"

"Agreed. Can you pick me up here at the bed and breakfast at 11:30? I'll treat you to lunch. And if you bring your laptop, I'll even swallow my pride and take some of those virtual tours while we eat."

"Yes!" she wanted to shout. She'd be able to pay her mortgage in November. Instead she answered in a calm voice that she'd see him at 11:30.

"Thanks, Carole. I really appreciate it. You won't regret it."

Carole checked the clock on her desk. She had just enough time to brush her teeth and go to the bathroom before leaving to meet Win. This time when she pulled her purse out of the file drawer, she added her .22.

Just in case, she thought.

CHAPTER THIRTY-TWO

Wednesday, 10:30 a.m.

King whined, pawed Aurora's knee. Little Guy barked and ran to the door. Intent on finishing a particular segment of the Lexington travelogue, she ignored the dogs. Little Guy jumped in her lap and licked her chin. King pulled on her shirt sleeve. She looked at the Lab and the Jack Russell terrier and laughed.

"Okay, guys, you have my attention. You want to go out?" Both dogs barked. "Don't get into any trouble," she called after them as they bounded down the hill toward the lake.

Back at her computer, Aurora edited video scenes of a horse-drawn carriage pulled by a dapple-gray mare clip-clopping down Lexington's Main Street. She and Sam had taken the same tour a few years ago. Shots of the storefronts and historic homes from the carriage would be perfect for the travelogue, especially with the rhythmic sound of the horse's hooves in the background. She made a note to drive to Lexington later in the week while the fall colors were still vibrant.

On Smith Mountain, Hessie Davis was hungry and cold. And terrified. Nothing looked familiar to her, but nowadays not much made sense. She knew she was losing her mind, but who was left to care? She wanted her Momma and Poppa. Where were Momma and Poppa and home? A child shouldn't be lost in the woods. She wondered how she had gotten so turned around. Maybe if she kept moving away from the bad man who hit her, Momma and Poppa would find her before he did. But she was so tired, so cold. And the bad man wanted her. She didn't want him to hit her again.

Her red flannel bathrobe snagged on a tree, jerked Hessie backwards. She fell, struggled to pull herself up, tumbled back to the ground. A branch scratched her cheek.

And then he was there, licking her face, pawing her arm, whining.

"Hey, Doggie," she said. She patted his head.

King barked, yanked at Hessie's robe, freed it from the branch.

"Doggie." She sat up, hugged her knees. She was safe now; Doggie would protect her from the bad man. She liked Doggie. "I'm hungry, Doggie. I want Momma."

King sniffed the hundreds of scents riding on the mountain breezes. Gently he grabbed Hessie's wrist as he tried to pull her up and lead her down the mountain.

"No, Doggie." She slapped his head, yanked her wrist from his mouth and curled into a fetal position on the ground. Tears ran down her cheeks. King licked her tears and snuggled up against her. Little Guy stretched out next to her on the other side. In the distance, a coyote howled. Both dogs lifted their heads and sniffed. King sighed and rested his head on Hessie's hip. He wanted Aurora, but he would not leave Hessie.

Aurora worked on the travelogue until her stomach rumbled a lunch-time tune at noon. Opening the door, she stepped outside and called for the dogs. She heard no answering bark. Back in the kitchen, she spread some tuna salad on whole wheat bread, topped it with romaine lettuce and a slice of tomato, peeled and sectioned an orange, and set the plate on the table. She checked again on the dogs. Where were they? She'd let them out over an hour ago. King never missed Aurora's meal times where he stretched out under the table at Aurora's feet just in case crumbs dropped to the floor. Little Guy had learned to do the same.

When the doorbell rang, she looked up. Robert Reeves waved to her through the glass door. She pushed herself away from the table and motioned for him to come in. She searched his face as he crossed the room. A sense of peace and calm seemed to envelop him. They hugged. He held her tight for a minute, then relaxed his hold. He burst into tears.

Aurora led him to the sofa, sat down with him, held him in her arms. Sobs racked his body. Aurora bit her lip to keep from crying, too. Robert raised his head, smiled. "I'm sorry, Aurora. I don't know what . . . ."

"Jill and the baby . . . ?" she interrupted.

"They're both doing well. I can't believe it, but for some reason my family survived the wreck." Robert took the tissue she handed him, blew his nose. He reached for another and wiped his eyes. "Don't know why I broke down like that. I'm sorry."

"Don't apologize, Robert. That was your body's way of reacting to the stress you've been under since Monday. I understand. I've been there myself. Could I fix you a sandwich? I was about to eat lunch. Tuna sandwich okay?"

"Whatever you're eating is fine." Aurora fixed another sandwich identical to hers, poured two glasses of tea, and joined him at the table.

"So where are the dogs?" he asked.

"Outside. I let them out nearly two hours ago. I'll check on them after we finish eating."

"Since Jill and the baby are out of danger, I decided to follow Jill's orders and come home for a good night's rest. Those chairs in the hospital rooms aren't the most comfortable. Thought I'd take Little Guy home to keep me company, then if you don't mind, I'll bring him back here tomorrow morning before I leave for Roanoke."

"That's fine. If you have things to do, I can call you when he and King come back." She looked at her watch. "Shouldn't be too much longer."

"That would be great. I need to check in with the office. My secretary returned to Washington on Tuesday and forwarded files to my laptop. I need to work on them. Couldn't concentrate while I was in the hospital."

"I can understand that."

"Thanks again for your help. I'll catch up with you and Little Guy later." He waved and headed out the door.

After Robert left, Aurora cleaned up the kitchen and attempted to work more on the travelogue. No use. Her creativity had vanished.

She hadn't talked to Carole since Monday, and wondered if Win had bought a house. She called Carole's cell.

"Hey," she said when Carole answered. She heard a man's voice in the background. "Are you with a client?" She hoped the voice didn't belong to Win.

"Hello. Yes, I'm with a client."

"Are you with Win?"

"Yes. May I call you tonight, around seven?" she asked, glancing at Win. He smiled at her from the passenger seat.

"You know I don't like that man, Carole. I don't like you spending so much time with him. I don't trust him."

"Neither do I. Like I said, I'll call you tonight."

"Are you in his car or yours?"

"Mine. I'll talk to you later."

Aurora hung up. At least Carole was driving.

CHAPTER THIRTY-THREE

Wednesday, 1:00 p.m.

In Sheriff Rogers' office, Conner and Johnson handed over the information they'd collected about the black van.

"Good work, guys." The sheriff studied the contents of the folder.

"So a kid is the one who placed the van at Ms. Davis' home." He read on, chuckled. "Leave it to a teenager to be up at 2:30 in the morning, and still have enough nerve to sneak in his parents' room and take his dad's high-tech night vision goggles. Glad he thought to get the license number. Smart boy."

"Yeah, he is," said Deputy Conner. "He's pretty sure it's the same van he saw at Tom Southerland's house that night. He didn't get the license number that time, however."

"Interesting thing is," said Deputy Johnson, "a black van was seen at the Southerland house. Tom Southerland disappeared that night. A black van nearly ran over Hessie Davis, and Kurt saw a black van at Hessie's house. Then Hessie disappeared, too."

"The license number of the van at Hessie's house is the same as the van that nearly ran her down," said Conner.

"So do we know who owns the van?" Sheriff Rogers shuffled through papers.

Conner bent over the file, pointed to the registration. "It belongs to a Wallace Smith, called 'Butch' by his buddies. He's in construction, worked for a while at Sweetwater Cove a few years ago. He's been arrested for petty stuff a couple of times, but there was never enough evidence to convict him."

"We need to talk to Smith. Find him and bring him in."

The conversation moved to the car that hit Jill Reeves. "We don't have much. We know it was a dark vehicle, one low to the ground, not a mini-van or an SUV. The license number started with either an 'I' or the number '1'. My witness said it was definitely a Virginia plate," said Johnson.

"Tell you what. Get one of the gals in the office to contact all the car rental agencies in the area, see if they have any vehicles matching what little description we have with our meager license number."

Conner and Johnson looked at each other. "Getting that information won't be easy, Sheriff. The rental folks are just gonna laugh."

"I don't care if they roll on the floor laughing. Just get that info. I know it's a long shot, but we've gotta try. DMV would have way too many plates to check, so there's no point in calling them until we either know the whole number and/or what make the vehicle is."

"Yes, sir."

CHAPTER THIRTY-FOUR

Wednesday, 1:10 p.m.

In the hospital in Charlottesville, Blanche studied the tubes running from her husband's nose, mouth, and arms to all kinds of medical equipment. Monitors told how well—or badly—he breathed, how his heart beat. She didn't fully understand all these gadgets, but she did know that when an alarm went off and the nurses and doctors came running in Tom's room, he was about to die. That had happened twice since she'd been here. Somehow he had survived.

The drive from the lake with Estelle yesterday had been a nightmare. Her chit-chat had been almost constant, so unlike the submissive Estelle she knew. Blanche had wanted to scream at her to shut up, maybe even stuff a rag down her throat, anything to stop that grating voice. But it was the actual driving that really upset Blanche. She hated the way Estelle gripped the wheel, ran off the road onto the shoulder continually. Where had the woman learned to drive? Blanche had wondered if she'd even live to see Tom in the hospital.

Before Estelle had driven the car into the hospital parking garage, Blanche had strongly suggested that she needn't stay, that she could just turn around and head back to the lake. Estelle had refused, had insisted she wanted to be with Blanche "in your time of need." Thank goodness for the nurses. They finally convinced Estelle to go home after four hours that had seemed more like 40.

She looked at Tom, wondered how they'd stayed together all these years. Could he still love her after the way she'd treated him? She stared at her reflection in the mirror over the sink. Could their marriage survive?

Blanche had first met Tom Southerland 40 years ago at a Washington and Lee dance in Lexington. A classmate of hers from Sweet Briar College, who had dated Tom for nearly a year, had asked Blanche to go on a double-date with one of Tom's fraternity brothers. Tom couldn't take his eyes off Blanche. The next day he called her, asked her out. After one date, Tom was hers. Her friend never spoke to her again.

Everybody at their schools said Blanche and Tom made the perfect couple. They attended house parties at the beach, danced at the best clubs on the east coast, skied the mountains in Austria together. Paparazzi covered all of their jet-setting travels and pre-nuptial parties. International newspapers plastered pictures of their wedding and honeymoon on the society pages.

She had loved Tom then. Or had it been the idea of love and reveling in the glamour and fame that their two big-money political families attracted?

Had her feelings for Tom changed when he insisted numerous times that they have a child and she had refused each time? At first she tried to make him understand how much pain women went through when they bore a child, how dangerous childbirth could be. When she was 15 years old, their family's housekeeper had gone into early labor. Blanche had heard her screams coming from the kitchen. Blanche's mother had called the rescue squad, but by the time the ambulance had arrived, the baby had died in childbirth on the kitchen floor. She remembered hearing the medical personnel saying what a shame the baby was breech. The housekeeper never recovered emotionally. Eventually, Blanche answered Tom's question with one word—never.

From then on, their life together had changed. Tom threw himself into his different jobs and hobbies, never staying long enough with one company to become really efficient at anything. For Blanche, happiness and fulfillment came with acquiring high status in the community. Money and her organizational skills had earned her the sought-after rank those trying to climb the social ladder wanted to achieve. Blanche had thought she had everything. Now she wondered.

"Tom, I'm sorry for the way I've treated you." She leaned over him, kissed a spot on his forehead not bruised or covered with bandages. "Don't die, Tom."

"Mrs. Southerland," said the nurse as she slipped quietly into the room, "why don't you go get something to eat?"

"I don't want to leave him."

"You need to eat. You didn't have lunch, did you?"

"No."

She glanced at her watch. "It's lunch time. Go eat something. If you don't take care of yourself, you won't be any help to your husband. I'll be with him."

"You're right. Thank you. I'll be in the cafeteria if you need me. I won't be gone long." She touched Tom's cheek before she left the room.

When Blanche walked past the ICU waiting room, a figure in green scrubs glanced up and down the hall, and hurried in the opposite direction.

CHAPTER THIRTY-FIVE

Wednesday, 1:30 p.m.

In Tom Southerland's room, his private duty nurse looked at her watch. She knew that handsome young intern would be coming on duty any minute, would check in at the nurses' station before starting his rounds. Yesterday he had winked at her, and he'd smiled at her the day before. She'd thought about him all night, thought what a catch he'd be. She frowned. She'd seen two other nurses flirting with him.

Private duty was boring, especially when the patient was unresponsive. She checked Tom's ventilator and vitals, assured herself that she could take a five-minute break, walked out of his room and closed the door.

Tom struggled to clear his brain, wondered why he couldn't open his eyes. His whole body hurt like hell and his limbs refused to budge. Something was stuck in his throat and he couldn't swallow. In vain he tried to scream his frustration to anyone who could hear him. Nothing. Where was he? What had happened to him? His mind was so foggy. If only he could remember.

He heard footsteps, felt a hand on his shoulder, then on his cheek. Maybe the hand would remove the terrible thing in his throat. He'd like that. A voice whispered something near his ear. He'd heard the voice somewhere before. The voice laughed. Tom opened his eyes, stared into the face leaning over him. Hands closed around his neck, squeezed. No! I can't breathe! Don't do this. Please.

The nurse was right, thought Blanche as the elevator door opened. I needed to eat. I feel much better now, better able to help Tom.

She stepped into the hall as a Code Blue alarm blared from the speakers. Medical personnel scurried past her.

For a moment she stood still as her mind sought to make sense of what was happening. "Tom!" she yelled, and began to run. "Nooo!"

She hardly noticed the figure in scrubs walk briskly by her and into the open elevator.

"Mrs. Southerland, you can't go in there right now," said Tom's nurse. She took Blanche's elbow, steered her to the ICU waiting room.

"What's happened to Tom? I want to see him." She struggled to escape the nurse's grasp. "Please. I want to see my husband."

"I know you want the best for him, right?"

Blanche nodded.

"At this moment, the best thing you can do for your husband is to stay out of the way and let the doctors and nurses do what they're trained to do." She pointed to a plump chair. "Why don't you sit there while I get you a cup of coffee. Or would you prefer hot tea?"

"Coffee, please."

"How do you like it?"

"Black, no sugar."

The nurse walked to the coffee pot in the corner, poured the steaming brown liquid into a Styrofoam cup.

Blanche sagged into the chair and looked at her. "What's your name?"

"Wanda." She smiled. "Is there anyone I can call to be with you? Any children or other family?"

"I have no family except for my parents in Rhode Island. I think they're still in Africa on safari. I don't know how to reach them." Blanche pulled a tissue from her purse, blew her nose. "I should try calling their cell, leave a message."

"Friends, then?"

"Not really." My only friends are those who want or need something from me, she thought. "Well, actually, I could call the girls in my bridge club. It would take them a while to get here, though."

"I think that would be a good idea. While you're calling them, I'll contact the hospital chaplain to stay with you for awhile." She handed Blanche the cup of coffee. "I'll be back in a jiffy. You won't go anywhere, will you?"

"No, I'll stay here. But I'd like you to get an update on Tom for me."

"I'll see what I can find out." She started down the hall.

"Wanda," Blanche called after her. The nurse stopped.

"I forgot all about notifying Tom's family. They're not my favorite people, so I guess I just put them out of my mind. I don't know if they're in Aspen or Kennebunkport. They have homes in both places." She searched in her purse, pulled out a list of phone numbers and handed it to Wanda. "I really don't want to deal with them right now. Would you please . . . ?"

"Call them? Of course."

Blanche pressed a hundred dollar bill into Wanda's hand.

"I can't take this, Mrs. Southerland." She handed it back. Blanche watched her hurry down the hall.

CHAPTER THIRTY-SIX

Wednesday, 3:30 p.m.

Driving up Route 29 North, Lillian thought about home and the purple mums waiting to be planted. And the pumpkins in their small patch were ready to pick. Why had she offered to drive to Charlottesville?

She glanced in the rearview mirror at Estelle fidgeting in the back seat. She's a nervous wreck, thought Lillian. I'm glad she couldn't talk us into letting her drive. Mary Ann and I've ridden with her before. Under the best of circumstances, Estelle's the worst driver I know.

She looked over at Mary Ann and smiled. Mary Ann smiled back. "How much longer, Lillian?"

"Depends on whether or not you and Estelle want to stop in Lovingston for a potty break and to get a quick bite to eat," answered Lillian.

"Yes, yes! Let's stop for a potty break. Lillian, can we stop? And I'm starving, too. No, I'm more than that. I'm absolutely famished. Really I am. If we don't stop soon, I'll wet my pants. You wouldn't like that, would you, Lillian? What would that do to these nice leather seats anyhow? What do y'all think?" asked Estelle. "Maybe I should call Dave and ask him." She dug in her purse for her cell phone.

Mary Ann and Lillian raised eyebrows at each other.

"I don't think I'd call your husband and ask him that, Estelle," said Mary Ann. "I bet you can find the answers to your questions at the information desk in the hospital when we get there."

Lillian looked at Mary Ann and mouthed, "You're awful." Mary Ann grinned and nodded.

"Good idea, Mary Ann. That's what I'll do. I'll ask the information desk to give me all the information they have on pee. They should be able to do that or they shouldn't be called an information desk. Right?" She dropped the phone back in her purse.

"Right."

"Estelle, how do you feel?" asked Lillian. "You seem more nervous today than I've ever seen you."

"You don't really know me, Lillian. You either, Mary Ann. Whenever you're with me, Blanche is with us. I keep my nerves under control when I'm around Blanche. After all, her husband is Dave's boss. I wouldn't want Blanche to get mad at me and make Tom fire Dave. Dave needs this job and he's good at it."

"Tom wouldn't fire Dave just because Blanche told him to," said Lillian. "Tom's a nice man."

"Easy for you to say, Lillian. Your husband's job isn't dependent on Tom like our husbands' jobs. Dave is Tom's foreman. And Mary Ann is well aware that Tom buys all of Sweetwater Cove's appliances from Carl. Right, Mary Ann?"

"Right."

"I've really gotta go. If we don't get to Lovingston—or whatever that town is—soon you'll have to pull off the road and let me find a corn field or something. Or we'll find out what pee does to leather before we get to that information desk."

Lillian liked her leather seats just the way they were. She checked the rearview mirror for cops, and pushed on the accelerator.

In the hospital, Blanche tried at first to blot out the chaplain's monotone voice and prayers. She knew he meant well, had her interests at heart, wanted her to "know the Lord" before it was too late. He'd asked if she was a Christian, a believer, if she went to church. She told him she'd studied different religions at Sweet Briar, that none of them had interested her, and that no, she did not attend church. "But I do believe in a higher power. I guess that qualifies me as agnostic."

He'd sighed, nodded. Then he asked her the same questions about Tom. Her answers to those questions were more positive, answers the chaplain seemed to like. Yes, Tom was a Christian.

No, she didn't know when he became a believer, but she knew he was. Yes, he attended church regularly. What denomination or church, she had no clue. Either Episcopal, Presbyterian or Baptist, she thought. She never went to church with him. He asked if Tom's parents were Christians. She didn't know.

Wanda interrupted her thoughts. "Mrs. Southerland, you can see your husband now, but only for a minute."

"Tom's alive?" Blanche heaved herself up from the chair.

"He is. The doctors say it was touch and go there for a while. He's still not out of the woods, however."

Blanche pushed the door open to Tom's room and stared at her husband lying in the hospital bed. He's so still, so pale, she thought. She stood near the door while a nurse checked his tubes. A doctor watched the heart monitor, listened to Tom's heart beat.

"Your husband's a lucky man, Mrs. Southerland," said Dr. Blackman. "He came real close to leaving us."

"What happened? I thought he had improved, might come out of his coma any second."

"So did we. He seemed to be doing reasonably well, but suddenly he stopped breathing. Where were you when it happened?"

"Me? I'd gone down to the cafeteria to get something to eat— hadn't eaten a thing since early this morning—had finished, and was just stepping off the elevator down the hall when I heard the Code Blue alarm, saw medical people running to this room."

"So you weren't near your husband's room when he stopped breathing?"

"No. I told you where I was. Weren't you listening to me? And why are you asking me these questions?"

"One of the nurse's aides got a glimpse of someone coming out of Mr. Southerland's room seconds after the alarm sounded. She couldn't tell if it was a man or woman." He took a deep breath.

"Sit down, Mrs. Southerland." The doctor pointed to the chair, waited for Blanche to obey before he continued. "Mrs. Southerland, I think someone tried to kill your husband. That person almost succeeded. I've called the police."

Blanche thought she might faint. She leaned her head against the back of the chair and closed her eyes, waited until the dizziness passed. In a barely audible voice she said, "I can't believe that. What makes you think such a thing?"

"He has suspicious marks on his neck as though he'd been strangled. And the tube running down his throat was damaged. Ironically, I think the tube actually saved his life."

"I can't believe that someone would want Tom dead. Everybody likes him. Tom doesn't have an enemy in the world. It's me people don't like."

Dr. Blackman started to speak when he heard a light knock on the door. A man wearing a coat and tie entered the door, flashed his ID.

"I'm Detective S. Holmes. No, my first name isn't Sherlock. Everybody tries to call me that. They think it's funny. I don't. So call me either Detective, Detective Holmes, or by my first name, Sid. Is that understood?"

Dr. Blackman, Blanche and the nurse nodded. Dr. Blackman stifled a grin.

"So what's going on here?" asked Detective Holmes.

"I'm pretty sure someone tried to. . . ."

"Uh, Mrs. Southerland, would you mind stepping out of the room for a few minutes? I'll let you know when it's okay for you to come back."

Wanda came in, took Blanche by the arm and led her back to the waiting room.

Lillian and Mary Ann stood in line at the fast-food eatery in Lovingston. "Did you see how Estelle galloped to the ladies' room?" asked Lillian. "I don't think she was kidding about needing to go."

"I agree. I'm glad she made it."

"Me, too. My car's only two months old; I'd hate for the seats to get messed up so quickly." They laughed.

"Lillian, do you think Estelle's acting a little strange? I've never seen her like this. Today she seems to be a different person."

"You know, Mary Ann, it's almost like she's on something."

"On something? You mean like drugs?"

"Yeah, I. . . ."

"Shh, here she comes," whispered Mary Ann.

The three women picked up their orders and carried them to a booth by a window overlooking Route 29. As they ate their burgers and fries, Estelle pulled a small bottle from her purse, opened it and swallowed a pill. Mary Ann and Lillian looked at each other.

"What did you just take, Estelle?" asked Mary Ann.

"Oh, that was just an aspirin. I have a little headache," said Estelle, smiling sweetly. She dropped the bottle back in her purse, leaned her head against the back of the booth and closed her eyes.

CHAPTER THIRTY-SEVEN

At the hospital in Charlottesville, Blanche greeted her friends. "Thank you so much for coming," she said when they entered the waiting room. "You are all such good friends." She hugged each of them.

Lillian and Mary Ann raised eyebrows at each other. Blanche had never acted this way before.

"How is Tom?" Estelle asked.

"He's doing better, was sleeping when I left his room."

"Could we see him?"

"Not now. They ran me out of his room twenty minutes ago. A detective wanted to talk to Tom's doctor. They didn't want me listening.

"Fix yourselves a cup of coffee if you want some." Blanche pointed to the coffee pot across the room. "And there's an excellent cafeteria in the hospital if you're hungry."

"We stopped in Lovingston and grabbed a quick bite," said Lillian, "but I will have some coffee. Anyone else want a cup?" They shook their heads.

"Why is a detective talking to Tom's doctor?" Mary Ann asked.

"Sit down. You're not going to believe this. The doctor and the detective think someone tried to murder Tom." The women stared at her.

"You can't be serious," said Lillian.

"Why do they think that?" asked Estelle.

Blanche told her friends that a nurse's aide saw someone leaving Tom's room seconds after the alarm sounded. "I'd just stepped off the elevator after eating in the cafeteria. I heard the Code Blue."

"Do they suspect you?"

"I don't know, but the doctor asked me lots of questions. The detective probably will, too. Oh damn! I just realized a person hurried past me when I was running down the hall to Tom's room."

"Was it a man or a woman?" asked Estelle.

"I don't know. I barely noticed the person. I do remember the person was wearing green, you know, like they do in the operating room. At the time I was intent on getting to Tom."

"Blanche, you need to tell the detective this. It could be important," said Lillian.

Estelle's cell phone rang. Wanda stuck her head in the waiting room. "You're not supposed to use cell phones in this part of the hospital," she said to Estelle. "Please turn it off immediately."

"Sorry." Estelle noted the caller's identity and turned off the phone.

"If you need to make a call, there's a pay phone over there near the coffee pot. There're also specific places marked where you can use your cell." Wanda pointed down the hall.

"Girls, that was Dave," said Estelle. "I need to return the call. Be back soon." She left the waiting room and walked quickly down the hall.

Detective Holmes stuck his head in the room. "Mrs. Southerland, could I have a word with you?" He glanced at the other two women. "Alone."

"We'll just wait in the hall," Lillian said as she and Mary Ann stood up and walked out of the room.

"This won't take long," said Detective Holmes.

Fifteen minutes later, Blanche looked at the completed sketch a police artist had made of the person she'd seen in the hall. Detective Holmes compared it to the sketch made from the description the nurse's aide had provided. The aide's was more detailed than Blanche's, but both showed the same build and type of clothing. Neither showed facial features.

"Wish I'd paid more attention, but at the moment I was concentrating on Tom." Blanche looked up as her friends entered the room.

"We'll take the sketches to the other rooms on this floor, see if anyone matching that description was here visiting another patient. We're pretty sure it wasn't a doctor.

"You're exhausted, Mrs. Southerland. Why don't you let your friends take you home when they go?" Detective Holmes turned to the other women. "You wouldn't mind, would you?"

"Of course not," said Lillian, "but we came prepared to spend the night if necessary."

"I don't want to leave Tom alone," Blanche said.

"Believe me, he'll be fine tonight. The doctor says he's improving steadily. And if you're worried about the attacker returning, I've already stationed a guard at Mr. Southerland's door. He'll be fine, Mrs. Southerland."

"A guard is so impersonal. I'll stay," said Blanche.

"I've got a better idea," said Estelle. "I'll stay. The rest of you can go home, get a good night's sleep, and come back in the morning refreshed. That'll give you chance to get a change or two of clothing, too, Blanche."

"I'll stay with Estelle to keep her company," said Mary Ann. She dug in her purse and pulled out a deck of cards. "I brought these with me in case the four of us wanted to play bridge. Estelle and I can play gin rummy or hearts. Won't that be fun, Estelle?"

"A blast."

CHAPTER THIRTY-EIGHT

Wednesday, 5:00 p.m.

On the mountain, Little Guy stood and nudged King. The dogs touched noses. King whined. Little Guy wagged his tail and trotted down the mountain.

Still worried about the dogs, Aurora stepped outside and listened. Did she hear a faint bark? "King! Little Guy! Come now," she hollered. Irritated by the disturbance, crows screeched from the top of a skinny pine.

Aurora started back inside, then stopped and listened. She was sure she heard a dog bark. She pulled the door shut and ran down the hill to the dock.

Across the cove, buzzards circled Smith Mountain's shore. Aurora froze, called again for the dogs. Nothing. She looked back at Robert's house. Should she ask him to help? Wait, that was definitely a bark. It sounded like Little Guy—a frantic Little Guy. *If anything has happened to the dogs. . . .*

All thoughts of calling Robert gone, she unlocked the storage room on the dock, put on her life jacket and grabbed the oars to the rowboat. For a moment she stood on the floating dock and looked across the large cove at the buzzards. She shoved the rowboat into the water and headed for the opposite shore. She dreaded what she'd find.

When she discovered the buzzards were interested in a dead catfish instead of her beloved King, Aurora started to push the rowboat back into the water. Then Little Guy dashed out of the woods. He barked, ran a few steps, barked again. Aurora hesitated, looked at her watch. Should she follow him? Sam would be home soon. If she'd brought her cell phone she could call him, tell him to come in the pontoon boat, ask him to bring her jacket and a flashlight. She thought about going for help, but if she left to get Sam or Robert, she would lose valuable time, time that could be important to King's life. If she followed Little Guy now, he might lead her to King. She chose not to go back to the house.

"Okay, Little Guy. I'm right behind you." Dog and woman vanished into the woods.

Aurora slipped on dry leaves, grabbed a branch to keep from falling. Little Guy disappeared in the brush. Which way had he gone? She called; he didn't come.

Aurora had no desire to wander aimlessly through the woods and brush, especially in the dark. Darkness scared her, always had, and if she were out here much longer, night would overtake her. She knew wild animals roamed the mountain. She'd seen bear, bobcats, coyotes. Even mountain lions had been sighted by boaters, hunters and four-wheelers. She needed a plan.

Unless she heard or saw Little Guy again, Aurora decided she would stick close to the shore. That way, she could retrace her steps and eventually return to the rowboat. And if she needed help and if a boat happened by, maybe the occupants would hear her shouts and come to her aid.

Too many "ifs." But she had no choice.

CHAPTER THIRTY-NINE

Wednesday, 5:15 p.m.

At The View, Dixie Lee punched the stop button on the elevator and loaded the four bags of groceries she'd just bought. Friends often asked if she had trouble getting her purchases all the way to the top floor of her building. Usually all went well. She learned early on to carry an armload or two of groceries inside the building and deposit them close to the information desk. When she finished unloading all the bags from the car, she moved them beside the elevator and took them all up at the same time. Once on her floor, she'd unload them into the hall before relinquishing access to the elevator. Maybe she should buy one of those small pull-behind-you grocery carts. She'd look into that.

The two pumpkins she'd picked from the Morgan farm came next. She set the big one beside her door in the hallway to celebrate the fall season, her favorite. She liked the crunch of leaves underfoot when she walked in the woods, the brilliant colors in the leaves, the promise of a restful winter coming when she could snuggle up by the fireplace and read good books.

Books. She'd left the two books she'd bought earlier from Kitty's Little Book Shoppe in the car. She started to hit the elevator button and go fetch them, but remembered that she still had to finish David Baldacci's latest novel, and Charlie was coming for dinner. The books could wait until tomorrow. Right now she needed to concentrate on dinner.

Charlie. What great times she and Ernie had enjoyed with Charlie and Annie. Funny how things work out. She wondered if she and Charlie had a future together. She believed they did; she hoped he felt the same. Ernie and Annie were gone now, but she knew they'd want Charlie and her to be happy. She looked at her watch. Charlie would arrive in an hour. Should she use the small pumpkin to make her famous curried pumpkin/apple soup or her homemade pumpkin pie? By the time she'd reached the kitchen, she'd decided on the soup, which would go well with the pork tenderloin, twice-baked potatoes and fresh green beans. For dessert she'd serve a couple of scoops of vanilla ice cream with raspberry sauce dribbled over it.

CHAPTER FORTY

Wednesday, 6:00 p.m.

Usually the drive home from Bedford relaxed Sam. Not today. He felt stressed, worried. Was something wrong with Aurora? He dialed her from his cell phone. No answer. He looked at his watch. Normally she'd be working on dinner at this hour or reading in the sunroom. Regardless, she would be close to a phone. He frowned, accelerated. If anything had happened to her . . . .

Gravel flew as he spun into the driveway. He didn't see Aurora's Jeep, hoped it was in the garage. He pushed the garage door opener, sighed in relief when he saw her car parked in the usual spot. He pulled his car in beside hers and hurried into the house.

"Aurora, where are you?" he called. When she didn't answer, he called again. He searched the upstairs, the main level and the basement. No Aurora. No note from her. And no dogs, either. Her purse and cell phone sat on the shelf in the closet. Strange. He checked the oven to see if dinner was ready. Nope, nothing there. Maybe she'd fixed a salad for tonight. He opened the refrigerator; no signs of dinner were apparent.

Stepping outside, he called again.

"Down here," came an answering voice. The voice wasn't Aurora's; it belonged to a man.

Sam's spine tingled. Who was at the dock and why hadn't Aurora answered him? Fear for his wife sent him sprinting down the hill. When he reached the lake, Robert Reeves stepped out of the storage shed.

"What's going on?" Sam asked. "Where's Aurora?"

"Don't know. I came down here to look for her and the dogs about five minutes ago. I went to your house first to see if Little Guy and King had come back, but nobody was home." He explained to Sam that the dogs had run off before lunch. "I figured they'd be home by now."

"Did Aurora have any idea where they went?"

"No, only that they'd been anxious to get out. They headed straight for the lake when she turned them loose."

"That's weird. King's never gone this long." Sam paced the dock.

"The rowboat's gone," Sam said, "her life jacket, too." At least she's wearing one, he thought.

"Look," said Robert. He pointed to the buzzards circling the far shore.

Sam grabbed the binoculars from the shed. "That looks like our rowboat tied up across the cove. Something's wrong. I'm going over." He slid the canoe into the water, grabbed a paddle, tossed a life jacket in the boat.

"I have my cell phone with me. I'll call you as soon as I check out the rowboat and those buzzards. What's your phone number?"

Robert fished a scrap of paper and a pencil from his pocket and wrote down two numbers for Sam. "One's my cell, the other is the house phone. Don't you want me to go with you?"

"No, it's better for you to stay here where you'll be able to get help if I need it."

"Don't you think you should take a flashlight just in case? It'll be dark soon."

"Good idea. There's one in the shed. Grab it for me, please." In the canoe he buckled on the life jacket. Robert passed him the flashlight and Sam pushed off.

The doorbell rang as Dixie Lee turned off the oven. Smiling, she opened the door. Charlie stepped inside and hugged her, kissed her cheek, handed her a bouquet of freshly picked marigolds from his yard. "Hey, Dixie Lee," he said.

"Hey, Charlie. Thank you for the lovely marigolds." She sneezed twice. "Unfortunately, I'm allergic to many flowers. Looks like these are in my sneeze zone." She sneezed again.

"Honey, I'm sorry. I'll take them outside to the trash bins." He reached for the flowers.

"Oh, no you don't. They're too gorgeous to dump. I'll put them in a vase and take them out to the porch. That way I can enjoy them but not be exposed."

Minutes later they sipped red wine and munched on cheese and crackers. Charlie looked at the lady sitting beside him on the love seat. He reached for her hand. "Dixie Lee, I believe you came back into my life for a reason. I treasure every minute I've spent with you, will feel the same way in the future. I honestly believe that Annie and Ernie would be thrilled that we've found each other, that we've been given a second chance at happiness. I don't know if you feel the same way, but if you do, then I think. . . ."

Charlie's cell phone rang.

Don't answer it, Charlie, Dixie Lee thought. Please don't answer it. My answer to your unasked question is yes. Please, Charlie, don't answer the phone.

Charlie glanced at Caller ID and frowned. Sam had never called his cell before. Something must have happened to Aurora. Oh, Lord, he prayed, let Aurora be safe. Please. All thoughts of the marriage proposal he'd rehearsed flew away. Sam needed him. Precious Aurora needed him.

"What's wrong?" he said into the phone.

Sam hated to worry Charlie, but he prayed Aurora had talked to him earlier, maybe told Charlie what was bothering her, where she was going. "Charlie, have you talked to Aurora today?"

"No. What's wrong?"

"When I got home, she was gone. King and Little Guy aren't here either. Her purse and cell phone are in the house. Her car's in the garage. She took the rowboat; it's beached across the cove. I'm standing beside it right now. It's almost dark and Aurora is afraid of the dark. I'm surprised she's not home. Robert Reeves said that Aurora was worried about King and Little Guy. According to Robert, the dogs have been gone most of the day. King is a homebody, likes to be at Aurora's side. So I'm thinking that something has happened to either King or Aurora. Or both."

"Sam, I'm here at the lake, at Dixie Lee's condo in Sweetwater Cove. What can I do to help?"

"You're good friends with Sheriff Rogers, right?"

"I am."

"Do you think you could talk him into organizing a search party to look for her?"

"Maybe. I'll call you back when I know something."

"Thank you, Charlie. Thank you so much."

Robert Reeves checked caller ID and snatched up his phone when it rang. "Sam, have you found Aurora and the dogs?"

"No. And I need your help. Can you get my pontoon boat out of the boathouse and ready to go? Or do you need to head back to Roanoke tonight? If you do, I'll understand."

"I've talked to Jill. Both she and the baby are doing well. Jill will probably be able to come home tomorrow, the next day at the latest. I'm ready to do whatever you need me to do."

"Thanks. My plan is to go back to the house, pack a cooler with some food, and take it back over to the mountain. I'll leave it beside Aurora's rowboat. If she goes back to the boat while I'm looking for her, then she'll know that I'm looking and will at least have something to eat. I'll also leave a flashlight, her cell phone, and a note telling her folks are searching for her and to stay put." He explained to Robert that Charlie was in the process of asking Sheriff Rogers to send out a search party.

CHAPTER FORTY-ONE

Wednesday, 6:30 p.m.

"I'm positive you'll be glad you bought this house," Carole said to Win as she locked the door behind them. "It has the openness you were looking for, plus four bedrooms and four and a half baths. The main kitchen has everything anyone could want. And I love the granite countertops. The view is terrific, and the dock is big enough to house several boats and host a huge party." She smiled at him. "Yep, it's a really nice house. Good quality and tastefully decorated. If I could afford it, I would have bought it myself. This one's been my favorite ever since we first looked at it. I'm proud of you for making a decision, Win, and really glad you picked this one."

"Took me long enough, didn't it? Sorry I've had you running all over for days, and finally decided on the third house you showed me. I should have just bought it the first time I saw it."

"I can understand that you wanted to see what else was out there, look at all your options. I'd do the same thing if I were shelling out that much money for a house."

"You said that most of the furnishings could go with the house if I want them. I like the contemporary style and the colors. How soon would I have to decide if I want the whole package?" Win took her elbow, guided her around a flower pot at the edge of the walkway.

"Thanks. I didn't see that."

"Wouldn't be good if you hurt yourself, Carole."

"No, I don't need to break anything, that's for sure. About the house furnishings—I think the sooner you decide, the better. Do you want the offer to include them?"

Win looked at his watch. "It's 6:30. Want to get something to eat? We can celebrate as I sign the papers. By the time we're finished eating, I will have made up my mind if I want all the furniture or not. You have everything you need in your briefcase, right?"

Carole laughed. "Guess you've gotten to know me pretty well. Yes, I have all the necessary paperwork with me. And yes, a celebratory dinner would be delightful. You pick the restaurant."

She felt like a huge weight had been lifted off her. She could pay her mortgage for months off the commission she'd receive from the sale of the $1,299,000 home. She'd expected Win to quibble about the price; he hadn't. She now realized how tense she'd become. It would be great to unwind with a glass of wine.

"Why don't you relax and let me drive. I know exactly where I want to go, but it's a surprise." Win opened the passenger door for her. "Your carriage awaits, my lady."

Carole smiled as he closed the door, warned herself that he could be charming when he wanted to be. "Afraid this clunker won't handle like your Porsche, Win. Are you sure you want to drive?"

"Absolutely."

"I just realized that I didn't see the Porsche when I picked you up. Does the bed and breakfast have a garage where you keep it?" She buckled her seat belt.

"Yeah, there's a four-car garage behind the house for guests. I park my car there."

"Funny. I've walked all the way around that house. I've never seen a huge garage back there. Or even a small one."

"It's brand new. The owner said he just finished building it. I'm only the second guest to use it." Win braked to avoid a skunk strolling across the highway.

They rode in silence for the next eight miles.

Carole closed her eyes, dreamed of how she'd handle her commission. Maybe she'd save half, put the other half in checking. Luke was a good businessman; she'd ask him if investing some of the savings in a six-month or twelve-month CD would be a good idea. Guess that would depend on how much interest the savings account would pay and what her estimated expenses for the next year would be. Yeah, she'd ask Luke.

Luke. How good his name sounded to her. She could almost feel the warmth of his touch, the deep love in his voice, the way he held her when they danced. She could picture the smile in his eyes. She'd call him tonight when she returned home from dinner, tell him that the next week would be for him. No, for them. If he could afford to take some time off, they could drive up the Blue Ridge Parkway, enjoy the changing colors of autumn, behave like silly out-of-state tourists.

Maybe they could make some detours, stop at Gross Orchard for apples, tour the area wineries. She licked her lips in anticipation.

Aurora would be thrilled to hear that Win had bought a house and that Carole's dealings with him would soon end. She and Aurora had been friends since elementary school. Even though they'd not seen much of each other since they went off to separate colleges, they'd remained in touch. In fact, Carole had been a bridesmaid in Aurora and Sam's wedding. She grinned, remembering the times when Aurora's vivid imagination had landed the two of them in hot water. When Aurora had warned Carole about Win just because he had scary eyes, Carole had almost laughed. She was glad she hadn't. Before she called Luke tonight, she'd call Aurora, tell her that all was well, she now had some money and could pay her bills, and she could stop worrying.

Win looked at Carole. She seemed so peaceful, so happy. Well, she should be, he thought. Her commission on the sale of the house is responsible for that. I'm responsible for that. Carole should be grateful. She should be glad to show me just how grateful. Money. Everything boils down to money. I don't care how often women deny it, the fact is that money—the more the better—is all-important. More important than love, family, friends, religion, anything. And it doesn't matter how they get it. Carole thinks she loves Luke, that she wants to spend the rest of her life with him. Love is a bunch of bull. We'll see what happens when she's given a choice. For her sake, she better make the right one.

Most women he'd known chose money over the elusive "true love." In Win's circle, those who didn't choose money often ended up destitute—or dead. Like the real estate agent in Nags Head a year ago, or the realtor in Hilton Head two years before that. And there were more. There'd always be more. Women—naive, gullible, romantic, plain stupid. He sighed. Can't live with 'em, can't live without 'em.

If she would play by his rules, dinner tonight would be an incredible experience for both of them. Had Luke ever arranged for a private, catered dinner? He doubted it. Had Luke ever uncorked a $150 bottle of wine for Carole? On his income? Of course not. He pictured what Luke would consider an elegant meal in a restaurant and laughed.

Carole opened her eyes, looked at Win. "You laughed. What's so funny?"

"Oh, nothing. I was just thinking about something. Sorry I woke you. We'll be there in about five minutes. You can close your eyes again if you'd like."

"Where are we going?" Carole peered out the window into deepening shadows.

"I told you it was a surprise."

"I know, but I don't remember any restaurants in this neighborhood. To be honest, I don't remember this neighborhood."

Win slowed and turned onto a paved drive, stopped at an iron gate, pulled a remote from his jacket pocket, and punched in a number. The gate swung open, then closed after he drove the car through. Victorian-style lamp posts lined both sides of the drive for a quarter mile. A huge stone house stood at the end of the driveway. Parked in front was a white paneled truck with "Cabaret Catering" painted on the side.

"Win, where are we? This can't be just a restaurant."

He looked at her and grinned. "You're right. It's a private club owned by the caterer. I've rented a dining room for dinner. Carole, get ready to experience the night of your life."

"I agreed to dinner only." Don't panic, Carole, she said to herself. Be calm. Don't let Win know you're nervous.

"And dinner you'll get, my lady." And a whole lot more than that. Whether good or bad depends on you, he thought.

Carole forced a laugh. "My goodness, Win. You certainly cut no corners. Will you at least tell me where we are?"

"Why, Carole, you sound concerned. You're not scared, are you?"

"Don't be silly. I just always like to know where I am, especially a place this incredible. I can hardly wait to see what it looks like inside." She looked at him, faked a smile. A valet appeared, opened her car door and helped her out.

"So won't you be a good boy and tell me where we are? Pretty please?" Carole watched the valet drive her car around the corner of the house and out of sight.

"I'm pleased, Carole. I thought you'd like this place. It's special; so are you. We're on a 400-acre private estate that straddles the Franklin County/Pittsylvania County line. The sole purpose of the owner is to entertain the rich and famous from all over the world. And to make gobs of money, of course. Few locals know it's here."

Win took her elbow, walked her up the marble steps to the front porch and rang the doorbell. A butler opened the door and ushered them inside. The 14-foot high mahogany doors closed behind them with a soft thud. Uneasiness ran through Carole. She trembled.

CHAPTER FORTY-TWO

Charlie paced the floor while Dixie Lee put dinner on the table for the second time that night. He pulled out his cell, stuck it back in his pocket. He'd already called Sam twice; he should wait a little longer before trying again, but he couldn't help being anxious.

After much talking, Sheriff Rogers had agreed to send a search party to look for Aurora. The only problem was that Aurora hadn't been gone long enough to file an official missing persons report. For now, the searchers would all be off-duty volunteers.

"Supper's ready, Charlie, dear," said Dixie Lee from beside him. She put her arm around his waist, rested her head against his shoulder. "Are you ready to eat?"

He looked at the sweet lady beside him, her eyes full of concern, and nodded. "This is not what I had planned for our evening. I know I've been a wet blanket tonight, haven't given you the attention you deserve, even caused your wonderful meal to be cold so that you had to reheat it." Was that a tear in her eye?

"That's okay, Charlie. I understand. I'm worried about Aurora, too. Even though I've known her only a short time, I care about her a great deal. She's a nice person and a good friend. And if supper's too cold, we can just zap our plates in the microwave again." Dixie Lee guided him to the table. "Will you bless our food?"

Back at his house, Sam stowed peanut butter crackers, water bottles, two cans of sardines, pork and beans, saltine crackers and Vienna sausage into a cooler.

"Add these cookies, Sam," said Robert as he came in the kitchen, "and these candy bars. How about some blankets and a first-aid kit, too? And maybe some dog food for Little Guy and King?"

"Good thinking, Robert. We'll need to put the dog food in something other animals can't tear into. There's a big popcorn can in the pantry if you'll get it. Just dump the popcorn in the trash. While you're in there, look on the shelf on the right just inside the door and grab the box of plastic forks and spoons." He dropped a bunch of bananas and a few apples in the cooler.

Five minutes later the two men loaded Aurora's Jeep with the packed items. "Just thought of something else," said Sam. He dashed back inside the house and yanked Aurora's down coat, ski cap and gloves from the hall closet.

"Good idea," said Robert when Sam stuffed them in the back seat. Sam nodded, cranked up the Jeep and drove to the dock.

CHAPTER FORTY-THREE

Brilliant smears of red, gold, orange and gray shone over the distant mountains on the Franklin County side of the lake. Aurora watched the sun drop below the trees. Soon darkness would come. She couldn't remember if the moon would be full. She hoped so. She figured she'd better get her bearings while she could still see the mountain peaks on the horizon.

The dampness of late fall chilled her. A heavy jacket or at least a sweater would feel really good over her thin, long-sleeved shirt. How could I have been so stupid as to come to the mountain without preparation? Be prepared, her dad had always told her. She patted her pants pocket; at least she had her dad's Boy Scout knife. She hoped she wouldn't need it.

She stared at the skyline, recognized Turkey Cock Mountain in Franklin County, knew that if she turned left and kept the lake in sight she'd eventually wind up where she'd beached the rowboat—as long as she didn't fall in the water. The last rays vanished. In the darkness, the chances of stumbling over a root, stepping in a hole, or sliding into the lake soared. Not a fun thing to do this time of year.

As she trudged the rough shoreline, she wondered what Sam had thought when he'd arrived home and she wasn't there. She hoped this wasn't one of those evenings when he'd have a last-minute meeting and call home to say he'd be late for dinner, because she wouldn't be there to answer the phone. And if he called her cell, he wouldn't get an answer. He'd figure then that something was wrong. Surely he was looking for her. She hoped he wasn't too worried. After all, she told herself, this is *my* mountain, Mom and I rode horses on it when I was growing up. I'm in no real danger. Right?

A twig snapped behind her. The hairs on the back of her neck stood up. She wheeled around, twisted her left ankle and fell to the ground. Her hands felt around for a root, a branch, anything to grab hold of to stop her downward slide. She cried out when her injured foot hit a stump. Lying on the ground, she waited for the pain to subside. Look on the bright side Aurora, she thought. At least you've stopped moving.

A rustling in the brush four feet away erased all thought of pain. Something—or someone—is stalking me, she thought. She eased her hand into her pants pocket, pulled out the pocket knife, opened the blade, and waited. The rustling ceased.

"Who's there?" she called out.

No answer.

"Show yourself." Nothing. Lord, she thought, am I going to die? Please not like this, Lord. Please.

Something—was it human or animal—moved closer. Whatever it was, she wouldn't go down without a fight. Aurora raised the knife above her head.

A familiar whine stopped the downward thrust of the knife in mid-air. "Little Guy! Am I glad to see you." She put the knife back in her pocket and wrapped her arms around his neck. He licked her face. Funny how much safer she felt now. She wished she'd brought a leash. Again she chided herself for being unprepared.

"This time you won't run off and leave me all alone." She grabbed his collar with one hand and unbuckled her belt with the other.

"Down, Little Guy." He stretched out on the rocky ground. "Good boy. Now please stay long enough for me to hook this belt to your collar." She ran one end of the belt through his collar and pulled it taut. "Glad you're tall enough and my belt long enough so I won't have to bend over when we walk. This isn't perfect, but it will work. It has to. I can't let you run off again. Wish you could tell me where King is."

When she tried to stand, pain seared through her ankle. She winced. "Not good, Little Guy. Hope I haven't broken it. Don't think I'll be able to put much weight on it. Nope, not good."

I need a walking stick, Aurora thought. Still holding on to one end of the belt, she crawled through twigs and leaves until she found a stick. Using the makeshift cane to brace herself, she hauled herself upright.

"I need to go right, Little Guy, get closer to the lake, follow the shoreline to the rowboat. But I can't see the lake or the shoreline. And I don't want to fall in the water."

Holding onto the belt, she hobbled a few yards and stopped to catch her breath. "This isn't working. I can't limp along uneven ground for more than a few steps at a time."

Little Guy barked.

"Why do I keep talking to you? I know you're smart, but surely not smart enough to understand me."

The terrier barked again. "Guess hearing my own voice makes me feel safer."

Her progress would be at turtle-speed, but she had no choice.

"Standing around gabbing won't get us anywhere. Let's go." Putting her weight on the stick in her left hand, she held the belt in her right hand and started out.

Crack! The crude cane broke in two. Aurora tumbled several yards down the hill, hit her head on a log, and lost consciousness. Little Guy's improvised leash fell from her hand. The Jack Russell terrier nudged her arm, licked her face. When she didn't respond he let out a high-pitched bark.

Two minutes later, Aurora moaned, rubbed the back of her head, felt the knot already forming. Her head hurt like crazy. She hadn't felt blood, but she was a little dizzy.

Little Guy cocked his ears, barked again. He dashed into the woods, yelped, returned to Aurora. She reached for his leash but missed. He whined, ran a few feet, stopped, looked back at Aurora, and disappeared into the night.

"No! Little Guy, come back!"

But he didn't come.

CHAPTER FORTY-FOUR

Wednesday, 6:45 p.m.

Sam guided the pontoon boat to shore. Robert grabbed one end of the line, stepped onto land and tied the line around a pine tree.

The two hauled the cooler from the boat and set it down near the rowboat. Knowing that if Aurora returned to the boat she'd find the supplies, they loaded the blankets, first-aid kit, dog food and flashlight into the rowboat. Sam placed Aurora's coat, hat and gloves on top of the pile.

Sam jumped when his cell phone rang. "This is Charlie. Any luck?"

"Not yet. We just arrived at the mountain a few minutes ago. We've unloaded supplies for Aurora. I'm anxious to start searching. Have you talked to Sheriff Rogers recently?"

"He called a few minutes ago. The search party has reached the dirt access road running up the mountain. They plan to drive to the top of the ridge, separate into three teams and search on foot. You'll probably see some of their lights as they move across the mountain."

"Good."

"Almost forgot to tell you. The sheriff wanted you to know that he had no trouble finding willing volunteers. They all know Aurora's my niece."

"I appreciate that."

"I'll go help you look, Sam. I can be on the access road in 30 minutes."

"I'd rather you stay where you are, Charlie. Sometimes cell phones don't get a signal on the mountain. I think you'll serve us better if you act as a command post. Even if you can't reach everyone, surely you'd be able to communicate with some of the searchers, forward info to the rest of us as needed."

"I'd rather help search, but I see your point. If you find Aurora or need me for any reason, call me. I'll be at Dixie Lee's. She insisted I spend the night at her place, said I'd be closer in case— well, that I'd be closer. Of course, I could always stay at your house." Charlie looked at Dixie Lee sitting on the couch, raised an eyebrow.

She smiled and shook her head.

CHAPTER FORTY-FIVE

Wednesday, 7:00 p.m.

Carole stood in the 25-foot high foyer amid old-world elegance. Her apprehension temporarily forgotten, she turned slowly around, fascinated by the antique paintings on the walls. To her left and right, two magnificent wide marble staircases curved up turret walls on both sides of the foyer and came together to form a landing on the second floor.

"This way, Carole," Win said to her.

She didn't budge.

"Carole." He touched her arm.

"What?"

"The butler wants us to follow him to the pub."

"The pub?"

"Yes." Win laughed. "I can tell you're in a state of shock. This house is really spectacular. There's a lot more to see."

"I can't believe I've never heard of this place. Nobody I know—except for you—knows it's here. Well, I guess the two county treasurers must, but they're certainly tight-lipped."

With Win's hand on her arm, they followed the butler through a maze of rooms to the pub in the rear of the house. A bartender stood behind a massive mahogany bar. Across the room, a wall of floor-to-ceiling windows looked out onto a lighted terrace, garden and free-form swimming pool. Arranged around the room were a dozen tables, each with chairs for four. Persian rugs covered portions of the parquet flooring.

"If you're interested, we could walk down to the stable area in a little while. The horses here receive the best care possible and the stable is nicer than most homes. Cleaner, too."

"I'll pass on the stable. I like horses okay, but I'm not what you'd call a horse nut like Aurora is." Carole looked at her watch. "Speaking of Aurora, I should probably call her. I told her I'd call around seven o'clock. It's 7:20 now." She reached for her phone.

Win grabbed her wrist. "Can't it wait 'til later, Carole? Believe me, there's lots more for you to see. Aurora will understand."

"Well, okay."

After the bartender poured them a glass of wine, Win said, "We must make a toast." He held up his wine glass. "To the most gorgeous real estate agent I've ever met." Carole blushed as their glasses clinked. Win ushered her through an archway into another room on the back of the house.

"Do you come here often? You seem to know your way around."

"You could say that. I've done some favors for the owner, so he reciprocates by letting me use the facilities whenever I wish." Win looked at her. "Stick with me, Carole, and you can live like a queen, come here as often as you wish."

She said nothing.

"This is the billiard/game room. Do you play pool?" He swallowed a sip of wine, set the glass down, and picked up a cue stick.

"I played a lot in college, was pretty good back then. But I haven't played since. That's been a while." She sipped her wine. "This is excellent, Win. What is it?"

"Glad you like it. And it should be excellent. The bottle cost over $100.00." Win racked the balls and handed Carole a cue stick.

"I didn't come here to play pool, Win. I came for dinner only, remember. Luke's expecting me to be home when he calls at 10:00." She laid the stick on the pool table.

"Just one game, Carole. It won't take that long. Pretty please." He tried to hand her the cue stick.

"Monsieur Ford, Mademoiselle, the chef asked me to announce that dinner will be ready in ten minutes," said the maître de from the doorway.

"Can't he hold it a little longer?" Win asked.

"Oh, no, Monsieur. The dinner he is preparing for you must be served as soon as it is ready or the taste will not be so delicious."

Carole was glad they would eat soon. She looked at Win, didn't like the expression on his face. He was not happy. Did he have other plans for her this evening besides dinner, plans she wouldn't like, plans that dinner had temporarily foiled? She wanted to leave, but how?

When they reached the pub room, the maître de showed them to a table in front of the large window. He pulled out a chair for Carole, seated her, and with a flourish removed the white linen napkin from her plate, unfolded it and placed it on her lap. "Your dinner tonight consists of dishes famous in the East of France, in the Alsace region. Your soup is *Soupe aux abats d'oie.*"

"And the English translation?" asked Carole.

"As you Americans call it, goose giblet soup." Carole forced herself not to gag. "It is very delicious, a delicacy."

He motioned to the waiter who set filled bowls on gold chargers in front of Carole and Win.

"Smells wonderful," said Win.

"What's our entrée?" She was almost afraid to ask.

"Rognons de veau au Chablis, also known as calves' kidneys in wine and mustard sauce," said the maître de.

She opened her mouth to protest, thought better of it and said nothing. Carole looked around the room. No other guests were visible. "Are we the only ones here?" she asked the maître de.

"Oh, no, Mademoiselle. The others, they dine in other dining rooms, the guest houses, or in their suites tonight. That is good, *oui*? You and Monsieur will have more privacy."

Strange, thought Carole. She finished her wine and set the empty glass on the table. Admiring the sterling silver place settings, she picked up the teaspoon and traced her finger over the ornate scrollwork on the handle.

Win watched her until she set the teaspoon back on the table. He covered her hand with his.

"Look at this gorgeous china, Win." Ignoring his gesture, she pulled her hand away, picked up her plate and turned it over. "It says 'Theodore Haviland, Limoges, FRANCE.'"

"Carole, look at me."

"Win, can you read what's stamped here?" She pointed to the indentation in the plate. "It looks like an 'H' and then something and then 'L.' Wish I had a magnifying glass."

Scowling, Win turned and caught the bartender's eye. Carole put her plate back on the table and watched Win's and the bartender's reflections in the window. The bartender held up a small bottle. Win nodded. The bartender signaled Win with a thumbs-up, smiled, and dropped something in a glass of wine.

Carole forced herself not to turn around and stare at the bartender when he walked to their table with two glasses in his hands. He set the wine on the table, removed the empties. She knew one of the glasses contained more than just an expensive wine, and her instinct told her that that particular glass was meant for her. Win wanted to drug her. Somehow she had to get away from him, from this place. But how could she do that when she didn't even know where she was or where the valet had taken her car?

CHAPTER FORTY-SIX

Alone on the mountain, the sounds in the darkness seemed louder, more threatening than Aurora remembered. Was that a coyote or a dog howling in the distance? She'd felt much safer when Little Guy was with her. Now she had no one—not Sam, not Little Guy, not King, not even daylight. And she was cold and hungry and thirsty. And exhausted. Her eyes still couldn't quite focus. She buried her head in her hands and sobbed. Her nose started running and she reached into her pocket for a tissue.

"I can't believe it. I didn't even bring a tissue with me. I always have a tissue. So along with everything else, I can't even blow my nose." She wiped her nose with her shirt sleeve, glanced up at the dark, starless sky. "Sorry, Mom."

Leaning her back against a giant poplar, Aurora closed her eyes. Her strength, like her spirits and Little Guy, had deserted her. She would stay here until daylight unless Sam—or some wild, carnivorous animal—found her.

Sleep came and went. In her dreams, a hawk pecked out her eyes, a large buck ran his rack through her body while buzzards cleaned the flesh from her bones, bats bit her and tangled themselves in her hair, and Sam chose another woman as his dance partner. Nocturnal animals, intent on tearing her into little pieces, closed in. And now she was about to be gobbled up by a bear.

A bear?

Aurora's hands closed around fur. She opened her eyes and screamed. She felt his breath on her face. Screaming again, she hit at his head with her fist, groped the ground beside her for a stick to defend herself.

The bear licked her face, whined. Bears don't act like this, she thought. The bear barked, nudged her arm.

"Bears don't bark, either. King, it's you! I found you. Well, no, you found me. Oh, thank you, God. Thank you, King." Whining, King crawled onto her lap. She hugged him to her, stroked his head and back. For several minutes dog and woman rejoiced at finding one another.

Running her hands over his body, Aurora felt for cuts or any injuries on her beloved dog. In the dark she couldn't detect any problems, feel any blood.

"I think you're okay, King, but I'll check again when daylight comes. Okay, boy, this is the way it is. I'm kind of lost, my head hurts, my ankle is either sprained or broken, and I'm hungry and thirsty. So what would you suggest?"

King yelped, jumped to his feet, grabbed her shirt sleeve, sniffed it several times.

"Yeah, I know. There's yucky nose junk on it. But it'll wash out."

King barked.

"I know you want me to get up, but you'll have to help." The Lab lowered his head, nudged it under her arm. She put one hand against the tree trunk, the other hand on King's shoulders, pushed herself into a standing position. "Guess you're right. We can't stay here all night. But why not?"

King barked again.

With her left hand, Aurora grabbed hold of his red collar and put her weight on his muscular frame. "I'm ready, boy. Let's go."

CHAPTER FORTY-SEVEN

Wednesday 8:00 p.m.

Jasper Smoot popped a Valium and swallowed it without any water. All his life he'd been proud that he could down pills dry and his perfect baby brother couldn't. That was one of the few things he did better than his perfect baby brother. Jasper didn't take Valium often, but today he needed one. Depending on how the rest of the evening went, he just might take another.

The visit from the cops today had seemed to go well. He thought about how his lip had twitched during questioning, was pretty sure they hadn't noticed. Even if they had, they'd never suspect that the twitching was a nervous habit, one that had also given him away when he lied to folks who knew him well. Thank goodness only his parents and his perfect baby brother knew what the twitching meant. They lied a lot, too, except his mother called her lies prevarications. He figured she'd learned that word in college. He'd caught his kin folks in some really big ones—except for his step-dad who was the most honest, gullible person he'd ever known, a complete opposite of Jasper's biological dad.

The two cops were waiting on his front porch when he drove into the driveway late this afternoon. They asked more questions about Hessie, wanted the names and phone numbers of all her caregivers and the days and hours the women had worked for the past 30 days. They'd watched him carefully to see his reaction when they told him they would be calling and interviewing each person. He'd lied and told them his records were at his office, that he'd be happy to get them tomorrow. That seemed to satisfy them temporarily.

Jasper opened a notebook and ran his finger down the list of caregivers. His finger stopped at Etta's name listed under "Substitutes." She was the one who concerned him the most. From what Butch said about Etta, he was sure she'd blab everything she knew, give the cops Butch's name, tell them how Butch had hit Hessie. If they questioned Butch long enough, he figured Butch would tell them all about his orders to drop Hessie off on the mountain. Damn that stupid Butch.

Another horrible thought hit him. The cops would surely search Butch's black van if they hadn't already done so. Would they find any evidence that Hessie and Tom Southerland had been in it?

Jasper's lip twitched. Only one sure way out of this dilemma— Etta and Butch must die. And soon. And then he realized someone else needed killing. The cops had mentioned that the kid across the street from Hessie had seen three men (Butch, Shorty and Otis) loading appliances and who they now believed to be a dead Tom Southerland into a black van last Friday night, the same van the kid saw early Monday morning. The kid must die, too. Jasper had never thought about killing a kid. Now several people had to die all because of stupid Butch screwing everything up. He looked forward to killing Butch himself.

For this many killings he'd need help, though—intelligent, cold-blooded help. He couldn't enlist Otis to do it, either; he was Butch's huntin' buddy. But there was someone he could always count on. Jasper picked up the phone and dialed.

CHAPTER FORTY-EIGHT

With King's help, Aurora covered more ground than she'd expected. And her ankle didn't hurt nearly as much as it had earlier. In fact, she could now move without holding onto King, even though she moved slowly. Maybe she'd just twisted it a little instead of spraining or breaking it. She had no idea where King was leading her, but as long as she had him with her she knew she'd be safe. At first she thought he would take her to the rowboat, but that hadn't happened.

To keep her mind off her fatigue and the blackness that surrounded her, she thought about all the things that had happened in less than a week and made a mental list of them.

Friday night I met Blanche Southerland for the first time. On Saturday, I helped Hessie Davis and met Dixie Lee Cunningham. Sam tried to find Tom Southerland, Sam and I met Kurt and Carole's client Winston Ford—didn't like him! Found Tom's cap in toilet. Uncle Charlie came to lake. Dixie Lee phoned, said Hessie remembered license number. Uncle Charlie remembered a Dixie Lee.

Jill and Robert stopped by on Sunday. Jill's pregnant. On Monday morning, I heard that a body had been found in a freezer in the lake. (Learned Tues. that body was Tom Southerland.) Hessie disappeared. I stayed with Dixie Lee, saw Win without sunglasses, recognized his eyes. Kurt left message saying he saw black van at Hessie's house Sunday night. Car slammed into Jill's car, Jill taken to a Roanoke hospital. Brought Little Guy home. Kurt gave me license number of van—same number Hessie remembered.

> *King and Little Guy disappeared on Wednesday. I rowed over to Smith Mtn. to look for dogs. Found and lost Little Guy, hurt ankle, King found me.*

Aurora jumped when King woofed and yanked on her sleeve. He whined, barked. A familiar bark a short distance away answered him.

"Little Guy, here boy," Aurora called. She heard an answering yap-yap, but he didn't come dashing eagerly through the woods as she'd expected him to.

"King, get Little Guy." King only whined. "What in the world is wrong with you two dogs? Okay, King, if Little Guy won't come to me, you take me to him. Let's go."

With her hand resting on his back, Aurora and King forged ahead. Minutes later a dog reunion took place. Little Guy and King acted like they'd been apart for days. Little Guy seemed to feel no remorse for leaving Aurora alone several hours ago. She grabbed hold of him. Good, her belt was still around his collar. She'd worried when he ran off earlier that the belt would get caught on something, that he'd be trapped.

"Doggie," said a weak voice a few yards away.

Startled, Aurora hushed the dogs and listened.

"Doggie," called the voice again.

Aurora couldn't believe what she heard. "Hessie, is that you?" she called. "Where are you?"

"Momma, I want a cookie."

Aurora pinpointed Hessie's location and hurried to her as quickly as she could over the rough ground.

"Oh, Hessie, dear. You're alive. Oh my goodness. It's Wednesday; you wandered off Monday morning. Have you been on the mountain all this time?"

Aurora sat on the ground and held Hessie in her arms, stroked her matted hair, pulled Hessie's torn red robe tighter around her. She ran her hands over Hessie's body and legs. One foot was bare; a ragged slipper hanging together by threads partially covered the other foot. To Aurora, Hessie's feet felt like chunks of ice. "However in the world did you make it this far?"

King whined, nuzzled Hessie and Aurora. Aurora grabbed hold of the belt on Little Guy's collar and pulled him close to her. "King, get Sam. Go, boy. Find Sam. Hurry."

The Lab licked her chin, barked, and disappeared into the night.

Little Guy tugged against the belt. "No, you stay here with me."

With one hand holding Little Guy's makeshift leash, Aurora removed her sneakers and socks. As gently as she could, she put one sock on Hessie's bare foot and replaced the mangled slipper with the other sock. Though not the cleanest around, Aurora's body-warm socks should feel good to Hessie's frigid feet.

Hessie sighed, snuggled against Aurora. "Momma," she said, and fell asleep cradled in Aurora's arms. In the distance Aurora heard King barking.

CHAPTER FORTY-NINE

Wednesday, 8:20 p.m.

"May I please speak to Kurt Karver?" asked the caller.

"I'm sorry, Kurt isn't here right now. He's at his digital camera class, should be home around nine. May I take a message? I'm his mother."

"What a coincidence. Kurt's digital camera class is the reason I'm calling." Jasper snatched up a sales insert from last Sunday's newspaper.

"Really? And why is that?"

What luck, he thought, as he stared at the digital camera ads right in front of him. He selected the most expensive camera on the page. "Your son—and you, Mrs. Karver, as a loving mother should be so very proud—has been selected to use, free of charge for six months, a Canon Rebel XT EOS digital camera. This camera has 8.0 megapixels, Mrs. Karver, and a 1.8" LCD. There's also a CMOS sensor and DIGIC II image processor. Isn't that amazing?"

"Mr. ...? I'm sorry. I didn't catch your name. I have absolutely no idea what you're talking about. And how is it that my son was, as you call it, 'selected'?"

"We drew his name from the list of people taking the digital camera class. Believe me, Mrs. Karver, there is no obligation to your son. Or to you. All we ask is that he evaluate the camera after using it for six months."

"Well, I guess that's okay. I'll have him call you. What's your phone number again?"

"It's hard to reach me. I'll give Kurt a call at, say, 9:15 tonight?"

"I'm sure he'll look forward to hearing from you. Goodbye."

"Goodbye, Mrs. Karver. And have a nice evening."

Jasper Smoot smiled and hung up the phone. He could hardly believe his good fortune—offering the use of an expensive digital camera to a camera buff would certainly not be refused. Soon Kurt Karver would be a dead camera buff. He grinned, wondered what kind of camera the cops would use when they snapped Kurt's picture.

CHAPTER FIFTY

At *La Grande Maison*, Carole tried to hide her fear. She'd heard a lot about drugs dropped in drinks, but had never experienced them herself. And she refused to be a victim. She must think, figure out how to get away from the man sitting beside her. She looked at his eyes. They'd changed. Even though a smile was on his face, his huge grays seemed sinister now. Aurora was right. Winston Ford was dangerous. She wished she'd listened to her friend. Now she'd have to play along with him, wait for her chance to escape.

"Carole, snap out of your daydream. Didn't you hear me?" Win reached over and caressed her cheek.

"No, I'm sorry, Win. It's just that this place is so overwhelming, so breathtaking." She smiled a smile she didn't feel. "I know there's not enough time before dinner for you to show me around—the chef would send someone to drag us back if we left the table—but will you please describe the layout of the house and grounds for me? Will you do that for me?"

"Why so interested, Carole?"

Playing to his gigantic ego, she said "Win, my little brain can't comprehend such a place as this. I love houses, especially estates like this one, although I've not had the good fortune to visit one this extraordinary. Don't forget that I'm in real estate." She leaned toward him, put her hand on his arm, said softly, "Will you bring me back here, Win? When I can stay longer?"

If the situation hadn't been serious, she would have laughed at the puzzled expression on his face. She wondered what he'd do now with the drugged wine he'd arranged for her to consume. She figured he'd go ahead with his plan.

"Now about the layout. . . ."

Win traced his finger across the linen tablecloth in an attempt to show Carole the floor plan of the house.

"I must be dense. I'm sorry. I could understand it much better, though, if you could draw it on a piece of paper. Would that be possible?" Carole smiled, giggled. "Oh, what a silly thing for me to say. Of course you could draw it. I've finally realized that, for you, anything's possible."

"I'll be right back." Win stood up and hurried toward the bar for a pencil and some paper.

Carole watched his movement in the window's reflection. When positive neither Win nor the bartender would catch her, she switched wine glasses.

When he returned, Win sketched a rough floor plan of the house on a piece of paper. "You haven't tasted your wine, Carole. It's delicious." He sipped his, set his glass down.

Carole took a swallow. "Yum, you're right. Delicious." She smiled at him. He grinned back at her, drank more from the Waterford crystal wine goblet.

Pointing to the house plan, she said, "Now where approximately is that stable you mentioned earlier? And are there any other outbuildings other than the guest houses?"

"There are four tennis courts, two 18-hole golf courses, a putting green, a clubhouse, and an exercise building with a spa and indoor pool. On the lake side is a marina with a boardwalk leading to a few buildings equipped with top-of-the-line clothing, gift shops, and nautical stuff." Win quickly drew them on the map.

"The lake you mentioned. Do you mean Smith Mountain Lake?"

"Yeah, but it's real private here."

Five minutes later, Carole stared down at a crude layout of the house, the grounds, and the waterfront. She now knew there were ten guest houses—two with five bedrooms, two with four, two with three, and four with two. All bedrooms had private baths, and all guest houses were equipped with designer kitchens and high-speed internet hookup.

The main building housed six suites, each with two bedrooms, two and a half baths, and a great room equipped with a luxurious kitchenette. All suites were on the third floor. Each suite had its own elevator and private balcony. Carole had already seen the billiard/game room, the pub room, and the enormous foyer. Win told her that a dining room with a banquet-sized table with seating for up to 60 people was behind the pub. The back wall in the pub could slide open when needed to host a larger crowd. The library, on the first floor to the left of the foyer and in the front of the house, contained volumes of rare books, along with the classics, contemporary novels and important nonfiction. A computer room equipped with eight computers, printers, a fax and high-speed internet adjoined the library. She studied the house's floor plan and the layout of the grounds. It didn't take her long to memorize the drawing.

"So what do you think, Carole? Is this place nice or what?"

"This is the most fabulous place I've ever heard of, much less experienced personally. What's it called?"

"*La Grande Maison*—The Big House. Which it definitely is, as you see."

"You were so sweet to introduce me to all this elegance. The 'commodities' you said you deal in must bring in loads of money in order for you to live like this."

"I earn enough." He smiled, drank from his wine glass.

Carole watched for signs that the drug intended for her was working on him. Nothing yet. She hoped she could stall his advances that she knew would be coming her way. She sipped her wine.

"This wine is fabulous, Win." She wanted to make him think the drug was beginning to work, so she giggled. "You know, I'm beginning to feel a little giddy. Why, honey chile, you've barely tasted yours. Drink up, *mon ami*."

Win watched her carefully and lifted his glass. "To you, Carole Barco." He drank deeply.

Carole looked at her watch. Timing was everything. If she remembered what she'd read and heard about this type of drug, the effects should be noticeable within 15-30 minutes, would last for four to eight hours. Would Win need to consume all of his wine, and would he be incapacitated for as long as she would have been? After all, he weighed probably 60 pounds more than she did.

She looked across the room. The bartender smiled knowingly at her as he dried glasses and put them away. Carole faked another giggle, smiled back at him and waved. Not this time, you jerk, she thought. I won't be the one sedated. But neither you nor he will know that until it's too late.

"You know, Win, I've changed my mind. Earlier you offered to show me the stables and I declined. But I would like to see the boardwalk and docks. Is there a place by the water where we could buy another glass of wine? Or maybe even a bottle?" She drained her wine and stood up. "Yum. That was good to the last drop."

Discretely folding the pencil-drawn map, she slipped it into her jacket pocket.

"I'd love to show you the boardwalk. It's not far from here." Win finished his wine. "Let's go, little lady." He took Carole's arm. She faked a slight stagger, smiled up at him. He waved to the bartender as they left the pub.

CHAPTER FIFTY-ONE

At exactly 9:15, Jasper Smoot dialed Kurt Karver's number. An ecstatic Kurt answered the phone. "My mom told me about winning the camera. She said all I have to do is use it for six months and review it. Like what kind of review do you guys want?"

"We'd want to know how easy the camera was to operate, how well you were able to understand the directions, what you thought of the quality of pictures you took, if you'd consider buying one just like it, that kind of thing."

"Yeah, I could do that." Kurt was excited. When he'd come home from his class and his mom had told him about the phone call, he'd immediately looked up the camera on the internet. He could hardly wait to start using it.

"How soon can I get it?"

Greedy kid, aren't you? Jasper wanted to say. Instead, he said, "Could you meet me in the Wal-Mart parking lot in Rocky Mount in, say, 30 minutes? I'd drop it off at your house, but I have another camera to deliver tonight."

"I don't know. Wait a sec while I go ask my parents." Kurt put the phone down, picked it up a minute later. "Hello?"

"Well, what did your parents say?"

"Sorry, mister, but both of them said no. Mom's too tired; Dad said he just got finished picking me up from my camera class and that it's too late to go back out."

"One of your parents would need to drive you?"

"Yes, sir. I don't have my driver's license yet. I'm only 13. You didn't know that?"

Damn. Jasper felt like hitting something, preferably Kurt or Butch or Etta. How could he have known the kid was only 13?

"No, Kurt, the form I pulled out of the contest jar gave only your name, address and phone number." Jasper scratched his head, tried to come up with another plan.

"I catch the school bus in the mornings at 7:30. Maybe we could meet at the bus stop tomorrow. Unless Mom decides to pick me up after school, I'll get home around 4:30."

"How would I recognize you out of a bunch of kids, Kurt?"

"No problem. Only Alice and I ride in the morning, and most times her mother drives her to school 'cause Alice is always running late and misses the school bus. Usually there're five who ride the bus home; only two of us are boys. I'm the tall, skinny one."

"Then I think we can work it out. I'll meet you in the morning. Think you can get there about 15 minutes early so I can go over the camera details with you?"

"Yes, sir." He gave Jasper directions to the bus stop.

"Fine, see you at 7:15 tomorrow morning then. Don't be late. Goodbye, Kurt. Have a nice evening."

Your last evening, he thought, as he hung up the phone.

CHAPTER FIFTY-TWO

Wednesday, 9:20 p.m.

"Aurora. King. Little Guy," yelled Sam. He and Robert had hollered those same words for over two hours with no satisfying results. Two dogs they didn't know had come and gone: a red bone coon hound and a young treeing walker.

"Hold up, Sam. I need a drink, and I have to rest for a few minutes." Robert opened his backpack and pulled out a water bottle.

"Good idea," said Sam. "I'm pretty hoarse from all the yelling, could use some water myself."

Bone tired, Robert looked at his friend, wondered where he found the energy to press onward. He was about to ask Sam that question when they heard a shout.

"Hello, over there. Have you found any sign of her?"

"Hello. No, have you?" Sam shone his flashlight toward the voice. Another light shone back his way. More lights bobbed on the mountainside as other searchers looked for Aurora.

"Hey, man, you're the husband, right?" The man offered his hand to Robert.

Robert shook his hand. "No, I'm a friend. He's Sam, Aurora's husband."

Sam thanked the men for volunteering their free time. "My wife's a special person. I'm worried about her." His voice broke. Regaining his composure, he said, "How long will you keep looking?"

"Searching in the dark is nearly futile. Dangerous, too. We'd have more success if we went home and got some sleep. We'll come back when it gets light." The two other volunteers agreed. "Come on, Sam. We'll drop you and Robert off at your house. There's nothing more you can do out here tonight."

"If we git hurt we won't be no help to her no how," said one volunteer.

"We can't just leave her out there. She isn't wearing a coat and she's scared of the dark," Sam pleaded.

"They're right, Sam. I'm going back with them. You coming, buddy?" Robert said.

"No. I'm staying here. Aurora's somewhere on this mountain. I won't leave without her. But you go. You need to bring Jill home from the hospital tomorrow. Thanks for your help." One by one the men patted Sam's shoulder and trudged back toward the dirt road on the ridge.

Sam leaned against a stump and chewed on a peanut butter sandwich minus the jelly he liked so much. Usually he couldn't handle peanut butter without jelly, but tonight it tasted as good as a porterhouse steak. Well, not quite, but mighty good just the same. He thought about Aurora and how she must be starving. He prayed she wasn't helpless and injured.

A crashing sound from higher up Smith Mountain stopped him mid-bite. Was that a person? Couldn't be Aurora; she'd have more sense than to run at break-neck speed down the mountain in the dark. An animal tearing through the brush? Very likely. Whatever it was, it was coming closer fast. He pulled the pistol from the holster on his belt, pointed it into the night.

King's exuberant howl reached Sam only seconds before his black body bowled Sam over. His big tongue licked Sam's face.

"Am I glad to see you, King. And I'm even happier I didn't shoot you. Other than the fact that I like you a lot, Aurora would never forgive me." Sam hugged the dog, offered him the rest of his sandwich. King gulped it down in one bite, barked at Sam, and headed back into the brush.

Sam dug out his cell phone and punched in Robert's number. No answer. He figured either Robert and the others were in a pocket on the mountain where there was no reception. He hung up and dialed Charlie. King came back to Sam, tugged on his coat.

"Charlie, I've found King. He's fine." Sam threw his backpack over his shoulder, retrieved a leash from his coat pocket, snapped it onto King's collar. "He wants me to follow him. I think he knows where Aurora is. Will you call the search team and ask them to get back here immediately? I doubt they're off the mountain yet. Tell them King's heading up and to the right of where I was when they left me."

"I'll call right now. But promise me you'll let me know as soon as you find her."

"I promise, Charlie. And if you can reach the search team, tell them I'll keep blowing my whistle so maybe they'll have a better chance of tracking me. Gotta get moving. I'll call you when I know more. 'Bye. And thanks, Charlie."

Dixie Lee looked at Charlie. "Well? Don't keep me in suspense. What's happened?"

"Sam's found King. He thinks King knows where Aurora is. He's leading Sam somewhere, anyhow. That's one smart dog. And he worships Aurora. He'll find her. Just pray he finds her alive."

Afraid to move for fear of waking Hessie, Aurora squirmed and slowly stretched out her right leg. Ahh, much better. Now maybe the cramp in her calf would go away. Her back and shoulder muscles screamed "Massage! Massage!" If only a massage were possible. She promised herself that if—no, when—she made it off the mountain she'd shower, spend an hour warming up in their Jacuzzi, then fall into bed, sleep for 12 hours straight, and then eat a double—well, maybe a triple—helping of grits swimming in butter. This time she'd use honest-to-goodness real butter, not the healthier spread she usually used. She squeezed her eyes shut and envisioned her muscles gradually relaxing, the welcoming warmth returning to her frigid body, her aches and pains washing down the drain when she pulled the plug, her stomach full.

Hessie cried out, shook, dropped back into a fitful sleep. Aurora felt guilty for having complained, even though she'd complained silently. Hessie had been through, well, through what? No one knew. How long had she been on Smith Mountain? How did she get here? Surely not on her own. And if someone else left her here, that person either had a horrible sense of humor—or meant for Hessie to die. Her conversation with Dixie Lee about how Hessie's guardian treated her rang alarms in her head. What was his name? His first name started with a "J"; the last name was Shoot or Toot or Smoot—something like that. She'd find out the next time she talked to Dixie Lee.

Snuggled against Hessie's feet, Little Guy lifted his head and growled. "Shh, Little Guy. Don't wake Hessie," whispered Aurora. "Please don't wake her."

Alert now, she raised her head and listened for any night sounds. She tried in vain to will the hairs on the back of her neck to lie back down. What now? she wondered.

Little Guy growled again, louder this time, and eased his body away from the old woman. Hessie moaned, trembled, coughed. Little Guy stood next to Aurora, growled softly, stared down the mountain. Aurora grabbed his collar, wrapped her other hand around his snout. "Be still, boy, please." He whined.

Aurora strained to hear what Little Guy heard. Maybe he's smelling it, she thought, when she heard no unusual noises.

A branch snapped nearby. The hair on Little Guy's back stood up. He barked, pulled against Aurora's grasp as he attempted to break her hold on his collar.

"No, Little Guy! Stay! I need you here." She wrapped the belt around her hand and let go of the collar.

Hessie cried out, pushed herself away from Aurora and attempted to stand. She fell to her knees. Crying, she tried to get back up, fell again.

"Hessie, dear, come to me. It's okay, Hessie. Don't you worry, nothing's going to hurt you. I'll take care of you." She reached for Hessie's hand.

"I want Momma," said Hessie as Aurora's hand closed around hers. She nestled closer to Aurora, rested her head on Aurora's shoulder.

"I know, I know." Aurora tucked the bathrobe over Hessie's feet as best she could, then put her arm around her shoulders. "Go back to sleep, Hessie. I won't leave you. I promise."

As Aurora rubbed Hessie's cold hands, she thought of her own mother who had died of complications from Alzheimer's less than a year ago. This could have been my mother lost on the mountain, she thought, glad that Margaret hadn't experienced these same hardships that Hessie was now fighting.

Little Guy licked Aurora's face and pawed at the belt attached to his collar. He cocked his head and nudged his nose under her arm. "I know you want me to turn you loose. But I need you with me. I feel safer with you here, Little Guy." She jumped when he barked.

Then, in the distance, she heard a whistle and Sam's voice calling her name.

"Here! I'm over here, Sam!"

"I'm coming, Susie-Q!" he called. King howled, pulled on the leash. Sam turned him loose. "Okay, boy, go to Aurora."

"Bad man! Bad man!" cried Hessie. She shoved herself away from Aurora, tried again to stand. Aurora grabbed her waist, locked her arms around Hessie and held her.

"No, Hessie, not the bad man. Good men, very good men, are coming for us. You're safe now, nobody will hurt you." Whimpering, Hessie sagged to the ground.

From higher on the mountain, Aurora heard men's voices, recognized Robert's. "We're coming, Aurora," he yelled. Lights bobbed in the dark as the search party scrambled down the mountain.

"King, it's you! I'm so glad to see you," said Aurora as the big dog whined, licked her face, and plopped down in her lap. Little Guy yapped his excitement and tried to squeeze his body beside King's. Aurora laughed, hugged both dogs.

To her right, a voice said, "Aurora, my sweet Aurora, we found you. Are you hurt?"

"Sam, oh, Sam." Aurora pushed the dogs off her lap, gently moved Hessie off her, and limped to Sam.

Sam kissed her. Aurora touched his face, felt his tears. Husband and wife laughed and cried together.

When Robert and the others reached Aurora, she said, "I'm not hurt. But Hessie needs help badly."

"Hessie?" asked Sam and the others. They shone their lights on the old woman. She shielded her eyes with her hands.

"I can't believe this. How did Hessie get here and how did you find her?"

"I'll answer your questions later. Right now she needs medical attention. She's thirsty, hungry, and nearly frozen. Probably has cuts and bruises all over her body. Maybe a broken bone, too. I'll fill you in on what I know later. Do you have any blankets with you?"

A man said, "Not on us. We're a search party. There're two blankets and a first aid kit back in my four-wheeler, though."

"How long would it take you to get there and back?" asked Sam.

"I'd say about an hour, maybe an hour and a half."

"My boat's stocked with food, water, blankets, and first aid supplies, even dog food," said Sam. "That's much closer. I'll get them."

"Can you find your way back there?"

"Yeah, I have my trusty Boy Scout compass, my flashlight, and my GPS." Sam looked at Aurora and winked. She squeezed his hand. "The compass belonged to Aurora's dad."

"I'll go with you," said Lou, one of the volunteers, "help you bring supplies back."

"I've got another idea," said Robert. "If Aurora's able to walk, she could go with Sam. A couple of you could go, too, bring the supplies back. Sam could take Aurora and me back by boat."

"I can walk," said Aurora. "Can we take Hessie with us?"

"I don't think so. We need to call the rescue squad, get an EMT over here ASAP. It's possible she has an injury that would require immobilization," said Sam.

"You're right. I'll stay here. Hessie's scared, but she trusts me. I promised I wouldn't leave her," said Aurora. "But would you bring a blanket and some water for us, and maybe something to eat?"

"That's probably a better idea," said Sam. "I'd like the EMTs to check you out before you go hiking through the woods." He took off his coat and handed it to his wife. "Put this on. I'll be back before you know it."

Aurora stuck her arms in the sleeves. The lingering warmth created by Sam's body felt so good.

Lou draped his down jacket over Hessie's shoulders and hurried to catch up with Sam. Careful not to hurt Hessie, Aurora and Robert put the coat on her. When Robert zipped it up, Hessie moaned slightly. King rose, moved to Hessie's side and stretched out close to her.

"Her feet are like iceburgs," said Aurora. "I put my socks on her, and I've rubbed them, but that's not enough." She looked at the men around her.

A man stepped forward, removed his thick wool cap, and slipped it over Hessie's feet. "That should help warm them."

"Thank you, . . . ? I'm sorry, I don't know your name or any of your names."

"I'm Earl," said the man with the cap. He introduced the others. "Mrs. Harris, try to get some rest. We'll take care of things from now on."

"Thank you, I will." Aurora snuggled closer to Hessie and closed her eyes.

*

On his way down the mountain, Sam pulled out his cell phone, dialed Charlie. "We've found her, Charlie. She's okay." He could almost feel Charlie's relief. He felt the same way.

Dixie Lee looked at Charlie. "That was Sam?"

"Yeah." A tear dropped down his cheek.

"So has he found Aurora? Is she okay? What? Talk to me, Charlie."

Sam, well, he and King found Aurora. She's a little battered and bruised, but she's okay."

"Praise the Lord!"

"Dixie Lee, Hessie is with Aurora."

"What?"

"Sam said that when he found Aurora, she was with Hessie. He doesn't know yet the extent of Hessie's injuries. EMTs have been called."

"Praise the Lord again. Aurora is okay, Hessie is alive. And you know what, Charlie?"

"No, what?"

"I love you." There, she'd said it. Aloud.

"Dixie Lee Cunningham, I love you, too. Will you marry me?"

"Thought you'd never ask, Charlie Anderson. Of course I'll marry you." A frown crossed her face. "There's something about me that you don't know, though."

"What?"

"Follow me." Dixie Lee took his hand, led him into her bedroom, pointed to her nightstand. "I have sleep apnea, Charlie. I have to wear that stupid head thing every single night or I don't breathe. I look like something out of a science fiction movie when I have it on. And it makes noise, too." She looked at him. "You can back out now. No hard feelings."

Charlie laughed. "Dixie Lee, I have sleep apnea, too. And I also wear a mask." He pulled her into his arms. "So are we going to get married or not?"

"Yes, Charlie. Yes."

"You know what? I was about to pop the question when Sam called and said Aurora was missing."

"I know."

"You knew? How?"

"We females just know these things. Stop talking and kiss me, Charlie Anderson."

CHAPTER FIFTY-THREE

Back at *La Grande Maison,* Win and Carole walked the winding cobblestone path to the boardwalk. So far, Win noticed, the pill the bartender had dropped in her wine didn't appear to be working. Oh, sure, she giggled more than usual, and seemed to stagger a little at times, but he'd expected she'd be feeling the drug more by now.

"How you doing, Carole? Feel okay?" He stumbled slightly.

"I'm fine, just a little sleepy. Is there a reason I shouldn't be?"

"No, of course not, just wanted to be sure you were warm enough. This night air's getting chilly and your jacket's not very heavy." So why am I sweating? Win wondered.

"Thanks for your concern, Win." Watching him wipe perspiration from his brow, Carole prayed the drug was doing its job.

"Believe me, I'm—" She stopped, stared at the powerboat tied up in a covered boat slip. "I've seen that boat before—this morning, in the *Smith Mountain Eagle.* An out-of-state resident reported it stolen from his boathouse when he came to his lake home the other day."

"I'm sure you're mistaken. No one could hide stolen boats here." Win tightened his grip on her arm. "The boardwalk's that way. Let's go."

"No. I want a better look." All thoughts of Win and the drug forgotten, she broke free and dashed to the dock.

"Look, Win, this is a Fountain powerboat, definitely the one pictured in the paper. It's the same color, same style. Even the name Delilah painted on the side is the same. This is a stolen boat.

We should call the cops immediately." She dug in her purse for her cell phone.

"Don't be an idiot, Carole." He reached for her. "Let's go." She side-stepped him.

"I'm going aboard." Carole scrambled over the boat's gunwale.

"You know what I just realized, Win? We saw this very same boat docked at a house I showed you over the weekend. I remember how excited you were when you saw it. You even climbed inside. Surely you recognize it."

"Get out of that boat, Carole. I'm not kidding. You're sticking your head into business that doesn't concern you. Get out now or you'll get yourself in deep trouble. I mean it."

Surprised at his threats and his tone of voice, Carole saw the menacing eyes Aurora had described—eyes infinitely more dangerous than those she'd looked into at the dinner table. An awful realization dawned on her: Win stole the boat, brought it here. Was he planning on keeping it for himself or selling it? Were the "commodities" he dealt with stolen boats? Had he been using the excuse to buy a house as a means to search for high-end boats?

"You never had any intention of buying a house. I know that now. You used me. If you want me to get out, you'll have to come get me." Carole darted below deck, grabbed her phone and dialed 911. No signal. Dropping the cell back in her purse, she pulled out the .22. She heard Win's feet on the top step. He reached for her. She pointed the pistol at his chest.

"Don't come any closer or I'll shoot."

"You think that pea shooter will stop me? Don't kid yourself." Win swayed, steadied himself.

"I'm a good shot, Win. And this pea shooter as you call it may not kill you, but it will do some serious damage where you don't want damage done." She lowered her aim from his chest to his groin.

Win lunged at her. The gun flew from her hand and skidded across the room. She fell to the floor. Win stood over her and laughed. Carole screamed at the weight of his body falling on top of her. She screamed again, kicked, beat her fists against his shoulders and the sides of his head.

Win didn't budge. Carole stopped fighting, willed herself to be still, and waited.

"Win," she said, after 30 seconds of lying on the floor, "get off me." He didn't move. "Get off!"

But he didn't. And he didn't utter a sound. She heard breathing, nothing else. She figured the drugged wine had finally done its job, hoped he'd be out for several hours.

She shoved him off her body and retrieved her .22. A wicked grin covered her face. Resisting the urge to pump bullets into Win, she tied his shoelaces together before going above deck. She secured the hatch from above, exited the powerboat, and vanished into the night.

CHAPTER FIFTY-FOUR

Carole skirted the lit paths and crept toward the house. If she could find her car, she'd have a chance to escape. The diagram would help her locate the garage, but she needed light to read it. In her mind she pictured Win's drawing, looked up at the well-lit mansion, angled to the left and up.

From the top of the hill a dog barked, then another. Carol stopped and waited for another sound. If security had released guard dogs, she was in big trouble. But, she reasoned, if dogs were running loose, then Win wouldn't have taken her for the walk. She figured the dogs would be released only if there was a security problem, and the grounds' security could not possibly know Win was unconscious in a boat and that she was plotting her getaway. Or could they? Suppose the drug had not worked well on Win and he'd awakened and called them.

At the sound of a man's voice a few feet away, she jerked to a stop and squatted behind a thick Nandina bush. Peeping through the branches, she saw the man silhouetted against the dimly lit steps.

"Any sign of 'em?" the man called.

"Nope," said an answering voice near the lake. "I'll check the waterfront. Has anybody searched the stables and tennis courts?"

"They're checking now. Want me to turn the Dobermans loose?"

Normally unafraid of dogs, Carole was terrified. Being ripped to pieces by a pack of killer Doberman pinschers didn't appeal to her. Momentary relief spread over her when one of the men hollered to the other.

"Naw, not yet. If you see him, tell him to call his mom. According to the bartender, I don't think Mr. Ford would appreciate being disturbed right now."

Whew, saved by the bartender, thought Carole. She stayed hidden for fifteen minutes until the voices stopped and the dogs no longer barked. With the lights from the mansion guiding her, she inched her way around bushes and flowerbeds until she reached the left side of the house. Hearing faint sounds of music from inside, she peeped in a first floor window. In the ballroom, a small band played while couples danced to the Latin rhythm. She ducked when a man stared in her direction.

On the other side of the house, she pulled out her crude map and studied it. Judging by the direction the valet had driven her car, a monstrous garage should be to the right. She turned the corner of the house and stopped short. The garage she sought loomed straight ahead. Spotlights flooded the detached, six-bay building. No shrubbery grew near it. How could she manage to get inside without being seen?

Carole decided to work her way to the back of the building, see if there were other entrances and less chance of someone catching her. Keeping close to the ground, she reached the rear.

Three more garage doors faced her. Two regular three-foot wide doors flanked the garage doors. To the side of each was a window. Carole reasoned that behind one door was an office; the other probably contained an apartment or automotive shop. Because a light shone from one window, she sneaked toward the other door. The door opened and two men stepped outside.

Carole darted around the corner of the building, flattened her body against the wall. She held her breath and prayed the men wouldn't come her way. She heard voices, the strike of a match. The men laughed and walked off in the other direction. Carole smelled marijuana. She forced herself not to cough.

Peeking around the building, she saw no one. Silently she moved to the door and tried the doorknob. When it turned in her hand, she nearly yelled for joy. Holding her breath, she stepped inside almost total darkness. There was a faint light. She waited until her eyes adjusted, then walked across the room and looked through a glass-topped door into a huge room. Dim bare-bulb lights dangled from the ceiling. She guessed this was the garage she sought. Now if she could find her car before someone found her.

Carole crept past a silver Rolls-Royce, two stretch limousines, a black Corvette, and a yellow Ferrari. Nice cars, but they didn't look nearly as fine to her as did her ordinary car when she found it behind the Ferrari in the last bay closest to a garage door. She figured she and Win must have been the last to arrive.

How would she get her car out? And were the keys in it? She opened the car door, slid in the driver's seat and reached around to the ignition. Hallelujah! The keys were there. Now she needed to open the garage door. But how?

The dim ceiling lights suddenly grew brighter. A door slammed. Carole climbed in the back seat and onto the floor. She reached for her .22, pulled it out.

"Whatcha reckon he needs the Ferrari for this late at night?" asked one of the men.

"Don't know. Don't care so long as I git paid for doing what I'm told and keepin' my mouth shut. Like not telling his wife he's headin' to Rock Bottom for a couple hours. Now open the door and move the crappy car so I can back out the Ferrari."

Crappy car? thought Carole. They have some nerve. She scrunched her body against the floor in the back and prayed.

Carole heard the garage door roll up. Her car door opened, a man got in the driver's seat, started the car, and backed out. The Ferrari followed.

"Might as well leave Crappy out, make it easier on us when Ferrari comes back."

Yes! Please! thought Carole.

Minutes later Carole was alone. Outside. In her own car with the keys. A faint sickie-sweet marijuana scent hit her as she crept back in the driver's seat. She scrunched down and waited until the inside garage lights dimmed, counted to 500, sat up and turned the keys in the ignition.

CHAPTER FIFTY-FIVE

Wednesday, 11:00 p.m.

Luke had given up all hope of talking to Carole. He looked at the clock for what seemed like the hundredth time in the last ten minutes. In the hope that she'd finally turned on her cell phone, he dialed her number again. No luck. "Where are you, Carole? Where are you?"

Maybe Aurora had heard from her. He called Aurora's house and left a message on the answering machine for her to call him no matter what time she got in.

"Calm down," he said aloud. "It won't do you any good to fall apart. Carole's probably with a client, forgot to turn on her cell. She's done that lots of times. So have I. Calm down, fix yourself something to eat." But why would she be with a client this late?

Hungry, he took a frozen chicken dinner from the freezer, rolled the lid back the proper amount, and stuck it in the microwave. When the timer sounded, he put it on a plate, opened a cold Bud Lite, dropped into his easy chair and turned on the TV to Channel 10.

The weatherman talked about the drought and how it looked as though there'd be no break anytime soon. The sportscaster discussed Virginia Tech's chances of beating UVA in the next football game. Luke took his last bite the same time the anchorman interrupted with a late-breaking story.

All chewing stopped when the announcer said, "We've just received word that a search party found and rescued two women from Smith Mountain. We don't know their condition or how they came to be on the mountain at night, but we do know the identity of one of the women. Her name is Aurora Harris, a resident at Smith Mountain Lake. The identity of the other woman, who is en route to Lynchburg General Hospital, is being held until relatives can be contacted. We don't know her condition at this time."

Luke choked on his food, spit it on his plate. His heart raced as though he were running a marathon. His hand shook.

"Carole. The other woman must be Carole. Oh, God, help her please." He dialed Aurora's house again, left another frantic message.

He called the emergency room, asked if Carole had been admitted. "I'm sorry, sir. I can't give out that information."

Luke knew he had to drive to Lynchburg and see for himself. He'd go nuts if he just sat and waited. He grabbed his coat and keys, and hurried to his car. Once again, he forgot his cell phone.

CHAPTER FIFTY-SIX

Thursday, 1:50 a.m.

When the emergency medical technician had said she should be checked again at the hospital, Aurora had balked. "I want to go home. I want a hot bath and a good night's sleep in our bed."

Sam had finally convinced her that trudging down a mountain in the dark on a bad ankle would not be wise, even though she didn't appear to have any serious injuries. After an emergency room examination showed a sprained ankle but no internal injuries or a concussion, the doctor had pronounced her well enough to leave.

Robert had offered to drive them to the hospital after dropping the boat off at Sam's house, but Sam had declined the offer. "You need to get ready for Jill," Sam had said. "Don't worry about us. We'll either call a taxi or Uncle Charlie. And I need you to take the dogs. They can't go to the hospital with us, and Aurora will kill me if we leave them on the mountain."

Now they were finally home. Sam paid the cab driver and helped an exhausted Aurora limp from the car and up the front steps.

"Where's King?" she asked when Sam opened the door and King didn't rush to greet her.

"He and Little Guy are at Robert's."

"Can you go get him now?"

"Aurora, honey, it's 2:30 a.m. Robert and the dogs are surely sound asleep. I'll fetch him first thing in the morning. I promise. Right now I want to get you to bed. Do you need anything to eat first?"

"No, thanks. I ate enough of the supplies you dragged up the mountain. I would like a bath, though. Well, maybe a quick shower instead." She limped to the bathroom.

Sam listened to messages on the answering machine. Three were from Luke, each more frantic than the first. He dialed Luke's home.

Luke jerked up the phone on the first ring. "Aurora, where's Carole?"

"This is Sam. We just got home. Aurora's taking a shower and then going straight to bed. She's had a rough day. What's up?"

"I can't find Carole. She should have called me by 10:00; I haven't heard from her. I've tried her cell and office phones, left messages. I hoped she was with Aurora or had at least told Aurora where she was going." He told Sam about his frantic trip to Lynchburg General Hospital.

"We may have passed each other. Aurora's fine, just a slightly sprained ankle and a few bruises. But we haven't seen Carole."

"I'm really worried about her. Please ask Aurora if she knows anything."

"Hold on. I'll see if she's still in the shower. She may already be sound asleep by now."

"Sam, this is important. If she's asleep, please wake her."

Aurora was brushing her teeth when Sam appeared. "That shower felt so good. See you in the morning." She put the toothbrush in the holder and started to bed.

"Not so fast. Luke's on the phone. He can't find Carole and he's worried sick."

Aurora grabbed the phone from Sam. "Carole's not home yet?" she asked. She listened as Luke voiced his concerns.

"I spoke to her after lunch. She was looking at houses with Win." Aurora heard Luke groan.

"Were they in his car or in Carole's?"

"Carole's. She said she'd call me around 7:00, fill me in on how the day went. If she tried to call, I wasn't here. But she would have left a message when I didn't answer. I know that she didn't want to spend any more time with Win than necessary. She was sure he was on the verge of buying a house." Aurora covered her yawn with a hand. "Wonder why she hasn't returned any of your calls."

"I'm wondering the same thing. My thought is that she's out of service range." Or unable to call, he thought. "On my way home from checking at the hospital, I drove by her place to see if maybe her phone was out of order. She wasn't there, Aurora." His voice broke.

CHAPTER FIFTY-SEVEN

Early Thursday Morning

Aurora couldn't stay in bed a minute longer. Her body craved sleep, but her mind demanded action. She crawled out of bed and hobbled to the bathroom. After splashing cold water on her face, she struggled into her bathrobe and made her way to the kitchen. She jumped when a hand touched her shoulder.

"Why aren't you in bed?" a sleepy Sam asked. He rubbed his half-shut eyes and focused on the wall clock. "Its 4:00 in the morning, Aurora. You should be in bed. I should be in bed." He pulled a chair away from the kitchen table and plopped down. "Everybody should be in bed."

"I couldn't sleep. I'm so worried about Carole." She put the filter in the coffee pot and measured out the usual number of scoops, then added one more. Today she'd need an extra jolt of caffeine.

"There's nothing you can do to help Carole right now. You need some rest. Go back to bed. Luke told you he'd call if he heard from her."

"I've thought this through, Sam. While lying in bed I mapped out a plan." Aurora poured the water in the coffee maker and flipped on the switch. "As soon as I get a cup of strong java in me I'll call Luke and get him to meet me at Carole's. He has a key; I don't."

She looked at her husband. "You're dog-tired. You're the one who should go back to bed. I'll wake you when I'm ready to leave." She leaned over and kissed the top of his blonde head.

"Susie-Q, you're not going anywhere without me. But you may want to make another pot of coffee."

"You need to leave for work in a few hours. Go get a little more sleep."

"After last night, I'd already decided to stay home today. I wouldn't be able to get anything done." He put his arms around her. "I'm yours for the whole day."

"Okay, if you're sure. I'll be happy to have your company and your brain." The coffee maker buzzed and Aurora poured herself a cup of the steaming, black liquid. "Yum," she said after the first sip slid down her throat.

"You get dressed. I'll fix breakfast." Sam pulled a carton of eggs and the package of nitrite/nitrate-free bacon from the refrigerator.

Fifteen minutes later the two sat down to a meal of orange juice, scrambled eggs, bacon, toasted cinnamon raisin bread, and coffee. Aurora quickly jotted notes on a pad as she ate.

"So what time are we meeting Luke?" Sam asked.

"We agreed on 5:30 at Carole's place." She spread butter on her toast. "Good breakfast, Sam. Thank you."

"You're welcome."

"I hate to ask, but do you think. . . ."

"Of course I'll get King. I'll call Robert right before we leave. Don't want to wake him too early, even though I'm pretty sure he'll be eager to get to Roanoke and to Jill."

"How'd you know what I was going to ask?"

"You had that I-want-King look in your eye. I know you pretty well, Susie-Q. Besides, I miss him, too."

The ringing phone interrupted their conversation. "That's probably Luke. Maybe Carole's home." She crossed her fingers and grabbed the phone.

"Aurora, I saw your lights on, figured you were up. Can I bring King to you? He's going nuts over here, probably knows you're back."

"Of course, Robert. Better yet, just open the door and let him out. He'll gallop straight home." Aurora explained why she wouldn't be able to keep Little Guy when Robert went to the hospital to pick up Jill. "Hope that won't mess up your plans."

"No, Little Guy will be fine by himself. Jill and I should be home around two or three. Four at the latest. So how'd it go in the ER? And how is Hessie?"

"Except for a sprained ankle, some bruises and minor scrapes, I'm fine. The doctors were still treating Hessie when I left. I'm pretty sure she'll be in the hospital for a while. Thanks for all your help last night. I don't know how we would have made it without you." A frantic bark outside the kitchen door made her smile. "King's already here. Gotta let him in. Talk to you later."

At 5:35 a.m., three exhausted and worried friends gathered around Carole's desk and brainstormed. Luke, unshaven, ran his hands through his hair. "I'm at my wit's end. I just know Carole's in trouble. I can sense it. And I don't know where to turn or what to do."

King whined, rested his head on Luke's thigh.

"We'll find her, Luke. And don't forget, Carole's one smart lady. She knows how to side-step trouble." But Aurora wasn't as certain as she tried to imply. Carole, her best friend, was in danger. And after having stared into his eyes twice, Aurora was certain that Win was responsible. And that they'd better find Carole soon.

"Carole won't like it when she finds we've messed up all these papers stacked neatly on her desk, but let's each grab a pile and go through them one by one."

"What are we looking for?"

"Anything, no matter how small, that could provide a clue to her whereabouts." Aurora glanced at a hand-written note, discarded it, picked up another paper. "Maybe there's something that will tell us where Win's staying. Check her notepads, her calendar. I'm sure she must have a client file around here somewhere." She yanked open the desk drawers, quickly thumbed through them.

Luke looked up from his paper stack. "She keeps a couple of file cabinets in the back room. Maybe client files are there. I'll go look."

"I'll help you," said Sam.

Aurora checked Carole's answering machine and listened to 11 messages. Four were from prospective clients who'd seen her listings in the *Smith Mountain Eagle*. Five calls came from Luke, one from Aurora, and the last was a hang-up. She sighed and finished searching Carole's papers. In vain, she looked for Carole's day planner, figured her friend must have it with her. The clock on Carole's desk read 6:02. Precious minutes had ticked away.

Luke rushed back into the office. "I just remembered that I memorized Win's license number the first time I saw his Porsche. I do that if I see Carole ride off in a client's car. I've tried to talk her into making a note of the license numbers, but she's not at all concerned."

"But Aurora said Carole was in her own car," said Sam, poking his head around the door. "What good will Win's license number be?"

"I don't know," said Aurora, "but it could be important. Maybe they changed vehicles. What's the number, Luke?"

"There're no numbers—it's all letters. His license number is 'I Win.'"

"You're kidding," said Aurora.

"Nope," said Luke. "He's an egotistical jerk. I'm not surprised he chose that one."

"Me, either," Aurora said.

"Carole met Win on Friday, October 13. I remember thinking it was a bad omen."

"I'm not superstitious. Don't you be, either," said Aurora.

"Geronimo!" hollered Sam from the back room. "I found Win's file. He's staying at a bed and breakfast a few miles from here."

"Do you have their phone number?"

"Uh, no. Sorry. But it's The Eagle's Perch."

"That's okay. I'll look it up." Aurora thumbed through the pages in the phone book, located the listing and dialed the number.

"What?" answered a groggy male voice.

"Is this The Eagle's Perch Bed and Breakfast?" asked Aurora.

"It is. Do you have any idea what time it is?" asked the voice.

"It's 6:15. I know I'm calling early and I apologize, but this is extremely important."

"Yeah? What's so important?"

"I'm trying to get in touch with Winston Ford. I understand he's one of your guests. Believe me, I would not be up so early myself if it were not imperative that I speak with him."

"Well, I don't think he came back last night. At least I didn't hear him come in. Wait a sec and I'll ask my wife, see if she heard anything. We don't keep close watch over our guests. I'm sure you understand."

"Of course," said Aurora. She said a silent prayer, waited for him to come back to the phone, wondered what was taking him so long.

"Miss," said the man at The Eagle's Perch, "my wife checked his room, said Mr. Ford did not return last night. His car's in the garage, though, so he must have ridden with someone else."

"Could I come by and look at Mr. Ford's car?" asked Aurora.

"I'm sorry, but I can't let you do that. All our guests' information is confidential. I couldn't violate their trust."

"Sir, a life could be in danger. Your guest could die if you won't release the information we and the police need." She knew she was stretching the truth, perhaps even making it up, but Carole needed her and she needed to search Win's Porsche. She prayed that the mention of the police would open the door she needed.

"Well, if you think somebody's in serious trouble and the police could come, I guess it'd be okay. How long before you get here?"

"Five minutes, maybe seven."

"Make it ten. We're not even dressed yet."

CHAPTER FIFTY-EIGHT

Thursday, 6:25 a.m.

Seated in the front seat beside Sam, Luke talked about Carole and
how much he adored her, how sorry he was he'd been unable to
help when she needed him so desperately. "I feel helpless, Aurora.
Utterly helpless."

Aurora glanced at Sam, saw his fingers tighten on the steering
wheel. She knew that he, too, believed Carole was in serious
trouble. Aurora tried to shake off the feeling of doom. King stuck
his head under her arm. She rubbed his throat.

"I've been thinking about Win's license number," said Sam.
"Didn't the TV say the car that hit Jill had a license number
beginning with either an 'I' or the number one? And I think I
remember hearing that the car was either black, dark blue or dark
gray. Isn't Win's Porsche black?"

"Yeah, it's black," said Luke.

"Oh, my gosh." Now Aurora was even more concerned for
Carole. "When we see Win's car, we'll know if the Porsche is the
hit and run vehicle."

"Unless he's already had it repaired."

"Not likely," said Sam. "I don't think many garages around here
work on Porsches. Besides, Win probably has a favorite shop he'd
trailer the car to. My gut tells me the car that hit Jill is Win's
Porsche and that it hasn't been fixed. When we know for sure, I'll
call Lieutenant Conner. I imagine he'll find the information quite
useful."

"We'll know in a minute," said Sam. "The Eagle's Perch is just
ahead."

When Sam drove into the driveway, a man and woman came outside. "This way," said the man. They followed him around back and waited as he pushed the remote. The garage door slowly ascended.

"Mr. Ford's car looks fine to me," said The Eagle's Perch owner as he examined the driver's side of the Porsche. He frowned. "I never should have listened to you."

Aurora ignored him, stepped to the front of the vehicle. "Sam, Luke, come look. The front end's all banged up, the passenger side is, too! And with that license number . . . . Sam, you were right. I'm certain this is the car that nearly killed Jill." She dialed Lieutenant Conner, left a message for him to meet her as soon as possible.

"I don't understand," said the owner's wife. "Mr. Ford seems like such a nice man, a real gentleman. I can't imagine him running into another car and not stopping. He's too charming to do such a thing."

"Ma'am," said Luke, "I'm afraid that's not all Mr. Ford has done. We believe he's kidnapped my fiancé, and her life is in danger."

"Oh, no, not our Mr. Ford. You'll never convince me of that."

Aurora and Sam exchanged looks. Sam put his hand on the woman's arm, guided her toward the house. "Mrs. ..., I'm sorry, I don't know your name. My name is Sam Harris. My wife is Aurora, and that's Luke. The dog is King." King wagged his tail.

"I'm Yvonne Bateman. My husband is Paul."

"May we wait inside, Mrs. Bateman?" asked Sam. "The police will be here shortly, and the three of us really should wait. I'm sure they'll want to search Mr. Ford's car and his room."

"Well, I don't know. Paul, what should we do?"

"Mr. and Mrs. Bateman," said Aurora, "if Mr. Ford is guilty of what I believe, then the press will be camping out at The Eagle's Perch to gather any information they can get their eager hands on. The publicity your establishment will receive will be invaluable to you, especially when the reporters write about how helpful you and your husband were during the investigation. I bet, too, if you had a few choice dishes for them to munch on, they'd mention that in some of their articles. The Eagle's Perch will receive national publicity—perhaps even world-wide—because of the horrible things Mr. Ford will be accused of doing. Even if he's innocent, reporters will be here asking questions and taking pictures of The Eagle's Perch."

"Well, all things considered, I guess it wouldn't do any harm for y'all to come inside," said Mrs. Bateman. "Except for the dog. I don't know about the dog."

"King is well-mannered, Mrs. Bateman. King, Mrs. Bateman wants to meet you."

King looked from Aurora to the woman standing beside her, trotted over to Mrs. Bateman, sat, and held out his paw.

"Well, I declare," she said as she shook hands with King. "I guess King can come in, too. And all y'all can call me Yvonne."

CHAPTER FIFTY-NINE

Thursday, 6:50 a.m.

Carole had spent hours trying to get as far as *La Grande Maison's* main gate. First she'd played hide-and-seek with the two security guards walking near the waterfront. That had taken precious time. Getting from the grounds in the front of the house to inside the garage had eaten up at least another hour. Then she'd hunkered down in the back seat of her car for another hour before the garage men backed Crappy out and disappeared. Because she couldn't risk turning on the lights, she'd driven at turtle-speed, occasionally pulling off the drive when she'd seen lights in the distance.

Finally she'd managed to drive Crappy as far as *La Grande Maison's* gates only to discover that she needed a remote to open them. Her first impulse was to step out of the car and scream her lungs out for the entire world to hear. But that would get her nowhere, and maybe even help Win find her. Should she ram Crappy through the gates? And if she even got through them, how far could she go? Her gas gauge read less than one-quarter tank, just enough to send the low-gas signal bleeping. If she made it through and then ran out of gas, *La Grande Maison's* security would find her car and know where to search for her. Same thing if the car got stuck in the gate. Right now, security had no idea where she was or they would've been on her trail. Not many choices, she thought. She tried her cell again. Still no service.

Her decision made, Carole drove off the road into the woods and hoped no one would find the car for several hours. She thought about crawling over the fence, but had noticed the electric wires running along the top. Were they meant to shock or to kill?

She didn't want to test it. Surely the wires wouldn't be along the entire length of fence. Probably her best bet would be to follow the fence until she found a break in the wire or figured out another way over.

Carole looked at her feet and her shoes, which were not good for hiking. She'd be traveling over rough terrain. She opened Crappy's trunk, reached into a cardboard box and pulled out a worn pair of sneakers. Good. At least with these shoes, she could move faster—and maybe her feet wouldn't hurt. She rummaged in the box again, dragged out her heavy, hooded fleece jacket. She slipped it on, stuck her feet in the sneakers, snatched up a partially-consumed water bottle containing water probably a couple weeks old, and looked back at the entrance gate before disappearing into the trees.

Seconds later she popped back out of the trees and stared at the iron gate. No electric wire ran across the top. If she could climb over, she could follow the road and eventually enter civilization. Or so she hoped.

On the way back from the bathroom to his post at the security station, Otis stopped and poured himself a cup of coffee. He eyed the sweet roll on the other guard's paper plate.

"Where'd you git that?" he asked the other guard, pointed to the roll dotted with raisins and covered with powdered-sugar icing. Just smelling it made his stomach growl.

"I stopped at the store on my way in this morning and bought 'em. Want one?"

"Yeah, I do."

"Look in that bag on the counter."

"Yum. That's good." Otis took a bite and headed back to his guard station. "I'll pick up something for us tomorrow."

"Great," said the guard. He looked at the video camera aimed at the entrance gates, watched a doe walk cautiously out of the woods and across the road a few yards from the gate. A crow flew in front of the camera.

On a pad, the guard jotted down the time. He started to rewind the video tape to see if he'd missed anything when he went for a bathroom break, coffee and the sticky bun, decided he'd not been absent from his watch long enough for anything to have happened. Instead, he picked up a book by Stephen King, opened it to page 43, and settled down to read.

CHAPTER SIXTY

Thursday, 6:55 a.m.

Kurt lifted his head from the toilet and blew his nose with toilet paper his mother handed him. He felt awful. This wasn't the right time to be puking all night. "What time is it, Mom?" he asked when his mother pressed a cold, wet washcloth to his forehead.

"Time for you to crawl back in bed if you think you're through throwing up for a while. I'll put the bucket beside the bed just in case you need it again."

Kurt stood, went to the sink and washed his mouth and hands. He stared at his ghostly white reflection in the mirror. "I've gotta meet the camera man at 7:15 at the bus stop." He sat on his bed, reached for the jeans hanging over the footboard. His mother took them out of his hand.

"I'm sorry, son. I know how much you want that camera. But you're not going anywhere."

"Aw, Mom."

"Your temperature is 102, and you've thrown up eight times since 2:15. You're staying home today, and I'm staying with you. I've already called the office and left a message that I won't be in.

"Here, sip some ginger ale." She held the glass steady, watched the pale liquid travel up the straw. "Only a couple of sips for now."

"My science project is due today." He watched his mother set the glass on the nightstand.

"It will have to wait. Your health is more important than a science project."

He remembered thinking how like a mom she sounded as he lay back on the bed and dropped into a fitful sleep.

At the bus stop, Jasper Smoot looked at his watch and frowned. He'd arrived at the appointed meeting spot at 7:10. The kid was late. If Kurt showed up right now, would Jasper have enough time to kill him before the school bus passed? The bus might even stop and wait a few seconds on the chance Kurt and/or the girl were running a little behind schedule. Jasper couldn't risk being caught. Furious that his plan hadn't worked the way he wanted, he slammed his fist against the steering wheel, started the engine, drove to Kurt's street and cruised by his house. Was Kurt home alone, or had he ridden to school with his mother before Jasper arrived at the bus stop? The closed garage door offered no answers.

Jasper pulled out his cell and called Kurt's home.

"Hello," said a woman.

Jasper said nothing.

"Hello?" she said again. "Hello? Who is this? Hello?"

He hung up. If his plan had gone as scheduled, the kid would have been dead by now. He needed another plan. The kid would still die, just a little later.

A grim smile crossed his face. Butch should be catching up to Etta by now. Soon she'd be out of the way for good, then he would get rid of Butch, make it look like a domestic dispute between Butch and Etta. He'd thought to kill Kurt first, then after Butch had knocked off Etta, Butch would die. Jasper didn't like kinks in his plans, but he would still have the same results.

CHAPTER SIXTY-ONE

Thursday, 8:00 a.m.

In the Cifax community, a frightened Etta emptied drawers of clothes into suitcases. If she stayed, Butch—or his boss—would kill her. Of that she was certain. She and Butch had shared some great times. She'd even hoped at one point that he would marry her. That would never happen now because she knew too much for him to allow her to live. Besides, she wouldn't want to marry a man who treated Hessie so badly.

She dragged the three suitcases to the front door, stopped and looked around. Had she forgotten anything? She had her cell phone, local telephone directories, a copy of the letter and pictures she planned to mail to her friend at work.

Etta had called her friend last night, and they'd worked out a plan. Once Etta made it to New Bern safely, she'd call her friend with instructions to go ahead and send the envelope to the local newspapers and television stations. If Etta didn't call within 48 hours, the friend would open the envelope and send the info to the cops as well as the news media. Because they'd want a hot story, she knew the newspapers would jump on the facts she'd sent them. In the envelope she'd named names, given dates. They'd publish an article, maybe put it on the front page. Even if the cops weren't interested, the media would push them to investigate.

She'd dialed her sister in New Bern, North Carolina, left a message on her answering machine saying she hoped she could get there that evening. But she hadn't slept at all last night, was starting out tired. If she had to, she would stop in some little town, spend the night in a cheap motel.

Etta loaded the suitcases, a pillow and comforter, maps, and a food-filled cooler in the trunk of her old red Capri.

She walked back inside her rented house at the far end of a mile-long gravel road. She loved this place, her home for the last four years. A few good neighbors lived along the road. If she ever needed help, she knew they'd come. But to tell them about Butch would put their lives in danger. She refused to do that.

Huge old oaks and poplars surrounded the tiny house, and there was a cleared space for a small garden. Her landlord plowed it for her every year. The rent was reasonable, the landlord kept the yard mowed and raked, and he maintained the home's exterior. And if Etta wanted to spruce up the inside, he'd always been happy to supply the paint and any wallpaper she selected. Etta, a good housekeeper, was proud of her little house and how neat and clean she kept it. Folks who visited always remarked on its appearance, said it smelled like homemade apple pie. Fond thoughts of friends, neighbors and fellow workers at Bedford Memorial Hospital ran through her mind. She wished she could take the things she'd accumulated over the last few years, things like framed pictures she'd bought at Wal-Mart, pretty knickknacks she'd acquired at yard sales, stuff that helped make a house a home, gave it that lived-in feeling.

Only knowing what Butch would do when he caught her could make her leave.

Etta heard a meow seconds before the yellow cat rubbed against her leg. She scooped him up, cradled him in her arms, rested her cheek on his head. She'd found him emaciated and lying on the side of the road the day she'd moved into the house, had nursed him back to health, had him neutered. The veterinary clinic let her pay a little each month until she'd paid off the bill. She couldn't just abandon him now.

Would one of her neighbors take him? She thought about the young girl down the gravel road and how much she loved on Mouser whenever she visited. Then Etta remembered that the girl's mother was severely allergic to cats. Was there anyone else who would take him? She looked at her watch. Every minute she stayed put Butch closer. She didn't have time to make phone calls. Trying not to cry, she set Mouser down on the floor, filled his food and water bowls, and walked out of the house. She'd call her landlord when she reached Oxford, ask him to find Mouser a good home.

Five minutes down the road she pulled onto the shoulder. She looked at her watch; precious time had passed, time she needed to survive. But she couldn't do it, couldn't desert Mouser no matter what happened to her. Butch hated cats. Etta knew Mouser would die an ugly death when Butch searched the house looking for her. She turned around in a driveway and hurried back the way she'd come.

Inside her little house again, she stuffed an uncooperative Mouser in the cat carrier, grabbed the cat food, treats, and his two bowls and loaded them in the car. Did she dare go back inside for his toys? Deciding against it, she started the car and drove down the gravel road. She prayed she could get to the main highway before Butch trapped her.

She reached 221, turned left toward Lynchburg. Normally she would have headed toward Bedford, but she knew Butch would come from that direction. In her rearview mirror, she saw a blue pickup truck turn onto the country road she had left less than a minute ago. The truck looked like Butch's. Etta stomped on the accelerator.

Butch's truck skidded to a stop in front of Etta's house. Her car wasn't parked in its usual spot. He'd figured she'd be ready to run, but had hoped she hadn't left yet. Etta wasn't stupid. She'd guess he would come after her. He ran to the front door, tried the knob. The door was locked. He retrieved the key she'd given him months ago from his key chain and opened the door.

He knew immediately the house was vacant. How long had she been gone? He looked at his watch—8:22. Entering the kitchen, he saw the unplugged coffee pot half-filled with coffee. He put his palm on the carafe. Still slightly warm. He smiled. She hadn't been gone long. Now all he had to do was figure out where she'd headed.

When he saw the blinking light on the answering machine, he hit the play button and listened to the message.

Etta, dear, this is your sister. It's 8:20. Sorry I didn't pick up when you called. I was in the shower. I'm guessing you're already on your way, but just in case you haven't left yet, I wanted to let you know that I think you should go to the police. If I don't hear from you, I'll assume you're on your way here. See you in New Bern tonight or tomorrow. Drive carefully now, you hear?

Butch laughed. He knew Etta would never go to the cops. They scared her, reminded her too much of her no-good cop dad. Butch knew her sister's name, but hadn't known where she lived. Maybe Etta had said, but until today he hadn't cared. Now he'd have no trouble finding the sister's address. Etta thought she could escape by running away. Not a chance. Even though he knew how to get to New Bern—he'd driven through the town on his way to Atlantic Beach a couple times—he punched in the quickest route to New Bern on his GPS.

CHAPTER SIXTY-TWO

8:25 a.m.

On the boat, Win groaned and rubbed his head. Groggy, he pushed himself into a sitting position and looked around. What happened? Where was Carole? And where the hell was he? He felt like he had a hangover, but why? He hadn't consumed that much wine. Carole should be the one with the hangover, a gigantic hangover. So why was she gone and he here alone? Wine. Drugs. Damn! Carole must have switched the glasses, waited for the drug to affect him, then left. But she couldn't have gone far; her car was locked in the garage. On foot she didn't stand a chance of escaping.

Win reached in his pocket for his cell phone, stood up and rang house security. "I'll get you, Carole," he said aloud, "and when I do I'll kill you slowly. Very slowly. And I'll record the whole thing, just like the other times."

"Hello," said a voice.

"This is Win Ford. The woman I came with . . ." He took a step, tripped and fell. I'll kill her, he thought as he realized Carole had tied his shoelaces together. He reached out to catch himself, stumbled again. His head hit the corner of the coffee table. The cell phone fell from his hand and slid under a chair.

"Hello? Mr. Ford, your mom wants you to call, says it's urgent. Hello? Mr. Ford, can you hear me? Where are you? Talk to me, Mr. Ford. Mr. Ford?"

CHAPTER SIXTY-THREE

Inside The Eagle's Perch, Aurora helped Yvonne carry the dirty dishes to the kitchen. "That was delicious, Yvonne. You know, I think this sausage/grits casserole is one you should have ready to serve reporters while they're eagerly getting your story."

Yvonne beamed. "Thanks. I have several in the freezer, wouldn't take long to defrost them."

"Do you have a good soup recipe?"

"I do. Why do you ask?"

"Well, we're into late October. We're already getting some frosty nights and we'll have a freeze any time now. Can you imagine how grateful those chilled-to-the-bone newspaper and television reporters will be when you offer them a cup of your homemade soup?"

"Excellent idea. I have some fresh pumpkins in the garden ready for picking. A pumpkin soup is one of my specialties. Aurora, are you into marketing, by any chance? You have such great ideas."

Aurora laughed. "Well, kind of. I'm a videographer. I produce travelogues, commercials, that sort of thing. I also design and sell cross-stitch kits." And somehow I get involved with mysteries and dead bodies, she thought. She prayed that Carole wouldn't be another dead body. She didn't think she could stand that.

Aurora was looking at her watch and wondering where Lieutenant Conner and Deputy Johnson were when the doorbell rang. Paul Bateman answered the door, ushered in the deputies.

Introductions were made, and Aurora told them about the damage to Win's car and his license plate. "We thought you'd want to check his room," said Sam. "We stayed out of it, so nothing's been disturbed." He crossed his fingers, hoped the deputies would allow Aurora and him to examine the room also.

Yvonne handed Conner the key.

"Thanks," he said. He didn't invite the others to join him.

After waiting 40 minutes, Aurora was on the brink of running upstairs and insisting they tell her everything they'd learned, when Conner and Johnson came downstairs. Aurora wanted to ask what had taken them so long, but kept her mouth shut.

"Interesting," said Lieutenant Conner.

"Did you find anything that ties him to the hit and run?" asked Luke.

"We did. But that's not all. Between what we found in his car and in his room, there's enough evidence to incriminate him in other crimes, even murders," said Conner. "Seems the man kept a scrapbook of newspaper articles, pictures, videos. The *Smith Mountain Eagle's* story on the hit and run was the last entry. He's a sick one, I can tell you that." He glanced at Luke. "We found pictures of women—before and after pictures."

"Before and after pictures of what?" asked Aurora.

"Pictures of women before and after they were murdered. We, uh, saw a picture of Carole, Luke. She was standing beside a For Sale sign. There're no pictures showing her dead."

Luke groaned. Aurora put her arm around him. "Carole's not dead," she said. "She's one of the most resourceful people I know, always has been. And she did not trust Win. She would have guessed if she were in danger and figured a way out."

"Are you sure your friend Carole is with Win?"

"She was when I talked with her yesterday afternoon. She said she'd call me last night." She looked around at the people in the room. "So what happens now?"

"I've already put out an APB on him with descriptions of Carole and her car," said Lieutenant Conner.

"I can't just sit around and wait," said Luke.

"Us either," said Aurora. "Let's go."

Outside, Luke, Aurora and Sam decided on a plan. Sam and Aurora would drop Luke off at the real estate office so he could pick up his car, then they would return home so Aurora could get her Jeep. They divided the Smith Mountain Lake map into sections; each would take a section to search. King would ride with Aurora. They'd keep in touch by cell phone every 30 minutes if they could avoid "dead zones."

CHAPTER SIXTY-FOUR

Thursday, 9:00 a.m.

Lillian dropped Blanche off at the front door of the hospital and drove into the parking garage. Hurrying into the building, Blanche rode the elevator up to ICU. By now she knew her way around the hospital well. Too well, she thought, and said a little prayer for Tom. Shocked when she realized she'd actually prayed, she shook her head to clear it and continued down the hall.

When they saw Blanche, Estelle and Mary Ann got up from their seats in the waiting room.

"How's Tom this morning?" Blanche asked as they walked to his room.

"We checked on him about 45 minutes ago. The nurse told me he didn't sleep well during the night. She wouldn't give me details. Estelle and I took turns poking our heads in his room every two to three hours. They wouldn't let us go in, though."

"I think they thought we'd try to kill him," said Estelle.

"Of course they didn't think that," said Blanche. "I'm shocked that you said that. Why would you say such a thing, Estelle?"

"Well, I tried twice to go to his bed. I wanted to speak to him, tell him I was there if he needed me. The nurse didn't like that and made me leave."

"You didn't tell me that, Estelle," said Mary Ann.

"I did. You just weren't listening."

Mary Ann rolled her eyes, admitted to herself that she often tuned Estelle out. "Blanche, you and Lillian must have left the lake early this morning. I didn't expect you this soon." She looked around. "Where is Lillian, anyway?"

"Parking the car. She dropped me off at the hospital. And yes, we left early. Lillian picked me up at 6:35."

"Were you able to get some rest last night?"

"Not much, but I'm glad I was able to change my clothes, shower, and pack a few things in a suitcase. Also gave me chance to make some phone calls and pay a couple of bills." They stopped outside Tom's door.

"I'd like to see Tom alone. You girls can see him later."

"Alone? You don't want us to go with you?" asked Mary Ann.

"Mary Ann, have you lost your mind? Blanche wants to see her husband. Alone. Without us. Period. So you and I will wait in the hall until we're told we can go in. Understood?" Estelle was tired of Mary Ann, tired of being at the hospital.

Mary Ann started to speak at the same time Lillian reached them.

"How's Tom?" Lillian asked.

"I'm going to find out right now," answered Blanche. The policeman sitting outside Tom's door recognized her, told her to go on in.

Blanche noticed Tom was still hooked up to all sorts of contraptions.

"Mrs. Southerland," said the nurse, "I hope you got some sleep." Blanche nodded. "Mr. Southerland didn't have a good night. His breathing was labored and his blood pressure was way up. The doctor thinks his foot's infected."

"His color doesn't look good," said Blanche. She put her hand on his forehead. "He's so hot. Is his fever high?"

The nurse nodded.

Blanche rested her hand on her husband's arm.

"Hey, Tom. I'm here." His eyelids fluttered, but he made no sound. "Is he in a coma?"

"No, your husband is sleeping. By the way, the doctor wants to talk to you when he makes his rounds, probably in about an hour or less, so please make yourself available."

"Of course. I'm not going anywhere."

At that moment the door opened and Dr. Blackman hurried in. "Mrs. Southerland. Glad you're here. I have bad news. I'm afraid your husband has taken a turn for the worse."

"What happened?"

"You know that mangled foot of his? Well, gangrene set in."

"Gangrene? How can that be? And why didn't you catch it earlier?"

"Mr. Southerland developed what we call gas gangrene. We didn't discover it right away because the surface of his skin appeared normal. When the skin on his foot turned purplish-red and he developed a foul-smelling discharge, I immediately suspected gangrene. I've given him strong antibiotics, done everything I know to stop the progression, but he's getting worse fast. I can't wait any longer. The foot must be amputated immediately. It's either that or his life." Dr. Blackman caught Blanche as she crumpled to the floor.

CHAPTER SIXTY-FIVE

Thursday, 9:11 a.m.

She'd been on the road only a little over an hour, but Etta was already a nervous wreck. She knew Butch well, figured he wouldn't quit looking for her until he found her and slit her throat the way he'd wanted to cut Hessie's. Every time a dark truck appeared in her rearview mirror, her stomach would tighten and she'd hold her breath until certain the truck wasn't Butch's. Her blood pressure must be sky high by now. Had she taken her blood pressure pill this morning? She couldn't remember. "Calm down, Etta," she said aloud. Mouser meowed.

A sign for Burger King appeared and she turned off the highway, pulled into the nearly empty parking lot. Etta frowned. If Butch drove past he would see her Capri. For the first time since she'd bought the car—used, of course—she wished she'd purchased a white or gray one instead of red. She needed a larger parking lot with more cars where she wouldn't be so conspicuous. Looking across the street she spied a sign for Shoney's. This time of day, lots of people would be eating breakfast there. Believing she'd be less conspicuous in their parking lot, she drove across the road and parked between two vans. From the back seat, Mouser voiced his dissatisfaction.

"Don't worry, sweetie," she said to the cat as she poured a little water from her water bottle in Mouser's dish and stuck it in the carrier. "I'll be back soon." She cracked open the windows, locked the car and hurried into the restaurant.

At her request, the waitress seated Etta in a booth so she'd have a clear view of the entrance and part of the parking lot. From her seat she might see Butch drive in, would surely see him the minute he entered Shoney's. She hoped he wouldn't come, but if he did she could duck down in the booth, maybe get out before he found her.

When the waitress returned to the table to take her order, Etta ordered the breakfast buffet and asked that the check be given to her immediately. The waitress raised an eyebrow.

"I'm in a hurry," Etta explained. When the waitress just stared at her, Etta smiled and said, "I got myself some serious man trouble. May need to leave in a hurry and I don't want to stiff y'all."

"Sugar, I shore do understand. I've had some man trouble lately myself." She tore out the check, placed it on the table. "You have yourself a nice day now." She patted Etta's hand and moved to another table.

Etta reached in her purse and pulled out nine one-dollar bills, placed them on the check, covered them with her napkin and hurried to the breakfast buffet. When she returned to her table with a heavily laden plate, she popped a forkful of scrambled eggs into her mouth and scribbled a note for the waitress telling her who to call and asking her to rescue Mouser from the red Capri if anything happened to her. She gave Butch's name and address. She'd place it on the table if she saw Butch. Even if she died, Mouser would have a chance at life. And maybe Butch would get what he deserved when the cops found him.

CHAPTER SIXTY-SIX

Thursday, 10:30 a.m.

Aurora looked at her watch and frowned. She'd hoped to be on the road before now, but she'd needed to put some food together to take on their search, make photocopies of a recent picture of Carole to hand out, and several messages on the answering machine had needed attention. When she'd arrived home, there was a message from Robert that sounded urgent, but wasn't. A call from Dixie Lee saying that Hessie had a broken arm but was improving required a call back. The last message was her doctor's nurse stating that her recent mammogram was negative.

Now she and King were beginning their search in Franklin County from Hales Ford Bridge down 122 to Scruggs Road, then on to 40. Sam would check roads off 122 from Scruggs Road to Route 40 in Rocky Mount. They would meet somewhere on 40. Luke would cover Bedford County beginning at Hales Ford Bridge. Police in all three counties were involved. Game wardens searched the lake by boat.

On the lookout for Carole's car, Aurora cruised country roads dotted with houses, collapsed buildings, house trailers, barns, and abandoned cars. No back roads would be left unsearched. She tried to remember what the deputies had said about the newspaper clippings in Win's room. All the murdered women had been found in desolate, heavily woody areas. Aurora sighed. Franklin County claimed thousands of square miles answering that description. So did Pittsylvania and Bedford Counties. Finding Carole alive promised to be a daunting task, perhaps an impossible one. She trembled at the knowledge of what would happen to Carole if she couldn't escape from Win.

Aurora drove down a two-mile gravel road until it ended. Four times she stopped pedestrians or people working in their yards and showed them Carole's picture. No one had seen her or her car. Calls from Luke and Sam proved they were having no success either.

When she reached Westlake, Aurora drove slowly through the shopping areas as she looked for Carole's car, made a quick pit stop for herself and King at Wendy's, then continued out Scruggs Road toward Route 40. All the time her concern for Carole escalated.

Furious, Win stood in front of the security guard's desk. "What do you mean you haven't found her? Where the bloody hell could she have gone? I know it was dark when she disappeared, and I didn't notify you until after nine this morning, but her car's locked up in your garage. She couldn't get far on foot."

The guard looked down at his desk, coughed, looked at Win. "Her car's gone."

"Gone? How'd that happen?"

"The only thing we can figure," said Otis, "is that the night people moved a couple cars out of the garage so the Ferrari could back out, then planned to leave the cars out until the Ferrari returned. After all, the woman was with you. At least that's what you told us." He patted the gun on his hip. "So don't you go gittin' so high and mighty with me, Mr. Ford. You didn't do so good keepin' track of her yourself."

Win tried to control his temper. "So what are you doing to locate her? Is there any way she could drive off the estate grounds without you knowing it?"

"None," said Otis.

"The entire 400 acres are fenced, most of the fencing has an electric wire across the top," said the guard seated at the desk. "All four gates have video cameras that we review every six hours. And if any of the gates are breached, an alarm there on the wall goes off. We're due to look at the tape of the East Gate Entrance at noon. My guess is that will be the one she uses since it's closer to the road leading away from the garage."

"Do it now."

"What?"

"I said do it now, damn you." Win slammed his fist down on the desk.

"Just who do you think . . .?"

"You'll be fired as soon as I make a phone call. Do you want to chance that? If you don't believe me, call your boss." Win raised his eyebrow and picked up the phone.

"Guess it won't hurt none," said the guard. He hit a remote, then pointed to a TV screen. "We'll scan the tape, see if anything but birds, deer and other wild critters crossed the road. Most times this is boring stuff, but if you want to watch, help yourself. This here button slows it down, this one speeds it up, and this one stops it." He stood up and stretched. "I'm gonna git a cup of coffee. Have fun."

Win slid in the guard's chair as the video played. With his eyes on Win, Otis leaned against the wall and watched.

CHAPTER SIXTY-SEVEN

Thursday, 10:35 a.m.

At the same time Win was reviewing the tape, an exhausted Carole sat on a fallen pine tree. Her left calf ached from where she'd cut it climbing over the iron gate. At least the bleeding had stopped. She tried to figure how long it had been since she'd last slept. She guessed about 30 hours. Right now it felt more like 300 hours, maybe closer to 3,000. How much longer could she keep going? Resting her head in her hands, she closed her eyes and nearly toppled off the log. Regaining her balance, she checked her cell phone; still no signal.

How could she have been so stupid to get involved with Win? Usually her judgment about people was excellent, a trait she'd inherited from her mother. Except that she hadn't done too well in the judgment department for a while. Win was a business interest, not a romantic one. But he could be so charming when he chose to be. She admitted to herself that the chance to earn big money— and the need to pay the mortgage—had caused her to ignore her intuition. Aurora had warned her about Win, but she hadn't listened to her friend. Never again, she thought. *If I survive this, I'll always listen to you, Aurora.*

She announced to the forest and any creatures within earshot, "You're stupid, Carole. After all you did to pay your bills, you'll never collect a single penny from Win. Too bad. That commission looked really good on paper. But that's all it was— paper. And empty promises from Mr. I. Winston Ford, jerk number one."

Carole reached in her jacket pocket, pulled the last cracker out of its wrapping and took a bite. The cracker was stale, but when she first found the package of six peanut butter crackers jammed in her jacket pocket, she wouldn't have cared if they'd been a year old. She stuffed the last of the cracker back in her pocket and opened her water bottle. Frowning, she screwed the top back on. She needed to conserve the little water that remained. Time to get moving again.

Most times she tried to stay about fifteen yards from the shoulder of the road in case the guards cruised the road searching for her. Twice she crawled through barbed wire. Cattle grazing in a pasture lifted they heads and looked briefly, then resumed munching. She wanted to move closer to the road, try to flag down a car coming from the opposite direction, see if they'd take her to the nearest town. But what if the vehicle was going to *La Grande Maison*, had heard that people were hunting for her? No, she'd better not show herself.

Had Win and the guards found Crappy yet? She prayed not. Every minute counted, meant a better chance to escape. She tried to calculate how many miles she'd walked and gave up. She just knew that it seemed like a gazillion.

"Keep going, Carole," she said. "One foot in front of the other. You can't afford to get caught."

In the guard station, Win stopped the tape, backed it up. He called the guards over to the desk. "Look at this," he said, pointing to the screen. "That's her car driving off the road. Why didn't the alarm go off? Oh, damn. There's Carole climbing the gate. Why didn't you see it? You idiots are supposed to be watching." He stood up, bent forward and shook his finger in a guard's face. "You really are idiots. You know that?"

"I don't know why the alarm didn't go off. It's set to warn us when someone tries to go through the gate. Besides, when the camera caught her and her car, you hadn't even reported her missing. Maybe you're the idiot. The guard had probably gone to the bathroom. Like all the other folks in the world, we need to do that occasionally, too. And did it ever occur to you that this woman is a whole lot smarter than you?" asked Otis.

The other guard picked up the phone, dialed a number. "Put the dogs in the Humvee," he said into the receiver. "We'll drive 'em to the gate, then turn 'em loose. And we'll need a driver." He looked at Win, wished Win were the one the dogs would corner, wished they'd rip him into shreds. "The dogs will find her."

"Will they kill her?" Win hoped not. He had other plans for Carole.

CHAPTER SIXTY-EIGHT

Thursday, 10:45 a.m.

In the Karver house, Kurt's mom took his temperature and read 99.6, down from 102 early this morning. His color looked better and he hadn't thrown up since around six, although he'd said once that his stomach felt queasy. Maybe he'd caught a 24-hour bug; she'd heard something was going around.

"How do you feel now, son?" she asked. "Think you could eat a little chicken broth?"

"Yes, ma'am, I could eat a little. I don't feel like I'm gonna puke anymore."

"Good. I'll fix a tray and bring it up."

"That's okay, Mom. I'll go eat at the kitchen table."

"You sure?"

"Yes, ma'am. I'll be there in a minute." He stuck his feet in his moccasins and put on a robe.

In the pantry, Mrs. Karver picked up the last can of chicken broth. She was low on a few other groceries, too, items she'd planned to pick up on her way home from work today.

She heated the broth and poured it into a large mug. That way Kurt could sip the soup instead of spooning it into his mouth.

"This is good, Mom. I didn't realize I was so hungry."

"You're eating the last of the chicken broth, and there are a few other things we need. If you're feeling well enough, maybe I'll make a quick run to the grocery store this afternoon."

"I'll be okay if you leave, but couldn't you just call Dad and get him to pick up stuff on his way home? He drives right by a couple stores."

"Normally, yes, but your dad's in an all-day meeting that includes dinner. I don't want to bother him except in an emergency."

The telephone rang. Kurt's mother answered it.

"I'm sorry. Kurt's home sick today," said his mother to the caller. "You'll have to call back or you can leave your number and he'll call you when he feels like it." Pause. "Yes, I know he's anxious to get the camera." She glanced over at Kurt who'd guessed the caller's identity. "He's signaling that he wants to talk to you, so I'll put him on, but just for a minute. We don't want his soup to get cold." She handed the phone to her son.

"Hello," he said.

"Kurt, buddy, I'm sorry you're under the weather. I waited for you at the bus stop this morning, thought maybe you'd forgotten or decided you didn't want the camera. Wish you'd let me know you weren't coming."

"You didn't leave a number. I don't even know your name. What did you say it is?" Kurt sipped his soup, wiped his mouth with the back of his hand.

"Uh, it's Smith, Arnie Smith. Listen up, Kurt. I've gotta fly out to the west coast tomorrow, to California and Oregon, won't be back for a couple weeks. You sound like a nice kid. I'd really like to give the camera to you and not to somebody else who doesn't deserve it. I think you will work with the camera, take the time to study the manual, learn how the camera operates. I think you'll shoot some amazing pictures."

"Thanks, Mr. Smith. I sure do want that camera."

"How about I drop it off in a couple hours, say between one and two. Will your mom still be there?"

"Yes sir, we'll both be here, except for when Mom runs to the grocery store."

"Anybody else be home? Your dad, perhaps?"

"No, sir. Dad's at work."

"I don't want to come when a parent's not home. I don't think that's proper. What time do you think your mother will be gone?" Jasper could hardly contain his excitement. Finally things were beginning to go right for him.

"Let me ask her." Kurt turned to his mom. "Mom, it's Arnie Smith, the camera guy. He wants to know when you'll be here so he can bring me the camera, says he doesn't want to come if you're not home."

"How thoughtful." She looked at her watch. "It's 10:50 now. I'll leave in five minutes, should be back by noon. That is if you're sure you feel well enough for me to go."

"Aw, Mom. I'm not a baby."

His mother laughed.

"Mr. Smith, Mom's leaving at 10:55, should be back an hour later. That okay with you?"

"Kurt, that will work just fine. And I look forward to meeting you and your mother, and showing you how to operate this incredible camera. See you around 12:15."

Parked down the street, Jasper hung up his cell phone and watched the Karver house through binoculars. He could hardly wait for Kurt's mother to drive off. His foot tapped to heavy metal playing on the radio. His cell rang. He checked caller ID, turned the music down and answered.

"Where the hell are you?" Jasper asked.

"In a rest station in North Carolina," said Butch.

"North Carolina? Why?"

"Because Etta's scared and she's running to her sister in New Bern." Butch tensed as a small red car turned into the parking area. He fingered the gun on the seat, then relaxed. The car was an Altima, not a Capri. He relaxed.

"You told me early this morning Etta was as good as dead. On the road to New Bern isn't dead. At least, it wasn't the last time I checked." Jasper picked up the binoculars, looked at Kurt's house, put them down. "Wanna tell me what happened?"

"I got to her house just minutes after she left. The coffee pot was still warm, so you know how close I came to catching her. Would have if I hadn't had to stop behind school busses, three of them yellow things. I would've passed two of 'em, but a cop was right behind me. Couldn't chance it. Damn those busses and damn the cops. It's not my fault, Jasper."

It never is, Butch, thought Jasper. But that will change soon.

"Did you hear me, Jasper?"

"I heard you." Jasper tried to figure out another way to incriminate Butch in three murders: Etta's, Kurt's, and Butch's. Suicide for Butch? Jasper would have to think about that one a little more. Originally he'd hoped to make Etta's death and Butch's look like a lovers' quarrel. But now. . . .

A minivan pulled up beside him. "I've gotta go," said Jasper. "Call me when you find her."

The driver waved, smiled, and rolled down the window. Jasper groaned. He recognized the nosey old battle axe who lived next door to Hessie. He rolled his window down, pasted a smile on his face.

"Mr. Smoot, how good to see you. So sorry to hear about Hessie. I know you must have been frantic when you discovered her missing and then found that she had wandered up on Smith Mountain. I trust she's doing well?"

"She is. And thank you for asking." Jasper had no clue how Hessie was doing. And he couldn't care less. He thought the Karver's garage door opened, but he couldn't be sure. He strained to see. Nope, he needed to use his binoculars.

"Interesting that you would be parked on the road instead of in Hessie's driveway. Hers is only a few houses away."

"Um, well, yeah. I'm waiting for a truck to come remove some of her furniture. Didn't want to get in the way. I'm sorry to say this, but with the Alzheimer's and all her other health problems, she'll need to live in a nursing home when she leaves the hospital. I'm sure you understand."

"Of course, of course." But she really didn't. She frowned.

"Well, don't let me keep you. I know a busy lady like yourself has things to do, places to go, people to see." He smiled his most charming smile, waved goodbye, and started to roll up the window.

"Yes, I need to get this book back to the library. Oh, did you know—."

"Don't let me keep you. Goodbye." He rolled up his window. He wondered if the nosey woman would ever get the hint. Probably not. Busybodies like her never did.

"Oh, right." She raised her hand in a half wave, put her own window up, frowned again and drove away.

"You have time to get a short nap before I get home and Mr. Smith arrives, Kurt. I think you should go back to bed. Or you could stretch out on the sofa. Oh, and keep the bucket with you in case you start feeling nauseous again." She picked up her purse and her keys.

"I can take care of myself." He didn't like being treated like a little kid. What was it with grown-ups, anyhow? "Mom, I'm 13." Kurt plumped a throw pillow, tossed it onto the couch.

"I know, sweetie, but to me you'll always be my little boy." His mother leaned over him, kissed his cheek. "I won't be long. I have my cell phone in case you think of something else we need. 'Bye, sweetie."

Exhausted, Kurt flopped on the sofa and put his head on the pillow. Not comfortable. He stood up and trudged up the stairs to his bedroom, crawled in bed and closed his eyes. He heard the garage door open and his mom's SUV back out. Thirty seconds later he fell asleep.

Jasper's penetrating eyes scanned the yards and houses on the street. Most of the people in the neighborhood worked during the day. Miss Nosey Neighbor had just left, and the house on the other side of Hessie's was vacant and up for sale. He figured that the women who stayed home would be glued to their television sets watching their favorite soap operas this time of day. Just like his ex-wife. She always complained about the house being a mess, said that Jasper never helped her clean. If she'd ever gotten that fat can of hers off the couch for even one hour a day, the bed could have been made and the dishes wouldn't have been stacked in the sink waiting for Jasper when he got home from work. And maybe she'd have had a chance to dab on some lipstick and comb her hair. He smiled, remembering how everyone had told him what a shame her brakes went out that morning, that she'd died such a horrible death. Accidental, of course.

Glancing around, Jasper wondered if passersby would notice his car in Kurt's driveway, then decided it wouldn't matter. He'd be in and out in minutes. He looked up and down the street and backed his car up the drive to the garage. That way he could get away fast if necessary, and if he had to, he could stuff Kurt in the trunk without being observed.

How nice of the missus to leave the garage door up, he thought, wondering if she'd locked the connecting door to the house. He tried the door. No luck. He slipped a credit card behind the lock, smiled when he heard the click. Jasper stepped into the mud room and softly shut the door. He pulled a silencer from his jacket and attached it to his pistol.

His cell phone rang. He jumped, bumped a shelf. Two empty wine bottles crashed to the floor. Glass flew in all directions.

Kurt struggled out of a deep sleep, reached for the phone. He heard a cell phone ringing, not his mom's or his. He sat up straight and listened. He heard glass break. Someone was in the house. He'd never admit it, but right now he wished his mom were home.

Jasper punched off his cell, stood stone-statue still and listened. Maybe the kid hadn't heard the ring or the bottles falling on the floor. Maybe he was sound asleep. After all, he stayed home today because he was sick. A minute passed. Jasper breathed easier.

He stepped through the shattered glass, walked quietly across the kitchen and entered the living room. No sign of the kid. Where was he? Had he ridden to the store with his mom? Jasper wondered. No, he was probably in a bedroom, either asleep or playing some game on his own computer. He sneered. Most kids these days were spoiled rotten, had their own bedrooms, TVs, computers, cell phones, iPods. Not like it used to be. Money wasn't everything. Jasper's family hadn't been rich, and he turned out just fine. Just fine? Some folks would argue with that. He covered his mouth with his hand to stifle a laugh.

Back to the present, Jasper thought. The question was which bedroom and what floor? He guessed the master bedroom was on the first floor, and in order to get to Kurt's sanctuary he'd need to climb the uncarpeted stairs.

Seven steps up he reached a landing that turned left. Only six more steps to go. *Squeak.* He stopped, his right foot poised above the next step. Damn. He aimed his pistol at the first door and waited—no sound, and no person. He hated to chance stepping on another squeaky step, but he had no choice. On up he went.

From the hall, he opened doors to two sissy bedrooms, each with a small, private bath. Guest bedrooms, he figured. He opened the closets, looked under the queen-sized beds. Nothing. The next door off the hallway was closed. He turned the knob and slowly pushed the door open. The unmade bed showed no sign of Kurt, but with the walls plastered with sports pictures, Jasper knew this was Kurt's room. A bucket rested beside the bed, moccasin slippers poked out from beneath, and a partially filled glass rested on the nightstand. Kurt must still be in the house.

Jasper looked at his watch. Too much time had elapsed. Kurt's mother could be home in 25 minutes, maybe sooner if she didn't run into a slowpoke, probably somebody driving a Jaguar capable of easily doing 130 mph. It always irritated him to get behind one of those. He reminded himself to get back to the present. All senses alert and adrenalin flowing, he made as thorough a search of the house as he could in the time he had left. The kid had vanished, had outsmarted him. He checked his watch. If he didn't leave now, the mother could arrive home before he escaped.

Neither the kid nor his mother knew his real name, had no clue what he looked like. Miss Nosey Neighbor had seen him, but not at the Karver house. He hurried through the family room, thought about smashing the large flat-screen TV for the fun of it, decided against it. No one had proof he'd been here; the mom would probably convince the kid that the bottles had fallen by themselves. Those things did happen occasionally. Yeah, he was safe.

At 11:45, a perplexed Miss Nosey Neighbor drove into her garage and punched the remote. The door rumbled to a close. She quickly exited the car, hurried into the house and peered through the blinds covering the laundry room window. She watched Jasper Smoot leave the Karver's garage across the street, climb into his car and drive away. Strange, mighty strange. What had he been doing in the Karver's garage when neither of their cars was home?

Blessed—some would say cursed—with an overactive imagination equaled only by her curiosity, she wondered if Mr. Smoot and Mrs. Karver were having an affair. Not likely. A classy woman like Ruth Karver wouldn't be the least bit interested in scrawny Mr. Smoot. There must be some other reason. She thought about all the recent break-ins and vandalisms in Sweetwater Cove. Maybe she should phone the police.

CHAPTER SIXTY-NINE

Thursday, 11:50 a.m.

Kurt silently cracked open the door to his hiding place and listened. Was the intruder still inside the house? He poked his head out and looked around. Nothing. He'd shut himself up in the wall for almost an hour. Surely it was safe to come out now. Slowly he pulled his body through the small door and tip-toed to his now-open bedroom door. He was positive he'd closed it before crawling into the storage area that ran past the three dormer windows and across the width of the Cape Cod house.

Behind the wall was the perfect secret place. If anyone opened the small access door and peered inside, he would still be hidden from view in the tight space below the dormer window. He remembered his mom saying that if anyone ever broke in when Kurt was home, he could always hide there. At the time, Kurt thought she was joking. Not any more.

He heard the doorbell chime. Before he could decide whether or not he should go open it, a male voice hollered from the front steps and someone banged on the door. Kurt peeped out the window, saw a county police car parked in his driveway. He hurried downstairs, opened the door.

"Your neighbor called in a possible robbery," said one of the officers. From across the street, Nosey Neighbor waved. "Is everything okay here?"

"Yes, sir, but somebody came in the house while my mom was gone."

"How can you be sure?"

"I was asleep in my bed upstairs and a ringing phone—not one of ours—woke me. After that I heard glass break and then a squeak on the stairs."

"That all? And why are you home today? Are you home-schooled?"

"No, I go to public school. Mom made me stay home because I was puking all night." The deputy backed up. Kurt smiled, thought about blowing germs on him.

"As for somebody being in the house, when I came out of my hiding place my bedroom door was open. I'm sure I closed it."

"Kurt, are you okay?" His mom rushed up to him, threw her arms around him. "Look at you. You're shaking. You shouldn't be out here in this cold air in your pajamas, especially when you're already sick. And where are your slippers? Get yourself back in the house right this minute, young man."

Kurt looked at her, shifted from one foot to the other.

"Who are you?" asked a deputy.

"I'm Kurt's mother, Mrs. Karver. I live here. What happened?"

"Your neighbor across the street," he pointed across the street to Nosey Neighbor who waved again and grinned, "made a suspicious-person call to us. Because of all the recent vandalism and thefts in Sweetwater Cove, we thought we should check it out. I'm glad we did; your son says someone was in the house."

"In our house? Oh my goodness. Kurt, I'm so sorry. I blame myself. I never should have left you alone."

"Aw, Mom. I'm okay."

"Maybe Mr. Smith arrived early. Kurt, do you think he's the person who came inside the house?"

"I don't know; I was hiding. I didn't see anybody, just heard noises."

"Who is Mr. Smith?" asked a deputy.

"A man who was delivering a camera to Kurt. I can't believe he would have come early; we agreed on 12:15. I had to run to the grocery store for chicken broth and a few other things. Mr. Smith said he'd come after I got home."

"What does Mr. Smith look like?"

"Don't know. We've never met him. He said Kurt had won the use of an expensive camera for six months." She smiled at Kurt. "My son's a camera nut."

"Kurt, I told you to get inside," she said.

The deputy scribbled notes on his pad.

From across the street, a single shot found its target. Nosey Neighbor toppled to the ground. A deputy dashed to her.

"Call 911!" he yelled. "She's been shot!"

Standing out of sight in Tom Southerland's side yard, Jasper Smoot slipped his rifle back in its case. Smiling, he hurried across the back yard, ducked behind a thick row of pines, and continued down the street to where he left his car. Now he had an appointment to keep in Charlottesville. Nosey Neighbor wouldn't tell anybody anything ever.

CHAPTER SEVENTY

11:55 p.m.

At the hospital, Blanche looked at her three friends.

"Do you want us to stay with you until Tom comes out of surgery?" asked Estelle. "I'm sure we'd all be willing. Right, girls?"

Lillian and Mary Ann agreed.

"You've all done so much already. Go home, get back to your families and your normal schedules. Tom will come through this just fine. And so will I. His parents should be here tomorrow if they can get a flight into Roanoke or Richmond. I'm not overly fond of them, but they need to be with their son. And having them here will give me a break."

"We can wait until he's out of surgery and in recovery if you want us to," offered Lillian, even though she was eager to go home.

"No, I'd like you to go," said Blanche. Just go, she thought. Vamoose, scat, give me breathing room before I go out of my ever-loving mind!

The three women gathered up their purses and tote bags, hugged Blanche goodbye with if-you-need-us instructions, and left.

At that moment, Detective Holmes entered the waiting room, dropped down in a chair. "Please sit, Mrs. Southerland," he said.

Blanche stared at him, perched on the edge of the other chair.

"I understand that you and Mr. Southerland had different, ah, interests." He raised his left eyebrow, looked at Blanche. "Is that true?"

"Well, yes. Tom's job with Sweetwater Cove is his priority, his life. Well, that and making money. Mine is bridge; playing golf comes second. Why do you ask?"

"You're away from home a lot, are you?"

"I am. Like I told you, I enjoy playing golf and bridge, and I do both of those at the club. I'm also involved in a number of charitable organizations that require a lot of my attention. Surely you've seen my name and picture in all the papers."

"Sorry, I haven't been that, ah, lucky." Detective Holmes put his fingers to his temples, thought a second and looked at her. "You and Mr. Southerland don't do much together, do you?"

"No. I told you, we have different interests. And what business is it of yours? Surely you don't think I had anything to do with the attack on Tom. You can tell there is no way I could stuff him in a freezer and shove it down the mountain and into the lake."

"You could have hired someone to do your dirty work. Can you look me in the eye and tell me you've never wished your husband dead?"

Blanche stood. "I don't like your insinuations. I will not discuss this with you further until my lawyer is present. Please leave."

Holmes smiled and walked into the hall.

CHAPTER SEVENTY-ONE

Thursday, Noon

The Humvee carrying the Dobermans, two guards, the driver, and Win slammed to a halt at the iron gate. Jumping from the vehicle, the dogs immediately picked up Carole's scent, barked, scratched at the gate.

"Quiet!" a guard shouted. "Sit!" Whining, the dogs obeyed, waited for the next command.

"You know we'll git in big trouble if anyone outside of *La Grande Maison* catches us. We could go to prison. You sure you wanna do this?"

"We'll go to prison if she escapes. She knows too much. She's figured out that I'm stealing boats and that *La Grande Maison* is fencing them. So yeah, I'm sure," said Win, "as long as the dogs won't kill her."

"They won't kill her, but I ain't sure they won't rip her up some if she tries to fight 'em."

"Oh, you can bet she'll fight." Win grinned, rubbed his hands together. "I wouldn't have it any other way. But I want to watch, so keep 'em on their leads until we're real close. Then you can turn 'em loose." Win smiled. He had his trusty camera and video camera, looked forward to adding more pictures to his collection.

Carole stopped and opened her almost empty water bottle, swallowed half of the remaining precious liquid. As she screwed the top back on, she heard a sound, like dogs barking in the distance. Cocking her head, she stood still and tried to gauge where the sound was coming from.

Her gut told her the dogs from *La Grande Maison* were hunting something. And I'm guessing I'm it, she thought. Somehow she summoned strength she didn't know was left. Without looking behind her, she took off at a jog. Trying to pick her way through the woods would slow her, but not the dogs. She decided to take her chances that someone on the road would see her, hopefully even help her. She veered toward the hard surfaced road where she could move at a faster pace.

A quarter mile down the road Carole stopped to catch her breath and listen again for the dogs. She heard nothing. Why? Somehow that worried her even more. Where were they? She patted her jacket pockets to make sure she hadn't lost her cell phone or her pistol. Satisfied, she downed the last of her water, tossed the bottle aside and began running. Her leg muscles ached, her legs buckled. She fell, pushed herself up, forced her tired legs to keep going.

The guards snapped the leashes on the dogs and opened the gate. At the command to track, the dogs strained at their leads, put noses to the ground, yelped and trotted into the woods. The men jogged behind them.

Seven minutes passed before Win called a halt. With hands on his knees, he bent over, tried to catch his breath. Even though the mid-October temperature was 50 degrees, beads of sweat covered his face.

"Whatsamatter, Mr. Ford? You havin' a heart attack or something?" a guard asked.

"No, I'm just not used to this. It's rough going in the woods, and Carole's got a head start." Win wiped his brow with a handkerchief. "Any suggestions?"

"We could just turn the dogs loose, but then you wouldn't get to watch them tear into her like you said you wanted."

"Okay, then let's keep going the way we were for a little longer."

Aurora and King made a right turn onto a road off Route 40. At the intersection, she saw a service station. She looked at her gas gauge; she'd used almost a whole tank. She'd fill up here and use the restroom. She pulled up to the pump, stuck her credit card in the payment slot, and started pumping.

Gassing up beside her, a young woman smiled at Aurora. "Don't I know you?" she asked. "You like look so familiar."

"So do you," said Aurora, "but I don't think we've ever met. Do you live around here?"

"Yeah, about five miles on down Route 40 toward Rocky Mount, but I like work at the end of this here road. Hey, your dog's real purty. What's his name?"

"King."

"I used to have a chocolate Lab mix, but she got hit by a car. My Daddy was drunk and Princess wouldn't move out of the driveway fast enough to suit him. He like just ran over her. On purpose."

"That's tough. I'm sorry."

"Yeah, thanks. That's when I ran away from home. After I buried my dog. Dug the hole all by myself, cried the whole time. My mom watched from the kitchen window. She wanted to help me, but she was scared of Daddy. She was always scared of Daddy. Anyhow, I was 17, almost 18. I been supportin' myself ever since. My boyfriend Otis helps some. He's the one who got me this job. I just started yesterday. I'm on my way there now. I'm trying to save up enough money to go to college." She laughed. "I'm 19, probably be like really old before I have enough." She beamed at Aurora.

"What kind of degree do you want?"

"I always wanted to like be a nurse."

"That's a good profession." Aurora checked the gas, figured she needed about 10 more gallons. She'd never seen such a slow pump. "What do you do now?" she asked the woman.

"I bus tables."

"There's a restaurant down that road?"

"A restaurant? Oh, my goodness, no. *La Grande Maison* is lots more than a restaurant. There's like a big, fancy-schmancy hotel what has lots of guest houses and a marina and some high-end shops that cater to rich folks. More than one restaurant, too. My boss said that if I do a good job, then I can like move up to waiting tables, earn lots more money. He said the tips there are real good. He said rich people from all over the world stay there." She described the estate. "You wouldn't believe the fancy iron gate I have to drive through. When I get to the gate, I like have to call the security guard—my Otis is one of 'em—from my cell and then he releases the gate. It just opens up like magic."

"Strange. I've never heard of *La Grande Maison*."

"It's kind of a secret. I'm not supposed to tell anybody about it. But I'm so excited about working there I just had to tell somebody. You won't like rat me out, will you?"

Aurora smiled. "You can count on me to keep your secret." She hesitated. "I'm sure there's no point in asking you, but have you by any chance seen a pretty lady with chestnut colored hair driving a gray Corolla? She might have been with an exceptionally handsome man, you know, movie-star type handsome."

The woman pulled the nozzle out of her tank, hung it back on the gas pump, examined the picture. "I don't remember seeing any folks like that. Why?" She looked at her watch, frowned. She didn't want to be late for work on her second day.

"My friend Carole has disappeared and I'm trying to find her. She's in great danger."

"I'm sorry. I ain't seen her." She started to drive away, then stopped. "I did see a gray Corolla, though. Like a kinda old one."

"Where did you see it? When?" Aurora could hardly contain her excitement.

"Lessee, it was last night when I was taking the garbage out. I like moved out of sight of the kitchen door to get a quick smoke—it's against the rules for the hired help to smoke inside—and I saw the valet drive by in this old gray Corolla. I remember because it looked so out of place with all the big expensive cars."

"You don't happen to know what time that was, do you?" Aurora crossed her fingers, said a silent prayer.

"I believe it was between seven and eight o'clock." She looked at her watch again. "Gotta go or I'll be late for work."

"What's your name?" Aurora asked.

"I'm Monique. Nice meetin' you. 'Bye, King." Monique waved as she pulled onto the road.

Not as nice as it was for me to meet you, thought Aurora. She let King out of the car to do his business in the grass next to the road. She tried to call Sam. No answer. She pulled out the piece of paper she'd written Luke's number on and dialed him.

"Aurora, any news yet?" Luke asked. "I hope so, 'cause I've hit nothing but brick walls. It's like Carole's disappeared into thin air."

"I may have a lead. How soon can you get here?" Aurora told him about her conversation with Monique, gave him directions.

"I'm on Toler's Ferry Road. I can drive straight to Route 40, meet you in about 30 to 45 minutes. What about Sam?"

"He didn't answer his phone. Probably out of range. Actually, I'm really surprised I got you. Maybe you can reach Sam. Please try. See you in a while." Aurora hung up, put King in the car, and raced to the restroom. Triple speed.

Back in her car, Aurora tapped the steering wheel with her fingers. She still had time before Luke arrived. She dialed Uncle Charlie.

"Uncle Charlie, have you ever heard of a place on the lake called *La Grande Maison*?" she asked.

"No. Why?"

"I think Carole is there, probably not of her own free will." She told him about her conversation with the woman at the service station.

"Let me make some calls, see what I can find out. I'll get back to you as soon as I can."

"Thank you, Uncle Charlie. You know I appreciate and love you."

"I know, Aurora. I love you, too. I'll get back to you soon."

"Okay, King," she said, "that took all of three minutes, maybe four. I can't just sit here and wait. How would you like for us to cruise that road, see if we can find the mysterious *La Grande Maison*?" From the back seat, King whined, nudged her neck. Aurora laughed and started the engine.

CHAPTER SEVENTY-TWO

Thursday, 12:20 p.m.

Behind her the dogs barked again, louder now. Carole pictured them galloping through the woods, then on the road, closing in for the kill. And she was the kill. Would Win allow that? Of course. Stupid question, Carole. Would the dogs go for her throat first? Would they kill her fast or enjoy ripping her apart bit by bit? She ran down the road toward somewhere. She didn't care where as long as it took her away from the dogs.

In the distance a vehicle came toward her. Carole stood in the middle of the road, waved her arms. The car slowed to a crawl.

"Git outta my way!" yelled the driver. "I'm gonna be late for work!"

"No, please, the dogs, they're going to kill me! Help me, please help me!"

"Move or I'll run right smack over you! I'm not kiddin'!"

Carole stepped out of the way, watched as the car drove on up the road. She heard the dogs, closer now. Once they came around the curve, they'd see her. Somehow she found the energy to pick up her pace.

"Stupid woman standing in the middle of the road like that," mumbled Monique. "I shoulda just run right over—. Omigosh. I sound like Daddy."

Monique stopped the car, looked in her rearview mirror as Carole, stumbling and weaving, disappeared around a curve. I oughta help her, she thought. But if I do I'll be late for work, lose my job. I cain't lose my job. Otis would git like madder than hell at me. He might git fired, too. And it would be my fault. Then he'd git real mad. If she hurried she'd reach the iron gate on time. She pushed on the gas.

The Dobermans bounded out of the woods in front of her car. Monique slammed on brakes, missed the dogs by inches. The dogs never even stopped. Looking out her window, she watched them race down the road. Now she understood what the woman meant—dogs were going to kill her. She couldn't let that happen. She turned the car around.

"Stop!" a man screamed. Two other men dashed out of the woods toward her. "Give us your car!"

Monique looked from the men to the still-running dogs. All the men waved guns. One of them was Otis. She remembered what the nice lady with the black Lab had said.

"No!" she shouted. She turned the steering wheel to the left, stomped the accelerator. Something hit her car. What? She glanced in the mirror. Bullets! The men were shooting at her! Except for Otis. I love you, Otis, she thought as her car leapt forward.

Carole forced herself to concentrate on the slap-slap of her shoes hitting the pavement. She must keep going. Run, Carole, run. Funny, that sounded like a first-grade reading book. She smiled at the thought. Run, Carole, run. But she was so tired. What was the point? The dogs would tear her to pieces. And she prayed as she hadn't prayed since she was a freshman in college.

She stopped running, sat down in the middle of the country road that had no yellow line. Never in a million years would she have guessed she'd die this way. She worried about Luke, Aurora, all the people who loved her. For their sake and mine, please, God, just let it be quick.

The Lord is my Shepherd, I shall not want; he makes me lie down in green pastures. He leads me beside still waters; he restores my soul. He leads me in paths of righteousness for his name's sake. Even though I walk through the valley of the shadow of death, I fear no evil; for thou art with me; thy rod and thy staff, they comfort me.

What was that noise? A horn? Go away, she thought. But the noise wouldn't stop. A hand grabbed her arm, pulled her to her feet. A voice hollered at her.

"Come on, lady! Hurry up! The dogs will kill us both unless we git in the car!"

"What?" Carole struggled to walk, felt herself shoved into the passenger side. The door shut. Dogs, close now, snarled, growled.

Carole looked out the window, saw the young woman trying to get to the driver's side of the car. Two Dobermans, their teeth bared, inched closer.

"I have a gun!" Carole said. "Stick your hand through the window!" She stuck the .22 toward the open window. "The safety's off. All you have to do is point and shoot. Take it!"

"I can't reach it!" screamed Monique.

Carole opened her door, hollered at the Dobermans.

"Here, boys. Come and get me. Yoo hoo!" Up the road, two security guards and an exhausted Win ran toward the car. "Yoo-hoo, doggies! Here I am. Come get me."

The dogs circled the car looking for Carole. Monique jumped in the driver's seat, locked the doors and started the engine. The head of one of the dogs appeared at the window.

"That was close. Thanks. You okay?" Monique asked.

"Yeah. And thank you. What's that noise?"

"Only bullets. Those guys are like shooting at us," said Monique. "My car ain't gonna look too good. They don't like you much, do they?"

"Nope. And thanks again for helping me." Bullets slammed into the car.

"We ain't like out of the woods yet. Are you Carole?" Monique asked.

"How'd you know that?"

"A friend of yours told me."

"What friend?"

"Don't know, but she's looking for you. She's like really worried. Oh, yeah, she has a black Lab."

"Where was she?"

"The gas station at the intersection six miles from here."

"In the direction we're going?"

"Yep." She looked in the rearview mirror. A vehicle popped around the curve a quarter mile behind them. "Uh-oh."

"What?" asked Carole.

"A Humvee just stopped, picked up the three guys. Now they're calling the dogs."

Carole turned around, stared out the back window. "The dogs are standing beside the Humvee."

"Maybe they'll like turn around, go back where they came from."

"Not a chance. I know Win."

Carole glanced at Monique. "Oh no, the dogs jumped in the Humvee! Can't this car go any faster?"

"Not on this road."

"They're coming this way." *Ping. Ping.* "Oh, no. Here we go again."

Bang! A rear tire blew. Monique's car lurched toward the shoulder.

"Look out!" she shouted. "I can't control it!"

Carole reached over, grabbed the steering wheel. Both women struggled to keep the car on the road. *Kerthunk. Kerthunk. Kerthunk.*

"How long can we keep on like this?" Carole asked.

"Don't have a clue. Like 'til it quits, I guess."

CHAPTER SEVENTY-THREE

Thursday, 12:35 p.m.

Dr. Blackman tapped Blanche's shoulder.

"What?" she asked, struggling to pull herself from a sound sleep.

"Mrs. Southerland, your husband is out of surgery. He's in recovery and will remain there for several hours. I'll let you know when he's back in his room."

Blanche looked at the book on her lap. She was still on page one. "I didn't get very far, did I?" She smiled. "Guess I fell asleep almost as soon as I sat down."

"That's understandable. You were tired; you've been under a lot of stress. I think now, though, since we've removed the source of infection, we'll see fast improvement in your husband."

"That's good."

"Do you have a car in Charlottesville?"

"No, friends brought me. I'll rent a car to go home when Tom's better."

"You'll have ample time to go to the cafeteria, eat a leisurely meal. I suggest you do that. I'm sure that's not happened for a while." The doctor's beeper sounded. "Gotta go. Get some food and rest, Mrs. Southerland."

On the road to *La Grande Maison*, Aurora rounded a curve, jammed her foot on the brakes. Her Jeep skidded to a stop. From the back seat King barked. Aurora stared. The car ahead looked vaguely familiar. She had prayed to find Carole or her car, but this wasn't it. King barked again, growled. Monique! Of course. The car stalled in the middle of the road belonged to Monique! But two people, not one, were inside. Was that gasoline leaking from the vehicle? Puffs of black smoke rose from under the hood. Farther up the road, a vehicle barreled toward the smoking car.

King scratched furiously at the window, whined, growled. A woman jumped out of the car, waved frantically. "Help us!" she screamed. "They're going to kill us!"

Aurora couldn't believe that the woman screaming and waving in the road was Carole. Monique vaulted out of the driver's seat. Both women dashed toward Aurora's Jeep.

"Hurry!" yelled Aurora. She unlocked the doors. "Run!"

Carole and Monique dived inside the Jeep and slammed the doors. In the driver's seat, Aurora spun the car around and pushed on the gas seconds before the men in the Humvee fired. In the rearview mirror, she saw Monique's car explode into flames. The Humvee didn't even slow down.

"Lie on the floor! Pull King down with you!" Aurora looked out the window. The Humvee was close; she could see the driver and two men in the front. Another man and two Dobermans filled the back. She put her .38 on her lap.

Attempting to keep the Humvee from coming up beside her, Aurora swerved across the road.

"Ram 'em!" shouted Win as the Humvee gained on the Jeep. The front bumper slammed into the Jeep's rear end. The Jeep slowed, allowing the Humvee room to pull up alongside.

"Shoot her!" Win hollered at Otis. "What the hell are you waiting for?"

"No!" screamed Otis. "My girlfriend's in that car! I might hit her!"

"That's the idea, you idiot!" screamed Win.

Aurora stomped on the brakes. The Humvee shot past the Jeep, ground to a stop. Aurora waited. Carole and Monique peered over the seat. Carole cocked her .22.

"Monique, can you use a gun?" asked Aurora.

"You betcha. And I'm a good shot."

"Take my .38, see if you and Carole can hold them off if they come toward us." She grabbed her cell phone, dialed Sam, prayed he would answer.

"Where are you? Why didn't you answer my call a minute ago?" asked a frantic Sam.

"Four guys are trying to kill us. One of them's Win. I've got Carole and Monique. Uh-oh. They turned the dogs loose."

"Dogs loose? Where are you? What's going on? And who's Monique?"

"Hold on." Aurora asked Monique the name of the road and relayed the information to Sam.

"I'm only a few miles from you. Luke's here, too, and the police are coming now. I can see their lights. We'll be there in a few minutes. Hold on, Susie-Q."

The Humvee's door opened. A man jumped out, ran toward the Jeep. When a bullet ripped into his back, he screamed and collapsed to the road.

"That's Otis! They like shot Otis!" Monique unlocked the door, reached for the door handle.

"No!" said Carole. "Don't be a fool! They'll kill you!" She struggled with Monique, tried to keep her in the car. The .38 fell to the seat. Aurora reached over the front seat, grabbed the gun. King jumped at the window, roared, bared his teeth.

"Monique, listen to me! Look! The dogs are circling the car. They'll attack you if you get out. Monique, use your head!"

"But what about Otis? If the bullet didn't kill him, the dogs will."

"No, they won't. The dogs are after me," said Carole, "and you. They won't attack Otis." She hoped she sounded convincing.

"Why would the men shoot Otis?" asked Aurora.

"Because he was trying to protect me. He's protected me ever since I ran away from home." Monique sniffed, wiped her eyes. "He's a good man most of the time, just got in with the wrong people."

"Uh-oh. They're turning around," said Aurora.

"What are we going to do?" Carole asked.

"I don't know. We're certainly no match for a Humvee. That monster could flatten my Jeep easily."

"Can we outrun it?"

"Don't know. We don't want to head back toward *La Grande Maison*. And driving past them without being shot or rammed would be difficult without running over Otis."

"Maybe we could like run, reach the woods before they catch us." At that moment, the Dobermans leapt against the car, slobbered on the windows, barked and growled. King barked back at them.

"Guess that's out," Monique said.

CHAPTER SEVENTY-FOUR

"They're leaving," said Aurora.

"I don't believe that. They're not the type to like just quit." asked Monique.

"They've cranked up the monster. Why?" said Carole.

"The dogs quit attacking the car," said Aurora, "and now the Humvee's picking them up."

"Down!" screamed Carole. Bullets slammed into the side of Aurora's Jeep as the Humvee roared past.

Aurora rolled down the window, poked her head up over the seat, fired back with her .38. The Humvee sped toward *La Grande Maison*.

"What was that all about?" asked Monique. "I cain't believe they just gave up."

"Me either," said Carole.

"There must be a reason," said Aurora. "Maybe they haven't left for good."

Carole and Monique nodded.

"Let's see if this Jeep will start." The engine started on the first try. "That's a relief. Let's get outta here."

"Wait! I have to get Otis!" Monique jerked open the door and ran to his side. Kneeling next to him, she called his name, patted his face, put her cheek to his nose. She felt for his pulse.

"How is he?" Aurora asked softly. She and Carole stood beside Monique, ready to help if needed.

Monique looked up at them. Tears streaked her cheeks. "He's not breathing and I cain't find a pulse. We have to start CPR."

"Monique, I don't know if CPR will help him. And it might even hurt. He's lying in a lot of blood, and it's spreading." Beside her, King whined.

"I have to do something. He cain't die like this. He's my Otis. I cain't leave him." Sobbing, she looked up at Carole and Aurora. "Otis ain't a bad person."

A deep growl rose from King's throat. He barked, ran to Aurora, barked again. Expecting the Humvee to pop back into sight, she stared up the road. She heard sirens, saw blue lights blinking in the opposite direction. Seconds later, three police cars and a rescue vehicle arrived. Luke and Sam followed.

"Help!" yelled Monique. Two EMTs emerged from the ambulance. She waved them over to Otis. "He's not breathing. Do something. Please don't let him die."

Aurora squeezed Monique's hand, patted her shoulder as the technicians examined Otis and loaded him into the ambulance.

Sam and Luke rushed to Aurora and Carole and held them close.

"What happened here?" asked the sheriff.

The three ladies gave him a condensed version.

"I'm so thankful you escaped," said Luke to Carole. "If anything had happened to you. . . ." He hugged her, kissed her, reluctantly released her. "I would have died if those men had killed you." His eyes searched her for injuries.

"Luke, I was terrified. I honestly think Win would have killed me." Carole gazed up at her fiancé. "I'm sure he would not have bought a house, either."

"Did Aurora tell you what we discovered about Mr. I. Winston Ford?"

"I haven't had a chance, Luke," said Aurora. "We were too busy trying to stay alive."

Monique stood in the road and watched the ambulance drive away as the siren blared and lights flashed.

The sheriff said, "I. Winston Ford isn't his real name. He's wanted for murdering two realtors, both women. From what the three of you have told me, I think Carole was supposed to be number three. Don't know why he picked lady realtors, though. But we'll find out."

"I think I know why," said Carole. "Win can be quite charming when he wants to be. He makes women feel special, like each one is the most gorgeous, important person on earth. I can see how females would fall for him. If I hadn't had such a special guy loving me, I might have succumbed to Win's charms myself." She looked at Luke, squeezed his hand. "My guess is that wealthy people from all over the world would put in orders through *La Grande Maison* for particular boats. Win pretended to be interested in buying property on the water, insisted on seeing boat docks, said he needed to be sure the dock would work for his big powerboat. Ha! He fooled me. I thought I'd sell him a house, get a big commission. All the time he was looking for expensive boats to steal. Then he would hide them at *La Grande Maison* and fence them. I bet those women he killed sold high-end waterfront property somewhere. Am I right?" She looked from Sam to Luke.

"Absolutely," Sam said.

"And Win nearly killed Jill when his Porsche slammed into her car," said Luke.

"Win's the hit and run driver?"

"Yep."

A wrecker arrived, hooked Monique's destroyed car up, asked where to take it. "I want to ride with you, if that's okay with everybody," she said. "I'll call my cousin to come get me at the garage. She'll take me to the hospital so I can like check on Otis."

"Fine with us," said the sheriff. "We'll catch up with you later." He jotted down her name, address and phone number.

"Call me when you know something, Monique," said Aurora. She pulled a business card from her purse, handed it to her.

"Where's your car, Carole?" asked Luke. "Do you need a wrecker for it?"

She laughed, said she'd need a wrecker to pull Crappy out of the woods. "But first the cops need to get through *La Grande Maison's* security and past the Dobermans."

"Dobermans? How many?"

"At least two, probably more they haven't turned loose. Yet."

"I think my car's okay to drive," said Aurora. "Looks pretty bad, though."

"I'll follow you to the garage," said Sam.

CHAPTER SEVENTY-FIVE

La Grande Maison, 2:30 p.m.

"I told you I need the chopper!" screamed Win at the security guards. They stared at him. "Now! Carole will blab everything to the cops. They know where to find me. I'm toast if I stay."

"What about us?" asked a guard. "You gonna leave us here to be handcuffed and hauled off to jail?"

"They won't arrest you. You were doing your job, following orders. You never did anything to Carole. And even if they did arrest you, you'd get a light sentence. Now get me a chopper and a pilot."

"The boss won't like it."

"You can tell the boss if I go down, he does, too. They'll take away his passport. He'll never be able to enter another country again. He'll rot in jail. And *La Grande Maison* will no longer belong to him and the other investors. Got it?"

"You shot Otis."

"You're damn right. And I'll shoot anyone else who gets in my way, including the two of you. You understand me?" The guards nodded. "Good. Now get me that helicopter and a pilot. Fast."

At the same time in Charlottesville, Jasper's frazzled nerves wanted pills. He fought the urge, promised himself that as soon as this job was finished he'd pop at least one, maybe two. He smiled. Unless he ran into major problems, he'd get his fix in approximately 10 to 20 minutes.

He rode the elevator to the floor just below ICU and stepped into the men's restroom. Setting his brown leather satchel down in the stall, he stripped off his clothes and replaced them with the green scrubs he'd donned just a day earlier in this same bathroom. This time, he promised himself, the outcome would be different. This time Tom Southerland would die.

Standing in front of the mirror, he adjusted the cap and mask. He raised a hand in a nonchalant greeting to a doctor who scurried into a stall. The doctor didn't bother to return the greeting. Jasper smiled. That was one man who wouldn't be able to identify him. Jasper retrieved a clipboard—complete with official-looking documents attached—from his satchel, tucked it under his arm, and walked to the elevator.

Doctors, nurses, and visitors crowded into the elevator with him. Most gazed toward the ceiling. One puzzled nurse's aide, however, stared, couldn't stop looking at him. When he stepped off the elevator on the ICU floor, she did the same. He shuffled the papers on the clipboard and headed in the opposite direction from where he wanted to go. As he was rounding a corner, he glanced back toward the elevator. The nurse's aide still stood there watching him.

He hurried into the men's restroom and leaned against the wall. Why had she stared at him, watched him walk away? No way could she have recognized him from the day before. The mask had covered much of his face. Maybe she just liked the way he walked or something. Anyhow, he had no reason to worry. And soon this job would be over and he could forget about the aide.

At the nurses' station in ICU, the aide told her supervisor about the doctor on the elevator. "Something about him didn't seem right. He just seemed, well, strange, nervous. And his eyes were different. You know, a person's eyes can tell you a lot. In fact, I'm pretty sure I've seen him before."

"When was that?" asked the supervisor.

"I don't know. I can't seem to get it all straight in my brain. But don't worry; I'll remember eventually."

"While you're trying to remember, I'd like for you to go to the waiting room and check on Mrs. Southerland, see if she's back from the cafeteria. Her husband just returned to his room from recovery. I'm sure she'd like to hear how he's doing."

"Happy to do it." As she walked toward the ICU waiting room, a doctor in scrubs slipped into Tom Southerland's room. He carried a satchel in his left hand. The guard hadn't stopped him, had just waved him on.

"Doctors almighty," she murmured. She had her own opinions of doctors, opinions she'd learned to keep to herself if she valued her job. She ignored their advances, always had. Her mother had taught her values, had drilled into her the Ten Commandments, all those "Thou Shall Nots." To be fair, though, she reminded herself that not all doctors were on the prowl. She shrugged, walked past Mr. Southerland's room toward the waiting room.

And then she remembered. The doctor she saw yesterday was carrying a satchel that looked exactly like the one she saw on the elevator, like the one she just passed. Yesterday she saw that doctor and that satchel come out of Mr. Southerland's room after someone had tried to strangle him to death.

She screamed for help and dashed into Southerland's room. The guard on duty pulled his revolver, ran after her. The doctor leaning over Tom Southerland looked up at them. He held a syringe in his hand.

"Leave this room!" he yelled. "You have no right. . . ."

"Stop him!" the aide yelled at the guard. "He's going to kill Mr. Southerland!"

"Drop the needle or I'll shoot!" said the guard. He aimed the gun at the doctor, moved closer to him. The supervisor came in the room, stood beside the guard.

"Okay, okay," said the doctor, "but I don't know what you're so upset about." Still holding the syringe, he edged closer to the door. "I was just doing my job."

"I want to see your face," said the aide. She stepped toward him, reached for the surgical mask.

"Back up, miss," said the guard. "You're too close to. . . ."

The doctor leaped forward, grabbed the aide, held the syringe at her throat. She struggled. He jammed the needle into her shoulder, pulled it out, laughed hysterically when she screamed. "Now stay still or next time I'll go for your jugular. And there's a drug in the syringe you really wouldn't like. None of you would, so all the rest of you folks back off or I'll kill her, maybe even pump some of this special cocktail into one of you." He looked at his captive audience. "You wouldn't want to be responsible for her death, now would you?"

"I'll shoot you," said the guard. "I swear I will."

"You start to shoot and I'll stab her before you squeeze the trigger. Move over beside the bed. All of you."

The supervisor inched toward the call button. With one arm around the aide's neck and the syringe tucked between two fingers, the man in scrubs kicked the supervisor in the stomach. She doubled over and fell to the floor.

"Hand me your gun, handle first," he ordered the guard.

"Not a chance in hell."

The door to the room swung open. Blanche stopped in the doorway, stared at the scene in front of her. "Tom! What's wrong with Tom?"

"Welcome to the party, Blanche. Join the crowd over there by your husband."

"You know my name. Who are you? And what are you doing to Tom?" She frowned. "Wait. I recognize that raspy, squeaky voice. And the scar on your forehead. You're. . .!" She grabbed at his mask, missed. His fist slammed against her mouth.

"What the hell do you think you're doing? Are you nuts?" She felt her lip, saw the blood on her hand.

Jasper moved fast, shoved the aide into the guard. Wrestling the gun from the guard, he pointed it at them. "Now I have four hostages, five counting Mr. Tom Southerland who's still sleeping like a baby after his successful amputation."

Jasper glanced around the room. "You," he ordered the aide, "yank the top sheet off Mr. High and Mighty Southerland there. Tear it into strips." He looked at the guard. "You help."

"You won't get away with this," said Blanche. "The cops will be all over you any minute."

"Don't bet on it, sweetheart." Jasper looked at his watch, frowned.

"The sheet's in strips like you demanded," said the aide.

"Aren't you just the sweetest little Southern Belle," said Jasper. "Now, you and Miss Priss there put your hands behind you and back up to each other. Cop, you tie their hands together. Tight, really tight. Understand?" The guard nodded, did as ordered.

"Now, stuff a sheet strip in their mouths, make 'em lie on the floor, then shove them under the bed. When that's done, tie Blanche in the chair and give her some sheet to chew on." Jasper looked at her and smiled. "Blanche, aren't you pleased that I thought of your comfort? Such a gentleman I am."

"Think about what you're doing. You won't get away with this," she said again. The strips of cloth tightened around her arms.

"Sure I will." Jasper ordered the guard to stuff rags in Blanche's mouth.

"I've done everything you asked," said the guard. "What's next?"

"Come closer." Jasper raised his arm and struck the guard hard in the head with the gun. "Sweet dreams," he said as the guard toppled to the floor.

Jasper shoved his body under the hospital bed and dropped the side rails. He picked up the syringe from the floor, jammed the needle in Tom's IV, and pushed the plunger.

Terrified, Blanche struggled against the sheets binding her. She tried to scream but couldn't.

"Blanche, you're the only one who knows my name and what I look like. You gotta die. The others, except for your husband, may live." Jasper pulled his gun with silencer attached from his satchel, aimed at Blanche's chest, and pulled the trigger. He picked up the satchel and the cop's gun, and walked from the room.

"How you doin'?" said a man hurrying to one of the bathroom stalls.

"Good," answered Jasper.

"Nice day, ain't it?"

"Um." Jasper headed to a vacant stall and shut the door.

"So what do you think about those Cavaliers? Think they'll win the ACC this year?" asked the man. Jasper didn't answer. "You like Virginia Tech or UVA?"

Jasper ignored him.

"You ain't very talkative, are you? Problems in the operating room, or is it a woman that's made you so unsociable?"

Jasper ignored the comment. He removed his mask, cap and scrubs, changed into his street clothes. He waited on the toilet for the man in the next stall to leave. So far the man hadn't seen Jasper's face. Good. Now if he would just leave without seeing the clothes Jasper had changed into. . . .

"Hey, whatcha doin' in there?" The man flushed, left his stall and banged on Jasper's stall door.

"Hey, man, I need to concentrate right now, don't need any conversation," said Jasper. "You were right; there was a problem in the operating room. My patient died. I'm trying to build up courage to go tell his wife. I'm sure you understand."

"Oh, sure. Hey, Doc, I'm sorry about your patient." He washed his hands and left the bathroom.

Ten minutes later Jasper dialed his mother from his car. Two police cars, their lights blinking and sirens blaring, passed him heading north.

"Where are you?" she asked.

"Route 29 South, about two miles south of Charlottesville. We have a problem." He told her what had happened in the hospital.

"Not good. Your brother's having a rough time, too. It's really hittin' the fan. And this time it's at my back door. I don't like this at all."

"So what are we gonna do?"

"You and your brother are going to get the hell out of Virginia. I've already talked to him."

"Where will we go?"

"That's your problem."

CHAPTER SEVENTY-SIX

North Carolina, 3:30 p.m.

Etta heard the tell-tale sound only a flat tire can make. She drove onto the shoulder and turned off the engine. Mouser, eager to escape his prison, screeched.

"Hush," she said. "I can't think with all that noise. This is not what I need right now."

Etta tried to remember the road sign she'd passed half a mile back. Had it said "Greenville?" If so, how many miles to Greenville? She didn't have a jack. But a jack wouldn't help anyhow—she didn't even have a spare to replace the flat. She'd been meaning to get a spare and a jack, but things—mostly a lack of money—seemed to get in the way. Besides, she never went anywhere except to work and occasionally to the lake to take care of Hessie. Well, she wouldn't be taking care of Hessie any more. By now Hessie was surely dead.

Etta opened the door, draped her purse over her shoulder, reached in the back seat and lifted Mouser and his carrier from the car. His purring and crying irritated her, even though she knew he craved freedom. She locked the doors and began her trek toward Greenville—wherever that was. She hoped it was close to New Bern. She also prayed that Butch wouldn't catch her walking.

Twenty-eight minutes later she heard a car pull onto the shoulder behind her. The hairs on her neck stood up. Certain that Butch had finally found her, she broke into a trot.

"Hello," said the male voice. "Can we help you?"

That wasn't Butch. Etta stopped, looked behind her. A man and woman stood a few yards away.

"Hello," the man said again. "Was that your red Capri parked on the shoulder a ways back?"

"I'm afraid so."

"Looks like you have a flat. I'd be happy to change it for you."

She took a few steps toward their car. "That's very kind of you. I don't have a jack or a spare. But thanks for stopping."

"Well, can we drive you somewhere?"

"I don't even know where I am."

The woman put her hand on Etta's arm. "I'm Sue, this is Mac. You're in Pitt County, North Carolina, only a few miles from Greenville. We want to help you if you'll let us." She took the cat carrier from Etta, handed it to her husband.

Etta looked into their eyes. These were people she could trust. "Thank you," she said. "Thank you so much." She climbed into the back seat of their car.

"Nice cat," said Mac as he passed the carrier to Etta. "What's his name?"

"Mouser. I'm Etta."

Mac started the engine, looked back at Etta. "Where are you headed?"

"New Bern. Is that far from here?"

"No, only about an hour," said Sue. "Where did you come from?"

"The Lynchburg, Virginia, area. I got all turned around. Somebody's chasing me, so I took back roads a person wouldn't normally take to get to New Bern from Lynchburg. I've been on the road since a little after eight this morning."

"I have a jack. We'll drive to your car and get the flat, then take it to a service station, see if they can fix it. If you're worried about leaving all your stuff in your car, we could probably squeeze most of it in ours." He turned the car around and headed back toward Etta's Capri.

"I don't want to be near my car long, only long enough to get my suitcase and Mouser's food. If Butch finds me. . . ."

"Is Butch the person chasing you?" asked Sue.

"Yeah. And if he finds me he'll kill me." She frowned, looked at Sue and Mac in the front seat. "You have to let me out. Now." She unbuckled her seat belt, reached for the door handle.

"Hold on," said Mac. "Don't try to get out while the car's moving. You'll get hurt. Why do you suddenly want to leave?"

"Because if Butch finds me with the two of you, he'll kill y'all, too. You've been really nice to me; I don't want you to die because you're nice. Please stop the car."

"Etta, we're not scared of Butch," said Mac. "What kind of car does he drive? We'll watch out for it."

"He drives a dark blue Ford 150 truck, no camper shell. It's got four-wheel drive. The tires are extra big, and there's a row of lights on the top of the truck."

"Does it look like that truck coming toward us?"

"That's him!" cried Etta. "I knew he'd find me!"

"Quick! Get on the floor!" said Sue.

Terrified, Etta slid down in the seat as far as she could and held her breath.

"You can sit up now," said Mac several seconds later. "He's gone on down the road. Probably thinks he'll catch up with you trying to hitch a ride. We'll hurry to your car, grab your luggage, and get out of here."

"Look at all that dark smoke down the road," said Sue. "Wonder where it's coming from."

"Omigosh," said Etta as they drove closer to the fire ball, "that's my car! Butch set my car on fire!"

"I've gotta call my sister, warn her that Butch somehow found out where I'm going." Etta dug in her purse for her cell phone. "I can't find it. It must still be in the car. My sister will die and I can't help her!"

"Do you know your sister's number?" asked Sue.

"Of course."

"Here, use my cell," said Sue.

Etta flashed Sue a grateful smile and dialed. When there was no answer, she left a message and passed the phone back to Sue.

"He'll kill her if he finds her," said Etta. "Maybe he already has."

"He hasn't had time to get to New Bern. We just saw him, remember? Calm down, Etta," said Sue.

"We need to get you to a police station, let you tell them what you know, tell them how dangerous this man is, what he's capable of doing," said Mac.

"No. I can't go to the cops. Butch will kill me if I do. And cops can't be trusted, anyhow."

"He'll kill you regardless. At least with the cops you stand a chance."

"I won't do it. Stop the car."

"First he'll kill you, then he'll go after your sister. You know that. Do you want to be responsible for her death?"

Etta slumped in the seat, looked out the window. "I can't take any more of this. Do whatever you think is best."

Mac nodded. "We'll take a different road into Greenville in case Butch is still searching for you on this one. I'll have you at the police station soon. And if it makes you feel any better, one of the detectives is a fishin' buddy of mine. Detective Stein will take good care of you."

"What about my sister?"

"The Greenville police will alert the New Bern cops. They'll protect her." Mouser meowed.

"My cat's hungry, and he needs more water."

"We'll take care of that," said Sue. She looked at Mac, raised an eyebrow. He nodded. "You and Mouser can stay at our house, Etta. You'll be safe there."

An angry Butch cruised the highway. When he found Etta—and he would—she'd beg him not to hurt her. He'd like to torture her, prolong her agony, but this had gone on long enough. Jasper wanted her dead, had ordered Butch to take care of "our little problem." Butch couldn't take his time killing her the way he'd like. Jasper had called his cell several times, but Butch had ignored the calls. If Jasper knew how far Etta had gotten, he just might come after Butch. Jasper didn't like it when things didn't go the way he'd planned.

He frowned. Etta's sister might be a big problem. Butch slapped the steering wheel. He'd give anything to know how much Etta had told her. And there was no way in hell Butch would let Jasper know about Etta's sister.

Butch looked at his watch. He'd set Etta's car on fire 10 minutes ago. Only one person had pulled over and asked if he could help put the fire out. Butch had told the man that he'd stopped to help when he saw the smoke, had checked the interior of the car, but nobody was inside. He told the goody-goody he'd already called 911. Of course he hadn't. The driver had waved and driven off.

Smiling, he remembered the rush he'd gotten when the Capri started smoking, then burning. The explosion and the leaping flames had excited him. He wished he could have just stood there and watched it burn, but the situation hadn't allowed that. The last fire he'd set had been in that new house in Sweetwater. The flames then had seemed to dance, kind of bend and twist to some type of rhythm. He'd forgotten how much he'd enjoyed watching. He wished he'd set Etta's house on fire. Maybe he'd start more fires just for fun. But first he had to take care of Etta and her sister.

CHAPTER SEVENTY-SEVEN

Thursday, 4:00 p.m.

Miss Nosy Neighbor blinked, opened her eyes, looked around the room. She watched the IV dripping liquid in her arm. "Where am I?"

"Ms. Patrick, you're in the hospital in Rocky Mount. How do you feel?" asked the detective.

"Like a horse kicked me in the head and then an elephant stomped on it. What happened?"

"A bullet struck you in the head. Fortunately it lodged in your skull instead of traveling through important stuff like the brain."

"I guess that's good. But I have a really awful headache. And who shot me?"

"We have no idea, but we're investigating. I'm guessing it was accidental. Probably somebody target practicing near by and missed. The guilty party most likely doesn't even know he hit you or that his bullet could have killed you."

"I disagree. I betcha anything my neighbor's guardian is responsible for shooting me. I bet he intended to kill me."

"Why would your neighbor's guardian want to kill you, Ms. Patrick?"

"Because he knows I saw him in the neighborhood. He was acting strangely."

"In what way?"

"Well, I left my house to take a book back to the library. I didn't want to get a late charge, you know. Anyhow, I saw my neighbor's guardian—his name is Mr. Smoot—parked on the road.

He was sitting in his car, said he was waiting for somebody to come pick up the elderly woman's furniture."

"Doesn't seem unreasonable to me." The detective glanced at his watch, stood up to leave.

"What would you say if I told you that when I came home, I saw his car parked in the driveway in front of the Karvers' garage? The garage door was wide open; Mr. and Mrs. Karver's cars were gone. I'm certain he's the man who entered their home. And I guarantee he's the person who shot me." The detective sat back down.

"You may have heard of the old woman. Her name's Hessie Davis. She disappeared, was found way over on Smith Mountain. She has Alzheimer's, but she couldn't have traveled that far in her bathrobe and slippers by herself. She had help. In my opinion, Mr. Smoot is responsible for driving her to the mountain and leaving her there to die."

The deputy stood, looked down at the woman with bandages on her head. "I'm familiar with the Hessie Davis episode and wondered how she got on the mountain. Ms. Patrick, we'll look into what you said, check out Mr. Smoot. You feel better, okay?"

"I just remembered," said Ms. Nosy Neighbor. "I snapped a picture of his car in the Karver's driveway."

"Where's the picture?"

"In my digital camera. I left it in the laundry room."

"When can I see it?"

"Get my purse out of the closet there and I'll give you a key to the house. I don't know when the doctor will release me and you need to see it. Actually, I took several pictures, one close-up that shows his car's license plate."

"Good girl," he said as he took the key. She beamed. No one had called her a girl for decades.

As soon as he left her room, he called his office. "You know that Mr. Smith we heard about from Mrs. Karver? The woman who was shot believes Smoot is responsible. And get this. She thinks he's the guy who entered the Karver house. She took pictures of his car in their driveway; one shows the license plate. After talking to Ms. Patrick, my guess is Mr. Smith is really Mr. Smoot. I'm on my way to her house to get her camera, then I'll head to the office. I'll fill you in when I get there."

CHAPTER SEVENTY-EIGHT

Thursday, 5:00 p.m.

Back home in his Sweetwater Cove townhouse, Jasper wanted to sit down with a beer and relax. But he couldn't now. Soon, though, he promised himself. His drive from Charlottesville had been nerve-wracking. Every time he'd seen a police car, he'd cringed, waited for the chase to begin. But now it looked like he was almost home free.

Quickly he packed two suitcases and set them by the door. Hurrying to his safe, he grabbed fake IDs, credit cards, and three passports—each with different names. He stuffed everything in his satchel. Unzipping a larger bag, he pulled bundles of fifty- and hundred-dollar bills from the safe and transferred them to the bag. Most of the hidden money he'd stolen from Sweetwater Cove and Tom Southerland—kind of cooked the books, some would say. He laughed. Initially, the deceased Southerland would be blamed. But auditors weren't stupid. Jasper was the accountant; they'd soon suspect him because he handled the money.

"What have I forgotten?" he said aloud. He'd called his brother Win, warned him that the cops would be coming soon, that he'd meet Win and the chopper in Altavista. He'd packed his passports, financial stuff, his laptop, computer backup, and contact book.

The front door opened. Quick footsteps sounded on the ceramic tile floor. Jasper froze.

"Where are you, Jasper? I know you're here."

Jasper relaxed, poked his head around his bedroom door. "I'm right here, Mom."

"You moron. Will you never learn to do as I say? You should have been out of the country by now." Mommy Dearest wagged a gloved finger at her older son. "What is your problem?"

"Hey, I'm not your only kid who's in trouble. I talked to Win. He expects the police to raid *La Grande Maison* any minute."

"Well, right now he's trying to commandeer *La Grande Maison's* helicopter. He won't be able to return to the bed and breakfast to get his makeup kit, passports and other papers. I assured him that you would take his backups with you. You do still have copies of all his papers, right? You will keep your baby brother safe, won't you?" said Estelle.

"Of course I have his documents, and of course I'll take care of him." Just like I always have, he thought. Jasper smiled. Part of him secretly hoped his handsome, perfect baby brother would be captured by the police, thrown into prison for the rest of his life. He certainly deserved it. But unlike Jasper, Win would talk, implicate Jasper and Mommy Dearest. The thought of spending the rest of his life in prison didn't appeal to Jasper.

What had happened to Butch? Jasper had called and left messages numerous times, but Butch never answered. Surely he wasn't still on Etta's trail. Somehow he had to find Butch and kill him before the cops did.

"Have you heard the news?" his mother asked.

"No, what?"

"I heard through the rapid-gossip line that the neighbor who lives next door to Hessie told the police about you coming out of the Karver's garage, said she thinks you're the one who shot her in the head."

"Impossible. She's dead. I shot her, watched her fall. You know I never miss." He zipped his satchel closed. "Naw, they're plain out wrong. Gotta be.

"'Bye, Mom." Jasper started to walk out the door.

"Where will you be? How can I get in touch with you?"

"Not sure yet. My guess is Win will want to run to Iran. I'll go with him. He's got important connections there. We'll call you when we get settled."

Estelle cupped her son's chin in her hands. "You're a good boy. Remember what I taught you and you'll end up a rich man." She kissed his cheek.

"Yeah, Mom, I'll remember what you always told Win and me—'Do unto others before they do it unto you.'" He patted her shoulder. "You take care of yourself."

"You, too. And remember, Jasper." She pointed a finger at him. "I'm counting on you to look after your baby brother."

CHAPTER SEVENTY-NINE

La Grande Maison, 5:35 p.m.

The long-awaited helicopter lifted off and headed north. From the air, Win watched the line of police cars snake along the curvy road to *La Grande Maison.* He'd escaped just in time. In a few minutes the cops would crash through the main security gate.

"I win again. I always do." Win smiled, settled back against the seat, looked below as the chopper skimmed the treetops. A large buck ran into an open field, turned, and dashed back to hide once more in the forest.

On a piece of paper, Win checked his to-do list: Pick up Jasper in an Altavista field off Highway 29; gas up the chopper at a private airstrip in Lovingston; rendezvous with Middle East cronies in New Jersey; shoot the pilot then blow up the chopper; fade into obscurity; get rich and live happily ever after.

He also needed to decide his next identity so that he could get that particular passport ready when he met up with Jasper. He hated to give up his I. Winston Ford identity, his favorite. The name suited him perfectly.

Win decided on the disguise that called for brown hair flecked with gray, a mustache, and brown eyes. He liked that one because even though it changed his appearance dramatically, it didn't hide his good looks; he'd still be handsome, a chick magnet. Before they reached New Jersey, he'd pop in the brown contacts and comb gray coloring through his hair and mustache. When he left the helicopter he wouldn't look anything like the man Carole knew. He figured Jasper had planned on an identity change, too, wondered what he'd picked.

Turning on his laptop, Win typed in his password and opened the site for I. Winston Ford's savings and checking accounts. Minutes later he'd transferred $700,000 dollars to the account of Ira M. Smartt, his new identity. He grinned. Even though this name wasn't as perfect as I. Winston Ford, he liked it. He'd go by I. Smartt, or Martin, or I. M. Smartt—and he was. He congratulated himself on his ingenuity.

Jasper drove his car onto the dirt road. He knew where to meet the chopper and his brother. Surrounded by thick forests that provided privacy, the farm field was a good choice, one they'd used before. He looked at his watch. He'd barely made it in time. He knew Perfect Baby Brother wouldn't wait more than five minutes. When Win hadn't come after 10 minutes, Jasper started worrrying. What if the police had raided *La Grande Maison*, captured Win before he could escape? Normally, he wouldn't really care if Perfect Baby Brother got caught. But if that were the case now, no helicopter would come to whisk him off to safety. Jasper wiped perspiration from his brow.

The distant drone grew louder. Relieved when he saw the helicopter, Jasper waited beside his luggage for the chopper to set down.

"You're late," he said when Win jumped to the ground and walked a few yards away. "And where do you think you're going?"

"I gotta pee. Load your stuff. I'll be right back."

Jasper hoisted his luggage into the chopper and hurried back to his car.

"Whatcha doing?" Win asked. "We're ready to take off."

"Almost forgot to get the license plates off the car. When they find the car it'll take them a little longer to trace it to me if there are no plates."

"Did you remember to empty the glove compartment?"

"Of course. Did that while waiting for you and the chopper. You were late." Jasper tucked the license plates under his arm and climbed aboard. Win tapped the pilot on the shoulder and nodded. The helicopter lifted into the overcast sky and disappeared in the clouds.

"Did you bring my stuff?"

"Of course." Jasper handed the bundle to Win.

"So what disguise will you use this time? And what should I call you?"

"Call me Martin, short for Ira Martin Smartt. Two 't's in Smartt." He grinned.

Jim, the pilot, had just delivered four *La Grande Maison* guests to the Boston airport when the head security guard contacted him and ordered him to return to home base immediately. Now he glanced back at his new passengers. He knew these guys, had never liked either of them, didn't trust them, would have preferred not to work with them. *La Grande Maison's* boss, a U.S. Senator with strong ties to the Middle East, hadn't given him a choice. He'd like to quit. But Jim knew better than to argue with a man who'd just as soon chop him up and feed him to the Dobermans as look at him. Death by Doberman didn't appeal. No, he never questioned the boss. If he'd known in the beginning that once you work for the boss, you *always* work for the boss, that the only way to quit was to die, he'd never have taken the job.

But now things were different. From all he'd heard, it sounded like *La Grande Maison's* days of secrecy were over. Soon cops would be swarming over the vast estate, arresting all the employees, scaring the high and mighty guests. Maybe he'd just keep going when he dropped off his two passengers, fly off into the sunset, start a new life. Good thing the boss was out of the country on a so-called fact-finding trip for the government.

Jim looked at his watch. In 40 minutes, he'd land the chopper on his buddy's private landing strip between Lovingston and Charlottesville. His friend Wade would be waiting at the airstrip to refuel the chopper. Jim knew he'd ask no questions, would never even see the two passengers.

CHAPTER EIGHTY

Greenville, North Carolina, 5:45 p.m.

"I don't feel safe," said Etta as they left the police station. "He's close, watching, waiting for his chance to kill me. I can sense him."

Mac scanned the parking lot and the on-street parking as best he could. He saw no dark blue truck like Butch's. "Etta, you're exhausted and jumpy. Stop worrying. My guess is that he's still searching the highway for you." He opened the car door for her.

A hungry Mouser voiced his outrage at still being in the carrier. Etta stuck a finger in the carrier to console him. "Ouch!" she said as a claw swiped her finger, drew blood. She sucked her wound, twisted a tissue around it.

"When we get home we'll put Mouser on our screened porch. Right now he's one irritated cat. Don't think I want him to have the run of our entire house when he's in such a foul mood," said Sue. "We can fix him a bed on the porch. It won't be cold tonight. That okay with you, Etta?"

"Of course. Whatever you wish. I appreciate you and Mac helping us. If you hadn't, Mouser and I would probably be dead. And a killer would still be loose. Actually, Butch is still free, and I'm not out of danger yet. Neither are y'all."

Butch felt a little conspicuous sitting in a stolen vehicle so close to the police station, but he had no other choice. Besides, the cops would never guess a stolen car would be parked at their doorstep. He thought about the woman who owned the car. He probably should have pumped a few bullets into her instead of just throwing her on the ground and driving off in her car, but he'd figured somebody at the shopping center would hear the shots and investigate. He hoped no one saw her hit the pavement. Nowadays, though, most people would be afraid to help another human being. They'd just stand around and gawk or pretend they hadn't seen or heard a thing. Now if an animal were in trouble. . . .

He couldn't believe his good luck when he saw Etta sitting in the back seat of some guy's car right beside him at a stop light. She hadn't even looked in his direction. Of course, if he hadn't ditched his truck. . . .

Mac drove away from the police station. "We'll be at the house in about 20 minutes, Etta. You can relax then, get Mouser settled in, eat a good meal." He glanced at Sue and smiled. "My wife's a great cook." He reached across the seat, patted Sue's hand.

"Thanks," Sue said. "Etta, sometimes Mac exaggerates. You can't believe everything he says." She twisted her head to smile at Etta in the back seat. "Mac, did you know there's a car close behind us?"

"Yeah, but don't worry. It's a small one, not a monster truck like Butch's." He frowned. He didn't want to worry Sue and Etta, but the car had tailed them ever since they left the police station.

Mac turned left, made a quick right at the next corner. The mystery car shadowed them. Three minutes and several unnecessary turns later, the car still hugged Mac's bumper.

"Sue, call 911. Tell them we're being followed. Give them our location. I think that's Butch behind us. No, Etta, don't look back. We don't want him to think we're suspicious." He glanced at Sue, saw her dial.

"I knew he'd find me. He'll kill me; y'all, too. Let me out, Mac." She tried to open the door, but Mac had already pushed the child lock button for the rear seat.

"They're on their way. Said they'd notify Detective Stein," Sue said. "I'm still on the line."

"Tell the operator I'm trying to double back to the police station, tell them what street we're on. I doubt Butch knows Greenville. If I take him down the back streets he won't recognize the station until we're there." At least I hope not, Mack thought.

Blam! Butch's car slammed into the rear bumper. Etta screamed. *Blam!* Mouser screeched, clawed the carrier's side.

"Get on the floor!" Mac said. He stomped the accelerator, ran a red light. At the last minute he hit the brakes, made a wild turn to the right at the next intersection.

Butch overshot the turn, stopped, backed up and followed Mac.

"He's still behind us!" screamed Etta.

"I told you to stay on the floor. Don't give him another target in case he has a gun."

"Oh, I guarantee he has a gun."

Coming toward them in the opposite direction, a police car turned on flashing lights. The siren blared. Butch stopped, put his car in reverse. Behind him another police car screeched to a stop. A second car followed. Police, their pistols drawn, ran toward Butch's car.

"Get outta the vehicle!" a cop shouted. "Now!"

Butch grabbed his gun and sprinted from the car.

"Stop or we'll shoot!"

Butch kept running, tripped over the curb. He fell to the sidewalk. His gun flew into the air and landed a few feet away. He crawled toward the firearm, stretched out his hand to reach it.

A foot stomped his fingers. A hand picked up the gun.

"Gotcha," said Detective Stein.

CHAPTER EIGHTY-ONE

Thursday, 5:55 p.m

Aurora slept on the sofa in their sunroom. Sam busied himself in the kitchen. He'd offered to take her out to dinner, but she refused, insisted they come home instead so she could shower and relax. Well, she would still enjoy a great meal. He scrubbed two potatoes and stuck them in the oven, washed and snapped the pound of green beans Aurora had purchased three days ago, and defrosted two bacon-wrapped filet mignons from Omaha Steaks. His mouth watered in anticipation.

Sam tip-toed to the sunroom and peeped at the love of his life. He couldn't seem to look at her enough, figured his brain had to satisfy itself that she was still there, still alive. After all, he'd come close to losing her.

Aurora's camera rested on the coffee table. He picked it up and snapped a shot of her stretched out on the sofa in her pink pajamas with black and gray Labs printed on the fabric. Her hand dangled off the edge of the sofa, her fingertips rested on King's head.

King opened his eyes, looked at Sam. Sam could have sworn the dog smiled and winked at him before drifting back off to sleep.

When the telephone rang, Aurora moaned and shifted her position. King raised his head. Sam snatched it and hurried to the kitchen.

"This is Luke, Sam. I'm calling to see how Aurora is."

"She's fine, just exhausted. She showered and is now sound asleep on the sofa."

"Hope I didn't wake her."

"You didn't. But it would have been okay if you had. I'll get her up anyway in about 10 minutes when supper's ready. How's Carole? She's been through a lot more than Aurora."

"You know, I can't get over that woman of mine. Carole's smart, resourceful, spunky. She told me that Win had the bartender at *La Grande Maison* mix a date-rape drug in her wine."

"You're kidding. So if she was drugged, how did she manage to escape?"

Luke laughed. "I told you she's resourceful. She switched glasses when he wasn't looking." He laughed again. "Win consumed the wine meant for Carole. She even acted like she was drugged. That's my Carole."

"You realize how blessed we both are, Luke?"

"Yeah, Sam, I do."

At the hospital, Monique tried for the third time to talk the staff into giving her an update on Otis. For the third time they refused.

"You're not family," they said. "We've told you that twice before."

"I will be family if he lives," she answered. "And I've told *you* that twice before." She struggled not to cry. "Otis saved my life. That should count for something."

"Sorry. You really should go home."

"I refuse to leave until I know his condition. Besides, I live with Otis."

From the hall, a nurse's aide motioned slightly to Monique and put her finger against her lips. The aide turned and headed away from the nurses. Monique followed.

"I can't stand what's happening to you, even though they're following procedure. My boyfriend means everything to me; I consider myself part of his family. If I were in your position, I'd want to know how he's doing."

"Thank you. I'm glad you understand."

"Miss, I shouldn't be the one to tell you this. The doctor should tell you. But he won't, not until they notify the immediate family. I really, really hate to be the bearer of bad news."

"What is it?"

"Your boyfriend died in the ambulance."

Monique collapsed to the floor.

Fifteen minutes later while Sam and Aurora were finishing their meal, the hospital called.

"I don't know if this is the right number, but a young woman gave me two phone numbers. I can't reach the first number, so I'm calling you. Glad you answered. The woman—her name is Monique—is in bad shape. Her boyfriend Otis died on his way to the hospital. She passed out when she heard. When she regained consciousness, she pleaded with me to let either somebody named Carole or you know. I have good intuition. Monique, in my opinion, might be suicidal."

"She saved my friend's life. And, ultimately, mine. I'm sorry her boyfriend died because of it. I'll get there as soon as I can. Will you be able to keep her at the hospital until I arrive?"

"I'll try."

"Bless you," said Aurora.

"I'll drive," said Sam. He set the dirty dishes in the sink, grabbed his jacket and Aurora's, and ushered her out the door. "Come on, King," he called.

Almost an hour later, Aurora and Sam helped a distraught Monique into their car. King jumped in the back seat and rested his head in Monique's lap. "Thanks for like helping me," Monique said between sobs. "I'd like sleep in the yard before I'd crawl in bed knowing my Otis would never come back to me."

"Plan on staying with us for a week or so," said Aurora. "We have plenty of room. Have you had anything to eat?"

"No. I couldn't eat a thing."

"Aurora and I finished eating right before the nurse's aide called. But I'll defrost and cook another steak for you, stick a baked potato in the microwave, zap the leftover green beans. You must be famished."

"I'm not hungry."

"I'll cook it anyway. If you don't want it tonight, you can warm it up tomorrow," said Sam. "Your choice. But think about it. Otis loved you. He'd want you to take care of yourself."

CHAPTER EIGHTY-TWO

Near Lovingston, the helicopter pilot circled the dirt landing strip twice. A familiar figure stepped out of the woods, waved him down. Jim landed the chopper, shut off the engine, jumped to the ground and shook hands with Wade.

"Appreciate the use of your strip." He looked back at the helicopter, said to his buddy, "This will be the last time I'll be landing here. Once I deliver those two goons to Jersey, I'm gonna drop out of sight. The entire operation at *La Grande Maison* is going up in smoke—maybe literally—and I don't plan to get caught up in it. If I were you, I'd be invisible for a few weeks, too. Go on an extended vacation with the wife and kids. Don't tell anybody where you'll be. These are dangerous guys we're dealing with. I don't trust 'em—never have. So after you gas me up, as far as you're concerned, you don't know me. You never heard of me. If asked, I'll say the same about you. Deal?" His friend nodded.

"So where in Jersey are you going?"

Jim told him, asked about Wade's family. Jim often wished he'd married that special woman who'd adored him, begged him to marry her and settle down like his friend had done, raise some kids. But he'd not wanted to drag a family into the evil that *La Grande Maison* represented. Once he finished running, invented a new identity, he'd call his old flame, see if she'd ever married. The prospect made him smile. He hadn't smiled in a long time. It felt good.

Jim refueled and started the chopper. "I'll be in touch, Wade!" he hollered and waved goodbye. He felt better knowing he'd soon be rid of his passengers, never work again for *La Grande Maison*.

*

"You want to take this one or want to wait 'til Jersey?" Jasper asked Win.

"I want New Jersey. This one's yours."

"Whatever." Jasper pulled his gun from his satchel, aimed and fired. Wade fell to the dirt.

"What the hell?" yelled Jim.

"Just fly," ordered Jasper. "Or you're next."

Jim wasn't dumb. The man had shot Wade, his friend. Jim didn't know if Wade had lived or not. He prayed he'd survived, but didn't have much hope. But why did they shoot Wade? Jim figured they thought Wade knew too much. Well, Jim knew a damn sight more about these people than Wade, a country boy, would have ever guessed. So, if you put two and two together and got a dead Wade, then Jim figured he didn't stand a chance according to the bad guys' thinking. Well, he'd give them a little surprise. He eased his hand into a storage cubicle, pushed maps aside, retrieved his .45 and tucked it in his jacket pocket.

On the eleven o'clock news that night, a newscaster reported the murder of Wade Mulberry. "He failed to come home this evening for dinner. His wife and four kids discovered his body at their private airstrip when they went looking for him. His wife said Mulberry had planned to meet a helicopter at the airstrip to refuel it." A short clip of the scene with the weeping family flashed on the screen.

"Wade was a good man," said his wife into the microphone. "He didn't have any enemies." She pulled a tissue from her coat pocket and blew her nose. "He was a good husband, a loving father, a Christian. Everybody loved Wade. Why would anybody want to kill him? Why?"

She stared into the camera, wiped her eyes with the tissue the reporter handed her. "I'm offering a reward of $10,000 for any information leading to the conviction of my husband's murderer." A phone number to call with information flashed at the bottom of the screen.

Aurora sat up straight in her recliner. "Did you hear that?"

"Yeah," said Sam.

"I know you'll think I'm crazy, but my gut tells me Win is involved in this killing. If I'm right, I'm involved, too. So are Carole, Monique, and even Otis."

King lifted his head from his dog bed, whined.

"Come on, Aurora. You're exhausted. Your imagination is doing double time."

"I agree with your wife, Mr. Harris." Monique stood in the doorway. "I couldn't sleep, so I turned on the TV in the bedroom. And when I saw the news, chills like ran all over my body. I really. . . ."

"Look," interrupted Sam, "there's a special report from this network's New Jersey affiliate."

Earlier this evening, an explosion rocked a private airfield in the Cherry Hill, New Jersey, area. Authorities there report that a helicopter is burning out of control. We have no word yet of how this happened. Authorities have not ruled out terrorism. Firefighters are on the scene. The aircraft housed in hangars are not in danger at this time. A news team is en route to the location. We expect live photos before this broadcast is over. Stay tuned for more details.

"Oh, my gosh," said Aurora. "This is too coincidental."

"I agree," said Monique.

"Let it go, ladies."

"Don't you get it, Sam?" asked Aurora. "The dead man in the Lovingston area was shot. He was refueling a helicopter."

"We can't prove that."

"His wife stated that he'd planned to refuel a helicopter. You heard her yourself, Sam."

"The key word here is *planned,* Aurora. So far there's no proof a helicopter ever landed."

"The key words in your statement, Sam, are *so far.* Don't you get it? It's a helicopter that's burning in New Jersey, too. I'm guessing there's just enough time for a chopper to refuel in Lovingston, and fly on to New Jersey in that same amount of time."

"Shh," said Monique. She pointed to the TV. "They're giving an update in New Jersey."

We just learned that the helicopter pilot jumped from the chopper the instant it touched down. Our witness, who doesn't wish to be identified, said the pilot hit the ground, rolled, and limped towards the forest surrounding the airfield.

He heard gunshots coming from the helicopter, thought one bullet may have hit the pilot in the shoulder. The pilot fired several shots back at the helicopter. The chopper burst into flames. The witness also said that two military-type vehicles drove onto the field, watched the helicopter burn, and drove away fast when they heard sirens. Our witness, who stayed hidden, fears for his own safety and the pilot's.

"Incredible," said Aurora. "Unless the witness didn't see anyone else jump from the plane, somebody died in the fire."

"Why do you think that?" asked Sam.

"Because bullets were fired at the pilot from the helicopter," said Aurora. "Now I'm even more convinced. I bet you Win was on the helicopter."

"I'll take that bet. What do you want if you should happen to be right?"

"Hmm. I've been thinking about getting a horse. Yep, if I'm right I want a horse."

"What would I get if I win?" Sam smiled at his wife.

"You won't win, but if by some miracle you do, I'll treat you to a weekend on Bald Head Island."

"You've got a deal." He looked at their houseguest. "Monique is our witness."

Monique laughed. "So like what kind of horse will you buy, Aurora?"

CHAPTER EIGHTY-THREE

Friday, 6:45 a.m.

In Greenville, Etta rocked on Mac and Sue's screened porch and watched the birds dive to the feeders. Mouser eyed the pair of cardinals on the other side of the screen.

"You're an early riser," said Sue as she joined Etta.

"Yeah, I usually am."

"I brought you a cup of coffee." Sue set a tray with three cups, coffee carafe, sugar, and skim milk on the glass-top table. "Mac will bring the bagels out as soon as they're ready."

"Thanks. It's so nice out here. I could live on this screen porch. Mouser likes it, too."

Sue laughed. "So do we. In the hottest part of the summer, the heat and humidity keep us from using it as often as we'd like. But spring, early summer and fall are perfect times to sit out here."

Mouser rubbed against Sue's leg. "Wraaa!" he cried.

"What's that mean?"

"I think he wants breakfast, too," said Etta as she dished cat food into a pie tin. "Thanks for stopping at the store last night for me to pick up cat food and cat litter. And I'm sure he liked his makeshift bed out here on the porch, too."

"He does seem happier this morning, more relaxed." said Sue. "It's nice to have a cat around again."

"Yeah. I'm real glad I brought him instead of leaving him in my little house. Butch would have killed him for sure."

Mac arrived with the bagels, butter and jams. "Dig in."

They did.

"Detective Stein called a few minutes ago, Etta. He asked if you could go to the police station this morning. He has more questions to ask you."

"I don't have a car, remember?" The thought of seeing all those police uniforms again made her tremble.

"Mac can drop me off at my office on his way to work. You can drive mine. Once you're through with the police, you can come back here and make yourself at home. A key to the house is on my key ring."

"I thought Mac needed to take his car to the garage. Butch put some bad dents in the rear end."

"I'll do that on the way. The garage will loan me a vehicle until mine's repaired."

"It's 7:00 now. What time do you need to leave? Since I don't know Greenville, I'll just follow you."

"That's fine. Would 7:45 be too early?"

"Nope. I'll be ready." Etta stirred milk and three spoonfuls of sugar into her coffee.

One and a half hours later, Sue's car idled in the police station parking lot. Etta stared out the window, worried about the inquisition the cops would give her. Mac had assured her that she needn't be upset, that all Detective Stein wanted was to ask her some questions, see if he could get more information on Butch.

But Etta's dad had been a cop, the kind folks called a bad cop. The fact that he accepted bribes was bad enough. What most folks never knew is that he took his frustrations out on his wife and their two daughters. That one winter night when Etta's sister had called the police to come protect them from their dad, the police had tried to ignore her frantic call for help. After all, he was a cop. Cops protect cops. When they finally came after a worried neighbor reported domestic violence next door, her dad had already stabbed her mother, beaten her unconscious, and tossed her out the door into the snow.

In Etta's mind, she could still hear his footsteps on the wooden stairs as he headed toward the bedroom she and her sister shared. Visions of her dad, butcher knife in hand, breaking through the locked bedroom door as she and her sister clung together still gave her nightmares. The sisters had screamed, held tight to each other.

"Drop it!" the police had ordered her dad. Etta could still remember the crazed look in his eyes and the sick grin on his face as he dashed toward their bed, his knife held high. "Stop!" yelled the police. Moments later her dad lay dead on the floor.

Maybe she should just drive away, forget about Butch, the cops, Sue and Mac. She could go to New Bern, live with her sister. She'd figure out a way to return the car to Sue. But what about Mouser? Even though she knew Sue and Mac would give him a good home, could she just walk away as though Mouser meant nothing to her? She closed her eyes, rested her head against the steering wheel.

No. She hadn't abandoned Mouser when she left her little house. She would not abandon him now. She sighed and shut off the engine. Determined to face her fears, Etta took a deep breath and walked into the police station.

CHAPTER EIGHTY-FOUR

Friday, 10:15 P.M.

Back on Spawning Run Road, Aurora finished her third cup of coffee, stuck the mug in the dishwasher, and dialed Uncle Charlie. She told him her suspicions about the helicopters. "I'm sure the murder of the man in Virginia and the burning helicopter in New Jersey are related. And I also believe Win Ford is part of it all."

"Aurora, you're not thinking clearly."

"Yes I am. Uncle Charlie, I just know I'm right. And I'm going to prove it."

"How?"

"First I'll call around, find somebody who knows how long it takes a chopper to fly from *La Grande Maison* to the Lovingston area. There are witnesses who say Win left the estate in a helicopter. We also know what time he left. Then I'll find out how long it would take a helicopter to go from Lovingston to the private airfield in New Jersey."

"You're a pretty stubborn lady, you know that? You always have been. Nothing I say will talk you out of doing this, so I may as well help," said Charlie.

"Remember when I ran into you, Carole and that Win guy in Dixie Lee's building? Well, I was positive his name was Anthony. He denied it. Remember?"

"I do."

"I'll check it out. His fingerprints will be on file."

"I was hoping you'd volunteer."

"Actually, Aurora, it would be faster to just run a print from Win, see if Anthony's name comes up."

"Yeah, it would. And his prints would be all over his car. The police have impounded it. They're probably checking it right now if they haven't already done so."

"I'll call Sheriff Roberts about the prints as soon as we hang up."

"And I'll get moving on the helicopter thing. Talk to you later, Uncle Charlie. Love you."

"I love you too, Aurora."

With local telephone books beside her, Aurora sat at the kitchen table and opened the Yellow Pages to listings under Aircraft Charters. Only a few companies listed helicopters. She jotted down their names and phone numbers.

Before she could start dialing, Sam called from his office.

"Just checking on you," he said. "You've been through a lot. I hope you're planning to take a nap today."

"Probably not. I really want a horse, so I'm working on the helicopter puzzle," Aurora said. "Just kidding. But I am trying to get info on helicopters because I want to know if I'm right." She told him how she planned to call helicopter charters to see if they could help.

"I can calculate the mileage and the length of time it would take a chopper to fly to the Lovingston and New Jersey destinations for you. Shouldn't be hard or take long. I'll work on it during my break. If I can't get what you want, you can start calling the numbers in the phone books."

"Thanks. Call me when you know something."

After talking to Sam, Aurora put on her sweats and running shoes, wrote a note for Monique, and called King. "Want to go for a run?"

King sprinted around the great room, yelped several times, nudged Aurora's leg and dashed to the door.

"I know we haven't run for a while. Sorry. We both need the exercise. Let's go." King barked.

Three miles and 35 minutes later, woman and dog walked back into the house. Aurora looked at her watch and frowned. They— well, she—hadn't made good time. King had stayed beside her as though he didn't want to let her out of his sight.

But at least I cleared the cobwebs from my head. I've got some ideas how to proceed with my investigation, she thought.

She showered, dressed in jeans, a fall-themed sweatshirt, socks and sneakers. When she walked into the great room, Monique was sitting at the kitchen counter munching on a bowl of shredded wheat topped with fat blueberries.

"These blueberries are really yummy," Monique said to Aurora.

"Thanks. I picked 11 quarts in late August from a local farm and froze them. They're especially good in the dead of winter. Glad you're enjoying them." She poured another cup of coffee and sat down beside Monique.

"Monique, do you mind if I ask you some questions while you're eating?"

"Nope."

"Will it upset you if the questions concern Otis?"

"All memories of Otis like upset me. I loved him more than I guessed."

"I know you did, but I must ask. People's lives depend on the answers."

"Okay. I'll try."

"Did Otis ever mention the names of the people he worked with or hung out with?"

"Yeah, he did. I like remember lots of nights when he didn't get home until really late. He'd tell me he'd been working—not his regular work at *La Grande Maison*—and he wasn't proud of what he'd done, said he'd done bad things to keep his job. Especially the last time."

"What kind of bad things?"

"Well, he and this guy Butch would like go into unfinished houses in Sweetwater Cove and vandalize and steal stuff. Most times they'd just like mess up floors, cabinets, walls. Once they almost burned a house down."

"I heard about the fire in Sweetwater Cove," said Aurora.

Monique nodded. "Well, he said the last time Butch like stuffed raw chicken in the heat vents in the master bedroom. Can you imagine how much that would stink, especially after the homeowners turned on the heat? Made me like gag when he talked about it. And they stole the brand new appliances that had been delivered that day."

"What'd they do with the appliances? Was one a freezer?"

"I think they like usually sold 'em. But the last time he said they like pushed a freezer off Smith Mountain. Then he like got really quiet, said he didn't want to talk about it ever again."

"Who is Butch?"

"Don't know for sure. But I remember Otis saying one time that their plans had changed 'cause Butch was gonna like meet Etta, whoever that is. Butch works for one of the head honchos, takes orders from some guy named Smoot. Funny thing is Smoot works for Sweetwater. He's like got some power, can do anything he wants. At least Otis said so. Oh, I just remembered that Butch drives a black paneled van. I know 'cause he picked Otis up in it a couple times."

Aurora couldn't believe what she'd just heard. She grabbed a pad and pen and started writing.

Butch drives a black paneled van. A black van almost ran Hessie down. Kurt saw the van at the Southerland house and at Hessie's house. The license number on the van that almost hit Hessie and the one at her house are the same. Appliances, including a freezer, were stolen from the Southerland house. Butch—or Otis—shoved a freezer off Smith Mountain. Tom Southerland was found in a freezer at the edge of Smith Mountain Lake. Hessie disappeared. King and Little Guy found her on Smith Mountain.

As Aurora was completing her Butch list, Sam called. "I got the info you wanted. Do you have something to write on?"

"Yep, I'm ready."

"Okay, then. What I discovered is that the average helicopter can fly 133 miles per hour, some at only 90 miles per hour, although one chopper is on record of going 331. As the crow flies, the distance from where *La Grande Maison* is located to the airfield near Lovingston, Virginia, is approximately 68 miles, which would take about 45 minutes. Does that sound right to you?"

Aurora studied her notes. "I'm guessing Win left *La Grande Maison* not too long after you and the police rescued us. Sheriff Rogers would know the exact time. I'll check with him. Now how about from Lovingston to the Cherry Hill area?"

"To the New Jersey airfield from the Virginia one is approximately 238 miles as the crow—or helicopter—flies, would take about two and a half hours."

"Did you add in the time it would take the chopper to refuel?"

"No. I'm guessing, but I'd say in the neighborhood of 15 to 20 minutes, depending on how many gallons the tank holds and if the pilot has several refuels ahead of him. You could check that out."

Aurora looked at the times she'd written down and made her calculations. "If you're right and it would take 20 minutes to gas up, then in my opinion it could be the same helicopter." She laughed. "How soon do I get my horse?"

"Not so fast, Susie-Q. You need to check out these calculations, and you still have to get the hard facts. Besides, you know my okay isn't necessary for you to buy a horse. I figured you'd buy one sooner or later."

An hour later, Uncle Charlie called Aurora. "His name is Anthony Smoot, not I. Winston Ford. And he was in my court once. I didn't like him. Thought he was dangerous. I was right. But with the evidence presented and a jury that didn't find him guilty, I couldn't throw him in prison for the rest of his life. Which is where he should be."

"Good work, Uncle Charlie. Monique mentioned the name Smoot a little while ago." Her fingers flew across the computer keyboard as she Googled the now familiar name.

"Sheriff Roberts reminded me that a Jasper Smoot broke into that kid's house. What's the name? You know him."

"You mean Kurt Karver?"

"Yeah. Jasper Smoot's also suspected of shooting Karver's neighbor. And he's the one who hired Dixie Lee to stay with Hessie."

"That's where I heard his name. So we have two bad Smoots in the area. My guess is they're related." Jasper's address came up on her monitor. "Oh my gosh. He lives in one of the Sweetwater Cove condos. I bet you anything he, Butch, and Otis are responsible for abducting Hessie and dumping her on Smith Mountain."

"Very likely," said Uncle Charlie.

CHAPTER EIGHTY-FIVE

One week later

Aurora set a tray of appetizers and wine glasses beside bottles of wine on the kitchen island. She smiled, enjoying the sound of Sam and their guests. She loved their chatter, their laughter. She liked being surrounded by family and friends; she wished her parents and Aunt Annie could take part in the festivities.

"Come pour yourself a glass of wine," she called to them. "There are sodas and water, appetizers, too. More will come."

King and Little Guy barked seconds before the doorbell rang. When Aurora opened the door, Lieutenant Conner and Sergeant Johnson stood on the front porch. Huge smiles spread across their faces.

"Mind if we come in?" asked Lieutenant Conner. He shook King's offered paw, patted Little Guy's head.

"Of course not."

"We have some information we thought you'd like to hear. But you have company. We can come back tomorrow."

"No, please stay," said Sam from behind Aurora. "You're just in time for a little celebration. Help yourselves to some appetizers and a glass of wine. I think you know everyone here."

The deputies looked around the room. "Actually, I think all of you would like to hear our news. We're on duty, can't drink anything alcoholic. A glass of water would be great, though."

Sam clinked a goblet with his spoon. "Everybody, I believe most of you know our friends, Deputies Ian Conner and Joe Johnson." A chorus of "Yes" and "Welcome" filled the room. "They want to share some information with us."

"Thought you'd like to know that Butch—real name Wallace Smith—confessed to hitting Hessie Davis and kidnapping her," said Lieutenant Conner. "Tom Southerland caught Butch stealing the new appliances from the Southerland house in Sweetwater Cove, so Butch and his buddies Otis and Shorty attacked Southerland and hit him over the head. Thinking they'd killed him, they stuffed him in the stolen freezer that was in the back of the van. Otis pushed the freezer off the mountain. Later, they also dumped Hessie on the ridge road on Smith Mountain."

"Nice guys," said Jill. She popped a baby carrot in her mouth.

Monique interrupted. "I like apologize to all y'all for what my Otis did. Basically, Otis was a nice person, just got in with the wrong crowd. And no matter what bad things all y'all think he did, he wouldn't shoot me. He saved my life. It ain't fair he died because of me. I miss him lots."

Sergeant Johnson walked across the room, sat next to Monique on the couch. "During our investigation, we discovered that Butch, Win and Jasper—we'll get to Jasper and Win in a minute—knew about something Otis did, used that information to force him to cooperate. They blackmailed him for several years."

"What'd they have on Otis?" asked Monique.

"Sure you want to know?"

Monique nodded.

"Well, a few years ago Otis got hold of some local moonshine, drank until he was out of his head, then robbed a convenience store and pistol-whipped the 52-year old clerk. She's still in a wheelchair, will probably deal with that for the rest of her life. Butch saw it all," said Lieutenant Conner. "The police never caught Otis."

"That like explains his fear of cops and goin' to jail."

"There's more. Butch thought Etta would rat on him after he hit Hessie. Even though Etta didn't know for sure that Butch dropped Hessie on Smith Mountain, Etta was smart. She wanted none of what was happening. Butch knew she'd turn on him eventually. He told me that Etta had morals and wouldn't keep her mouth shut," said Lieutenant Conner. "Besides, Jasper threatened to shoot him if he didn't get rid of her."

"Butch would have killed me if Mac and Sue hadn't helped me. And he torched my car," said Etta.

"What about Jasper?" asked Aurora.

"Jasper Smoot worked as the accountant and bookkeeper at Sweetwater Cove for the last few years. His stepfather Dave had worked as foreman for Sweetwater for about six years. Dave expected to be promoted to contractor. When the owner hired Tom Southerland—his old college roommate—instead of promoting Dave, Dave's wife Estelle—who is Jasper and Win's mother by another marriage—set out to destroy Southerland and his wife Blanche. On orders from Estelle, Jasper embezzled funds from Sweetwater and planned to blame it on Southerland if anyone discovered the money was missing. Jasper hired Butch, Shorty and Otis to vandalize houses under construction. Also on his mother's orders."

"Why did Jasper go after Kurt Karver?" asked Aurora. "And didn't Jasper shoot the Karver's neighbor?"

"Yep. He shot the neighbor because she could place him on the street near Kurt's house and parked in the Karver's driveway. And he intended to kill Kurt because Kurt could identify Butch, who could identify Jasper. Sorry, it's a little complicated." Lieutenant Conner sipped the glass of water Aurora handed him.

"Tell us about Win." Carole chewed on a ham biscuit.

"Although Win seemed charming, his mother had created a monster. Always babied by Estelle, told that he could coast through life on his looks, do anything he wanted, Anthony Smoot—alias I. Winston Ford—believed he could do just that. A bad seed—his biological father is in prison for life—he possesses no morals, most often gets what he wants. He loved the ladies; they usually reciprocated. Those who didn't play his games ended up mutilated and dead. We know of at least two. My guess is there are more." Lieutenant Conner looked at Carole. "Because of her instincts and resourcefulness, Carole managed to escape."

"I didn't trust him from the beginning. But the idea of a huge commission on the sale of an expensive house beat out common sense. Lesson learned here? Never put money over what you know is right, over values, over friends and family. If I'd listened to Aurora and Luke, I wouldn't have been in danger in the first place," said Carole.

Luke squeezed her hand. "Yeah, you still would have. You came really close to dying. But you're smart, suspected Win of stealing boats. And you switched glasses so that he drank the drugged wine intended for you. Then you ran."

"But I should have seen through him sooner."

"He thought you'd figured everything out. Besides, you turned down his advances. That alone marked you for death. Carole, you never had much chance of surviving." Luke hugged her.

"Who killed Blanche and Tom Southerland?" asked Sam.

"Jasper," answered Conner. "Unfortunately for him, the first attempt failed. He strangled Southerland, tried to make it look like he'd just quit breathing. He figured the man was in such bad shape that no one would notice the marks on his neck." He laughed. "In squeezing Southerland's neck, he damaged the tube in his throat. The doctor immediately suspected attempted murder and called the cops."

Little Guy and King darted to the door. Little Guy barked.

Sam let them out, laughed as King snatched up a tennis ball and dashed toward the lake. "Sorry about that. Please continue."

"Am I boring you?" asked Conner.

"No!" everybody said together.

"Okay, then," Conner said. "Posing as a caring friend, Estelle volunteered to spend the night in the hospital so Blanche could go home with their bridge friends and get some rest. Unfortunately for Estelle, Mary Ann insisted on staying, too, which thwarted Estelle's hope of slipping into Southerland's room and killing him."

The oven timer buzzed. Aurora excused herself and hurried to the kitchen.

"A nurse's aide foiled Jasper's second attempt when she and the guard burst into Southerland's room just as Jasper was about to inject something into Tom's IV. Then the head nurse and Blanche walked in."

Sergeant Johnson picked up the story. "Jasper disarmed the guard, who, following orders from Jasper, tied up the aide and the nurse with a ripped sheet, gagged them, and forced them under the bed. Afraid Jasper would start shooting if he didn't obey, the guard tied Blanche in the chair and gagged her. Jasper knocked out the guard, shoved him under the bed, and plunged a syringe filled with death into Southerland's IV."

"That's one evil family," said Aurora. "Even though I had no idea Win was related to Jasper, when I looked into Win's eyes at an intersection a few months ago, I thought I'd seen the devil."

"Was Estelle's husband Dave involved in all this?" asked Jill.

"No. Dave worshipped Estelle. He knew she'd been upset ever since Southerland was given the contractor job over him. He figured he just wasn't good enough for her. To compensate, he worked harder and longer hours and wasn't home long enough to figure it all out. As for his stepsons Jasper and Anthony—alias Win—Dave knew they were bad eggs. He didn't trust them, but what could he do? After all, they were Estelle's sons. And she adored them." Lieutenant Conner put a chunk of Havarti cheese in his mouth.

"So what about Blanche?" asked Sam. "How'd Jasper kill her?"

"He held his gun against her chest and fired. She died instantly."

"Yuck," said Monique.

"I'd like to know how Southerland's cap got in the portable john next door," said Sue.

"I can answer that," said Johnson. "Southerland surprised Butch, Shorty and Otis as they drank moonshine in the van. He confronted them. They grabbed him, knocked him down. Southerland got up, ran across the yard, and locked himself in the john. He hoped they wouldn't find him. They beat in the door and dragged him out. That's when he lost his cap."

Deputy Conner's pager beeped. "Sorry, folks, but Joe and I are needed on another call. If you have any questions, call me later. Good to see all of you."

"Wait. I have a quick question. Well, maybe two," said Robert. "First, what happened to Jim the pilot?"

"He survived. He had one bullet wound—not serious—and a few scrapes. Lucky man. The two guys on the chopper, Jasper and Win, died in the helicopter's explosion. Dental records proved their identities. And your second question?"

"What happened to the coon hunters who found Tom Southerland in the freezer?" asked Robert.

Both deputies laughed. "They're fine. Jude, who was impaled on the pine branch, spent time recuperating in the hospital. He's still getting physical therapy." Conner laughed. "His wife made a lamp from the pine branch that was sticking through his leg. Put a red lamp shade on it. She told me she set the lamp on the foyer table so Jude would see it every time he left the house."

"You're kidding," said Mac.

"Nope. She thinks his hunting days are over."

Before the deputies could leave, Monique asked, "Did you ever find Mr. Southerland's pickup truck?"

"Yeah. We raided a local farm, discovered the truck parked in a storage building."

"Think maybe I could have it? I need a car. Mine like burned up," said Monique.

Conner and Johnson looked at each other. "I doubt it," said Conner, "but we'll check."

CHAPTER EIGHTY-SIX

After the deputies left, Aurora removed cheese straws and ham biscuits from the oven, stirred the meatballs in the crock pot, and placed the food on the dining room table beside platters of shrimp, tea sandwiches, lemon bars and cakes.

She looked around at her old and new friends. Carole and Luke, Uncle Charlie and Dixie Lee, Robert and Jill, and Monique were there. Also there were Mac and Sue, who had grown fond of Etta and had driven up from Greenville with Etta and planned to stay a couple of nights. Hessie's doctor thought the visit would be too much for her. Because the huge amount of media coverage kept The Eagle's Perch filled and Yvonne busy in the kitchen, Yvonne and Paul Bateman sent their regrets. Kurt Karver sat at his parents' feet.

"Buffet's ready, y'all," Aurora announced. "Fill your plates and take them to the sunroom, or find a seat here."

"Before we spread out, could we make an announcement?" asked Luke. Everyone agreed. He put his arm around Carole's shoulder. "As you know, Carole and I are engaged. We've finally set a date—February 14th—and you're all invited. You'll receive an invitation in January."

Everyone applauded.

"We hope you'll all come," said Carole.

"I'd like to say something, too," said Uncle Charlie. He reached for Dixie Lee's hand, held it. "We're also making wedding plans." A radiant Dixie Lee held her left hand high, flashed the diamond and ruby ring. "Don't know the date yet, but it'll be soon."

"Will you live at the lake or in Lynchburg?" someone asked.

"We'll keep both places for now," Dixie Lee said. "And since I no longer have a job, I'll need something to do. Charlie stays pretty busy with golf and his volunteer work in Lynchburg, so I thought I'd volunteer for something, too. Any ideas?"

Suggestions flew through the room. "Before Mom's Alzheimer's disease, Dad participated as a driver with Bedford Ride," Aurora said. "Often the clients would have no other way of getting medical treatment. If you're interested, I'll tell you more about it later."

Dixie Lee nodded.

Etta stood, said that she and Mouser planned to live with her sister in New Bern. "It makes sense to me," she said. "I like my little house in Cifax, but I can never live there again. Too many bad memories. Mouser and I almost died in that house. And New Bern is close to Greenville, so I'll get to visit with Sue and Mac often."

"Monique, what are your plans?" asked Carole.

"Deputy Johnson like found me a part-time job as a live-in mother's helper. And he's also trying to get me a scholarship so I can go to nursing school."

"That's wonderful," said Carole. "You deserve it, Monique. If not for you, Win would have killed me if the Dobermans didn't rip me to shreds first."

Two weeks later, Aurora leaned on the board fence and stared at the pasture. Sam walked up behind her, touched her shoulder. She jumped.

"I didn't hear you drive up," she said.

"I know. My guess is you were absorbed in horsey thoughts."

"How was work today?"

"Fine. But I kept thinking of you, wished I were here with you instead of slaving in front of a computer. I love you, Aurora."

"I know you do, Sam. And I love you, too."

"So have you decided what kind of horse you'll buy?"

"I've made a decision, but you may not understand." She watched five turkeys cross the field. King barked. A large hen lifted her head and sprinted into the shelter of the woods. The others followed. "I don't know what breed I want."

"So you just can't decide?"

"The horse will decide," she said.

"What?"

"I've been Googling horse farms for the past week. I keep going back to horse rescue sites. Today I drove to a rescue site in Roanoke, met the horses and their caretakers. I cried all the way home. Sam, you won't believe the condition of some of those horses. Most were once fine animals that were abandoned by their owners and left to starve, or just plain mistreated. Some owners who could no longer keep their horses for one reason or another, gave them to the horse rescue before they became emaciated. Thank goodness for those rescue folks. They really care, Sam. They're doing all they can to help these animals." She looked into his eyes. "I want to adopt a rescue horse, Sam. The right horse will choose me. You think I'm nuts, don't you?"

"No, I don't think you're nuts. One of the things I've always loved and admired about you, Susie-Q, is the love and empathy you have for all living creatures." Sam kissed her, pulled her close.

"So when do we start cleaning out the barn?" he asked.